Sorry, Wrong Afterlife
A Novel
Susan Whiting Kemp

Also by Susan Whiting Kemp

The Climate Machine
The Time Philosopher
We Grew Tales

Acknowledgements

I would like to express my deepest gratitude to authors Evelyn Arvey and Nancy Bonnington for their thorough feedback on the early versions of *Sorry, Wrong Afterlife*. Their clever insights and boundless enthusiasm helped make this book what it is today.

Special thanks go to Don Webb, Editor of *Bewildering Stories*, who published "Sorry, Wrong Afterlife" back when it was a short story. I appreciate his faith in my writing, and am especially thankful for his title suggestion, which was a great improvement over mine.

Praise goes to my editor, Kara Aisenbrey of Just the Right Words, for her professionalism and expertise. Her guidance has been invaluable.

I extend my sincere gratitude to Ingrid and Gary Bruner for their enduring inspiration and unwavering support throughout my life. My life has been much richer because of them.

I would also like to thank Heidi Meade, walking partner extraordinaire, for her encouragement and friendship.

Last but not least, I'm enormously grateful for my husband and children, who inspire me and make this world a better place.

Chapter One

"We're dead, Morris. Deader than disco. Shovel-ready. From now on, we're going to wake up on the wrong side of the dirt." I hoped saying it out loud would help me adjust to our new normal.

My best friend and I were crouching on a massive tree branch, surrounded by nests of sticks, grass, and mud. No birds, just nests—some shaped like cups, some like gourds; some the size of my fist, some larger than laundry hampers.

Tropical warmth bathed the air. Vines with white flowers hung all about like discarded feather boas. They smelled like sweetened butter. This was a jungle, not the Cascade Mountains where we'd been hiking just a few minutes ago.

Morris twisted his lip piercing and plucked at his earlobe. "I guess so. We've been eighty-sixed, Leo, but it's hard to believe. It was so sudden. That avalanche came out of nowhere."

Luckily shock had tamped down my horror, because I remembered the previous moments all too clearly. The rush of snow and ice roaring toward us and burying me, Morris, and my wife, Lilly. The pain under the weight of all that snow, the panic at being unable to move, the frustration at being powerless to help my wife or my friend, the realization that death was imminent for all of us. Then finally, the fading of consciousness.

And now this. I never imagined that I would end up in a treetop after death. Where were the silken sheets and sumptuous banquets? Where was the workshop where I could build furniture to my heart's content? Where was the award ceremony in which my furniture designs could finally win first place?

"I'm too young to be dead!" said Morris. I nodded vigorously. It sucked to kick the bucket at thirty-two (Morris) and thirty-two and a half (me).

1

I fished in the pocket of my extra-breathable nylon-spandex hiking pants, digging out a small keychain with a green metal four-leaf clover and hangnail clippers. "So much for my lucky charm." I nearly tossed it away but then thought better of it.

Shuffling carefully on the tree branch, I turned around to see how my wife Lilly was doing with all this. She could probably use a comforting hug. Certainly I could use one. It was an excellent time for a group hug, come to think of it.

She wasn't there.

The woman who stuck I-love-you Post-its on the underside of the toilet seat for me to find. The woman who found forever homes for seventy-two dogs, fifty-eight cats, three horses, and a bald guinea pig in a single month. The woman who had a positive affirmation for any situation (example: *You can and you will*), which would be extra helpful about now.

She was dead too, so why wasn't she with us? The avalanche had pushed us right next to each other, our heads in a little air pocket, my cheek near her mouth. I could feel it when she stopped breathing. It was the worst moment of my life. It was also the last moment of my life.

My head swiveled like a barstool. My throat tightened into full-on squeaky toy. "Where's Lilly?"

Morris looked up, down, and around, then spoke with an energized rasp. "Not here. That means she's still alive!"

"No. She died right before I did."

He ran a hand over his buzz-cut fade while pondering. "Okay. Then she's got to be around here somewhere. If that's how it works."

His uncertainty made my skin prickle. What if that wasn't how it worked? What if she'd been put somewhere else? I tried to peer past the tree leaves, which were shovel-shaped, dark green, and glossy as plastic. "Lilly? Honeybunch, where are you?"

In his loudest outdoor voice, the one he used to call to his students on the other side of the playground, Morris shouted, "Lilly, come out, come out, wherever you are!"

There was no answer. I couldn't see her teal-dyed hair, cherry-red windbreaker, orange shape-sculpting leggings, or engaging smile. Yes, the leaves were dense, but she was colorful. If she had been anywhere close by, I would have spotted her.

Would my cell phone work here? I reached for it, but it had been in my backpack, which I'd taken off just before the avalanche hit. It was just as well, since as far as I knew, my plan coverage didn't extend to heaven.

I took a step, caught my toe on a twig, and stumbled. Luckily the branch supporting us was wide as a footbridge, so I didn't fall out of the tree, but I landed hard onto my elbow. I made a noise like a jilted marmot, then swore a few times.

"Leo! Are you all right?" My friend scooted over and examined me. "You're bleeding. You know what that means? You can get hurt here, even though you're dead."

I let that sink in. Life's pains and travails were over, but those of death had only just begun. We'd ceased to be, yet peril lived on, for me, my friend, and my wife.

"Lilly was carrying a heavy backpack to build muscle. It could have made her fall!" Holding on tightly, I peered down from the branch, but a mist—far, far below us—kept me from seeing the ground. I could tell, however, that our tree was at least as high as a water tower.

If she'd fallen, she could be hurt badly. We had to get to her fast, but the tree trunk below us was limb-free and smooth. "There's no way down."

My blunt statement seemed to trigger him. He squatted on the branch with his hands cradling his knees. "Leo, I can't believe we're sleeping with the fishes. My parents will be devastated. And my exes too."

Morris was the affable kind of guy who remained friends with ex-girlfriends. Luckily there was no current girlfriend, because she'd have died with us.

I grasped his shoulder with my good arm and tried to keep my voice steady. "What's done is done, and we'll see them all eventually when they come here. At least we've got each other. Right? We'll get through this, just like we got through puberty together." I admit that was an awkward statement, but as any adult can attest, it's truly an accomplishment.

He took a power breath in and let it out in three great huffs. "I guess. But I shouldn't be dead. It's not my time." He rubbed his knees, then stood. "So where are we?"

It was a good question. I realized that depending on the answer, Lilly might have been shuttled to somewhere else entirely. I had been brought up on Christianity, which prominently featured heaven and hell, but it really depended on which religion, if any, had described the afterlife correctly. If we knew more, we might be able to figure out where she was.

"Could this be heaven?" I ventured, although this was nothing like I'd imagined it to be. In fact, it should surpass anything the human imagination could dream up, and this place fell far short. Plus, Lilly's absence implied she'd ended up in hell, which was impossible. I was sure of it. Really sure. Pretty sure.

Actually, I wasn't sure at all. After all, Morris and I seemed to be in the wrong place, so that could mean mistakes happened.

Mistakes happen. Could it be that we weren't supposed to die? What if we were here mistakenly, while so many others were still alive, still had their families, still had their meaningful occupations and/or engrossing hobbies? A familiar feeling lit up my belly, like a cigarette lighter was burning my duodenum (just below my stomach). Why were they still alive, while I had ceased and desisted?

It wasn't fair. I deserved to have survivor guilt just as much as anybody.

No. I couldn't let myself be distracted by envy. I had to find my wife. I thought of her cross-eyed determination at a jalapeño-eating contest, and also her determination to eat the year's worth of jalapeños she won. She'd succeeded, and so would I. I resolved to be that formidable. I resolved to chew up my obstacles until I found Lilly!

There was motion in a nearby nest. It held three fist-size eggs speckled blue and brown; one of them was jerking. The bird inside was trying to hatch.

Nests. Bird eggs. Morris is a bird fanatic. A theory started to form in my mind. I pushed it aside as ridiculous. But was it?

A tiny crack worked its way along the egg, then a naked chick burst out. Beige, all beak. It gave a single squeak, like a tiny door opening.

"I name you Esmerelda," said Morris.

I didn't ask him why that particular name, since I knew he wouldn't have an explanation. Thoughts came to him and he voiced them, even while teaching, making him one of the most loved yet parodied teachers in his grade school.

I myself was a furniture designer. My day revolved around the blending of the tactile, the visual, and the experiential. And now, suddenly, it didn't. I had an idea why.

I decided I'd better just say it. "We're here because you're obsessed with birds. To you, this is heaven."

His voice rose an octave. "You think we're in this hot jungle because I'm a birder? That's ridiculous."

I kept my own voice in the same key. Almost. "We're in a tree filled with bird nests." I peered into a few of them. "They're filled with bird eggs. We made it to heaven, but yours, not mine. Morris heaven."

Morris grunted. "This isn't my idea of heaven. Not even close. No women. No beer. No avocado toast."

Certainly it was his fault we were here, but he could apologize later. In the meantime, I needed to unclench my teeth and find Lilly. I just didn't know yet how we were going to do that.

"Never mind." I tried to sound magnanimous but might have only achieved flippant. "Let's find Lilly. We can start up here, and if we don't find her, then we'll climb down. Somehow."

Morris wiped his face in a this-is-so-crazy gesture. I could tell he was still annoyed by my accusation. "We might lose each other. If only we could use crumbs or stones to mark our way. Or mark the trees somehow." He thought some more and said fervently, "I wish we had a roll of yellow caution tape." He held out his hands as if one would magically appear in his palms in response to his wish.

Honestly, if we had been granted wishes, it would have been more helpful to try, "I wish we hadn't been killed by an avalanche," or "I wish Lilly was with us," or even the old favorite, "I wish I had a hundred more wishes." In any case, it didn't work. No danger warning tape appeared in his hands.

"Let's just stay together," I said.

We clambered from tree branch to tree branch and from tree to tree, calling for Lilly, looking up, looking down. I looked for signs of her passage, but no branches were broken, because they yielded as easily as the swinging doors in a Wild West saloon. If there were any trails of blood (heaven forbid!) they were camouflaged by dapples of sun and shade.

Her absence reminded me too much of the darkest day of my life. We'd only been married a year when Lilly collapsed in our kitchen. She wasn't breathing and her heart wasn't beating when they took her away in the ambulance. At the hospital, a doctor informed me she was dead. For three hours, I thought she was.

Then I got the call. She was alive. Nobody understood it. She'd somehow revived. Well, I knew that you couldn't be dead for hours and come back from it, so it was obvious that she hadn't died in the first place. Somebody had made a big mistake, but all I cared about was that my Lilly was alive.

I'd gotten Lilly back that day, but now, after a couple hours of searching, I despaired of getting her back again. I squatted on a branch, head in hands. "We're never going to find her."

Morris punched me on the arm. "Snap out of it, Leopold." I preferred to be called Leo, so I knew he was still mad at me. "We haven't looked everywhere yet."

He was right, but he didn't have to be so rude about it. I snapped out of it, because I needed to, not because he told me to.

Being a natural explorer, Lilly could have climbed upward to look for us. I liked to joke with her that she was an alpine ibex (which climbs a cliff as if gravity didn't exist). She would respond that I was a flatland giraffe (which lopes across the savanna in an ungainly yet enthralling manner). How I wished she was there to tease me about my height!

Above us I could see nothing but tree canopy. "I'm going to the top to get a feel for the terrain."

"Man of action," said Morris sarcastically.

I considered making a snappy retort, but instead allowed him some leeway. It's not every day you find yourself taking a permanent dirt nap in a tropical canopy.

We climbed. It was much easier than it would have been when I was alive, although my elbow still hurt. "I'm stronger in the afterlife," I said.

"I am too. Good thing, this is hard work."

I brushed against a pitch glob and it stuck to my arm, making it look like I had an amber boil. I wiped it with some leaves, but it stuck fast, and now the leaves were stuck to me as well. "Watch out for the pitch," I told Morris. "It doesn't come off."

"Too late." His attempts to get pitch off his wrist looked like he was dancing a hula. Thinking how I would rather be attending a luau than pushing up daisies, I sighed and continued upward.

At the top there was nothing but jungle canopy as far as we could see. I kept turning, hoping that a different perspective would reveal something I'd missed the first time around, but after several 360-degree turns I had to allow that there was nothing around but trees.

As for Morris, he was looking upward, into a cloudless sky the color of blue bubblegum. "I was hoping that heaven would be up there. I was sure I'd see sunrays, like in the pamphlets." His lower lip began quivering. I searched for words of consolation, but could only think of "stiff upper lip," and it was his lower lip that was the problem. "Stiff lower lip" didn't have the right ring to it.

The poignancy of our situation compelled Morris to create a poem. He cleared his throat like he usually did before a performance.

> "Where are the lost souls?
> The emptiness fills with more emptiness
> Void of humanity.
> Me and my shadow
> Search for God and for Lilly
> And find egg."

The words made me feel like I was floating in a pleasantly warm sensory deprivation tank. Annoyed as I was with him, I couldn't help gushing, "That was one of your best. I would never have thought to make egg singular, but it completes the poem."

"Thank you," he acknowledged with a stiff bow of the head.

"She's not up here. We need to look for her on the ground."

The pitch was still stuck to my arm. It was strong stuff, which gave me an idea. "Let's make a stick-on ladder!"

We climbed back down to where we'd arrived and began breaking short branches off the tree. Using the pitch, we glued the branches onto the trunk, creating ladder rungs. It was hard work. Still, we made excellent progress, and I judged that we were about halfway down the tree when Morris asked, "What if hell is down there?" He held on to the ladder tightly, as if a sudden wind might propel him into a fiery inferno.

I imagined Lilly among demons, with their slathering jaws, slicing fangs, scarlet hides, extendable claws, and rude remarks. My skin crawled. She was good with animals—she was a professional dog skateboard instructor, specializing in bulldogs and their social media content. But I doubted that she would have the same touch with demons.

Of course, I'd traverse the fiery depths of hell to save my wife, but now work on our ladder was stopped, and I had to reassure Morris to get him moving again. "Oh, pshaw. Hell isn't down there."

I wasn't very convincing, partly because I'd never used the word *pshaw* before, and it sounded more like a leaking air mattress than a motivational exclamation.

"What if it *is* there?" His tone implied that I was being dismissive without considering the ramifications.

"What if it's not?" My tone implied he'd gone too far with his accusing tone.

"What if it is?" His tone implied that I was out of line and I should check myself.

I resumed building the ladder without him. My passive-aggressive grunts implied that he was a coward, and finally he joined me once more.

After a couple of hours we passed through the mist, giving us a view of the jungle floor. Well, not actually the jungle floor itself, because it was obscured by ferns and shade-tolerant bushes. It smelled like grated nutmeg and freshly turned earth.

"Lilly?" I called. "Are you down there?"

There was no answer. Just the sound of the breeze shifting the leaves of the undergrowth. I felt my brow knit together. If she was here but not answering, that meant she was hurt, and I needed to find her more than ever.

Working with renewed vigor, we continued pasting branches on the tree trunk. Reaching the ground a short time later, we began our search. I pulled the fern leaves aside tentatively at first, worried about snakes, giant jungle spiders, poison frogs, and human-eating Venus flytraps, but I encountered no bugs, animals, or thorns (and for the record, no demons either), so I sped up, tearing through the underbrush, calling for Lilly.

We'd scoured the area, and I'd nearly given up when I spotted something the red of Lilly's coat.

"Lilly? Lilly!" I ran. "I'm coming!"

Chapter Two

I jumped over round rocks and frilly fronds, hurrying toward Lilly. She had died to get here, but what if her fall had killed her a second time and her spirit had gone to wherever it was you went to after this place? The after-heaven, the after-hell, or the after-afterlife. I imagined a never-ending subway of afterlives, where she would always die one train car ahead of me and I would never catch up to her.

When I got there, I saw that it wasn't her. It was a section of log partially covered with red fungus. I hadn't found my Lilly! I knelt there, emotions crashing over me in waves. Relief! Dismay! Anger! Relief! Dismay! Anger! I moaned. Just a little.

Morris stomped through the undergrowth, calling, "Did you find her?"

"I thought maybe... but no." I bowed my head.

He put his hand on my shoulder.

"Lilly doesn't deserve to be lost and all alone," I said. "Just yesterday we were in line at the grocery store, and there was a man walking with a cane who seemed to be in pain. She insisted he go ahead of us."

"She's good people," said Morris. "That's for sure."

"She helped him do the self-checkout. She had something fun to say about everything in his cart. She was like, 'Potato bread? Potato head! Have an egg-cellent day! Bean there, done that.' She had him laughing like crazy."

I thought about the wry twist to her mouth and her little winks. She had a way of connecting to people that I'd never mastered.

Morris and I stepped away from the log, then he gave my shoulder an on-to-the-next-thing double pat. "I'm hungry. Let's climb back up to the nests and get something to eat. Then we can figure out what to do next."

"I'm not eating eggs." In life I'd loved eggs of every sort—scrambled, fried, pickled, deviled. *Deviled! Yikes!* But here the thought of eating them—or any of the birds that had laid them—made me nauseous. I supposed death had converted me into a vegetarian.

"No!" said Morris. "That's not what I meant. I saw fruit when we were up there. Let's get it."

I was crazy hungry. It had now been at least half a day since we'd eaten.

He added, "Besides, maybe there was a delay in her arrival. Maybe she's there now."

That did it for me. We climbed back up our ladder. My elbow ached from my earlier fall, but it didn't slow me much.

We reached the branch with nests all around, but Lilly wasn't there. I tried to be strong about it, but then the strings of feathery white flowers reminded me of New Year's Eve, when Lilly had dressed as a sexy chicken. Recalling her come-hither *bock-booock* made my eyes tear up.

We were about to continue upward to find the fruit when there was a *krick-krick* sound. Peering into a nest, we saw fissures in its eggs. There was more *krick-krick*ing all around us, like many different sizes of knuckles being cracked.

Morris announced, "They're all hatching at once!"

It seemed profound that new life was happening in a place of death. Within minutes the nests were full of featherless bundles of avian joy, with chirping and squeaking coming from all directions.

An adult bird—scarlet with charcoal wings—swooped down and landed on a branch above, its beak as long as my arm, curved like a scimitar. Morris threw his arms over his head for protection. I crouched and held my hands out in I-don't-want-any-trouble position.

Other oversize adult birds arrived. Soon the treetops were filled with hundreds of birds of all shapes and colors, making a cacophony of squawks and chirps. They all sported bone-cracking, eye-gouging types of beaks. The beating of their wings made the air whoosh this way and that like a malfunctioning wind tunnel. It smelled like sugar cookies.

A sleek crow landed on Morris's shoulder, cawing harshly. It had an unusual feature: A single brown feather nestled among the black ones on one wing. It extended its head slowly toward my friend's mouth, like a lover going in for a kiss in a romcom.

He leaned away. "Hey, back off!"

I scurried forward to shoo the bird away. After a quick, jerky twist of its head, it flew off with something shiny in its beak.

"Ow!" Morris's hand flew to his mouth. "It stole my lip piercing."

The crow landed on a branch above us, tilting its head as if to show off its new prize.

Morris used one of his standard classroom commands. "Stealing means taking something that doesn't belong to you. That is wrong. Please return that to its rightful owner."

For a moment I thought the crow might return, but no, it flew off.

His shoulders slumped. He'd had that lip piercing for years.

I tried to sound cheery. "We'll get you another one when we reach civilization."

There was a pleasant sound of rain on leaves, like the plinking pizzicato of a dozen cellos.

He held up his palms, looking like a supplicant in a medieval painting. "I hear rain, but it's dry."

We both realized why at the same time. *Bird poop*, we mouthed in unison. Sure enough, feathery tails were lifting. Splotches of creamy white and forest green materialized on the broad leaves all around.

"Kind of pretty," said Morris uncertainly.

It was, actually. The perfect pattern for sling chair fabric, with its subtle nod to pinto pony, but I would no longer be designing furniture. I was dead. I'd always known death would come someday, but this was too sudden.

A bird dove to one of the nests, picked up a chick in its talons, and flew off. Another followed suit. This continued for a crazy half hour until all the birds and chicks were gone.

A new bird arrived—the largest bird yet, three times taller than me. White feathers framed its face. Its muscular legs had a black-and-white zigzag pattern like a dress Lilly wore. (My sweet Lilly! Where was she?)

The feet of this stunningly majestic creature were large enough to wring my body like a washcloth. I backed up against the trunk of the tree, wishing I could disappear into it.

Morris whispered reverently, "Wow. A king-size harpy eagle."

"That thing could kill us," I whispered back.

"We're already dead."

"It could kill us deader."

Still whispering, Morris put his palms together respectfully. "I name you Lancelot."

"How do you know it's male?"

"Just a guess. The female is bigger than the male."

"So there's an even bigger one out there?"

He shrugged.

Lancelot stretched his wings wide as a paraglider. What were we to him? Friend? Foe? Dinner?

"What do we do?" I asked urgently.

"Back up slowly. Make a lot of noise. No wait, that's for a bear. I don't know. Look unappetizing."

I was trying to figure out how to accomplish that when Lancelot screeched. I could feel it in my bones, a vibration that began in my skull and traveled down my vertebrae to my pelvis, which magnified the vibration into a sound like a harmonic gong. That astounded me, as it never would have happened in life, but in heaven, who knew what acoustic rules applied?

The sound also startled the harpy, whose head feathers rose into a crown.

"Oh no," said Morris. "That means he's angry."

Lancelot dove toward us. He grasped one of my ankles with his talon, lifting me. I grabbed for a bough, but missed.

With his other talon, he snatched Morris by an ankle. My friend flailed, hollering, "Ay-yai, ay-yai."

I was now in my least favorite position: upside down. Blood rushed to my head, and I lost all sense of my three-dimensional positioning. And so, while we rose, I used my abs—what was left of them after years of sporadic weekend exercise—to pull myself up and grasp the bird's leg with both hands. His squawk told me he wasn't pleased by that—he dipped and swerved—but in the end he let me hammock underneath.

"Lilly!" I called as we left. "Lilly!" I tried to get one last look around for landmarks, but the motion and flapping made that impossible.

"He's taking us to be judged." Morris hung limp, like an upside-down marionette.

Of course! That was what happened in the afterlife. Judgment.

I generally considered myself to be a good person, and could defend any of my actions that might initially appear dubious; however, I remembered a time I'd been stopped by a cop for speeding. While waiting for him to call in my license plate and then amble up to my car, I'd prepared justifications and explanations in my head. By the time he'd reached me I had the perfect wording ready, and I imagined him listening to me, then smiling from behind his aviator sunglasses and telling me to be on my way, *safely now, you hear?*

But I'd been given no chance. He gave me a ticket without preamble. I'd been judged and sentenced. Done deal.

Was that going to happen now? My heart was pounding dubstep hard. "What if we've already been judged and sentenced, to the Prometheus torture?"

"What's that?" asked Morris.

"An eagle eats our livers out every day, and they grow back every night."

"Maybe yours," said Morris petulantly. "But I don't deserve torture."

"Are you saying I do?"

"You asked me to come on the hike. I'd be alive if it wasn't for you."

It took a moment for his words to sink in. *I'd be alive if it wasn't for you.* Was he right? I couldn't think with all that wind rushing up my nose.

A few minutes later, Lancelot dropped us into the bottom of a nest as big as a fishing scow. He perched on the edge, peering down at us with his penetrating raptor eyes.

A juvenile harpy eagle was in the nest with us. It was my size, with a black beak, white feathers, and black-tipped wings. It greeted us with a *squick-squawk*.

"Oh shit," said Morris. "We're breakfast."

Of course. Lancelot would now shred us to bits, then feed us to his progeny. Was that what had happened to Lilly? I hoped not, with all my might.

We scrambled up the sticks that formed the nest, but Lancelot butted us back down with the top of his head. And then, so quickly that I had no chance to react, he pried my mouth open with his black beak. A gloppy mess flowed into my throat, making me gag. It tasted of raw hamburger, which I'd only ever tried on a dare and wouldn't recommend even when doctored with Worcestershire sauce and given the misleading name of *steak tartare.*

Instead of ripping me to pieces, Lancelot was feeding me. It was too much, too fast. It felt like I was going to die again, this time from choking. When he finished, I spit out what I hadn't swallowed, then wiped my face frenziedly, making noises of disgust. I was surprised I didn't throw up—maybe one couldn't vomit in the afterlife. Time would only tell.

Lancelot did the same to Morris. I whimpered at the sight of his monstrous beak buried in my friend's mouth, filling him so full that his throat bulged.

Afterward Morris spit many times, made *ack* noises over and over, blew gunk from his nostrils, and wiped his entire forearm across his mouth. "That was probably dead sloth or dead monkey. That's what harpy eagles eat. Disgusting. Absolutely disgusting."

My nausea ballooned. "You shouldn't have told me that."

Lancelot fed the juvenile bird, then flew off, the wind from his wings pinning us against the side of the nest, as if gravity had suddenly gone sideways. I watched him grow smaller in the distance.

I was still reeling from that disgusting force-feeding, but I had to get past it, because this was our chance to escape. We climbed to the edge of the nest. As before, the tree trunk below us was limb-free and smooth, except for globules of amber-colored pitch. And what was more, we couldn't reach the boughs of the nearest trees to climb away.

"We have to build another ladder," said Morris.

"Yes. Then let's look for other humans. We can organize a search party for Lilly."

The thought of finding others to help us scour the jungle propelled me into action. I examined the nest. Its sticks were the right size for our ladder, but were too well woven into the nest to easily extract for use. Otherwise there were bits of animal fur, feathers, seedpods, and short pieces of green vine. At the bottom was feather fluff and a musty smell that I surmised was old bird poop. Nothing we could use here.

We began breaking branches to build the ladder. The young harpy eagle watched us in what seemed like a quizzical manner.

"You know what's weird," said Morris, "we're in a tropical place, and there aren't any bugs. No mosquitoes, no flies, no creepy-crawlies of any kind. We've only seen birds since we've gotten here."

Only birds. My stomach fluttered as a thought struck me. "We *are* in heaven, but the wrong heaven. Bird heaven instead of human heaven."

Morris's eyes widened, like a vintage troll doll minus the cheesy grin. "Oh my god, you could be right."

The resentment I'd been trying to suppress surfaced all at once. "If only you hadn't taught me so many bird calls."

He stiffened. "Stop blaming this on me."

I couldn't keep the surliness out of my tone. "Why not? We always talk about birds. Mating habits, migratory paths, endangered species status..."

He shook a branch in my face. His voice went icy. "It's your fault we died. You were the one who asked me to go hiking."

I bristled. Again I wondered if he could be right. But honestly, it wasn't like I'd personally ordered up a natural disaster. "It was a freak accident. There was no snow anywhere in sight. Not above us, not below us, not beside us. And it's not avalanche season... I don't understand it myself. There was no risk."

His words held venom. "And yet here we are, deader than doughnuts." He abandoned our task, jumped into the nest, and snuggled up to the young bird, giving me a look that implied I was a third wheel. "You go look for Lilly. I'm staying here."

I gaped. We'd been friends for years, together through thick and thin. Never once had we abandoned one another, or even threatened to. "Bro. There's no need for all that."

"I'm done with you."

That stony voice. He meant business. I'd lost my wife, and now I was losing my best friend.

I slipped into one of those states that are impossible to describe. *Bottom of the deepest, darkest well* comes close, as does *limitless maze with no exit*, but those were mere words that fell far short.

I shouted to God, or the manager of whatever sorting service had mistakenly shuttled us here. "Hello? We're in the wrong heaven! We're not birds. I'm Leo Cooper, and this is Morris Johnson. We're human. And we need to find my wife, Lilly."

The juvenile harpy eagle squeaked frantically, as if to warn me against such folly.

"I name you Dakota." Morris stroked the harpy eagle anxiously.

I called and called, imploring for help. Explaining the situation. Nobody answered.

It was only then I noticed something the size of a cantaloupe hanging from a branch, smooth and vermillion.

My reptilian brain abruptly took over. I spilled out of that deep, dark place like slop from a bucket. Up there hung something I could eat other than regurgitated meat, and I had to have it.

"Fruit, glorious fruit," I muttered as I climbed toward that beacon of sweetness. Would it taste like cantaloupe? Plum? Papaya? I wasn't hungry in a physical sense, but I needed something yummy to counter my emotional upheaval and get the taste of Lancelot's regurgitated food out of my mouth.

Morris shot upward. He was going to get it first! No way I would let him do that after he'd dissed me so badly. But he was already within a few arm lengths. I lit the afterburners, reached it first, and plucked it from the branch.

His eyes went dull. He climbed back down to the nest and sat slumped.

I sighed. Whether we were splitting up or not, I couldn't let it end this way. I descended and held it out to him.

His eyebrows slanted, signifying wariness. He gave me a look that said, *You're really giving this to me?*

I gave him a look that said, *I can't stand to see you so miserable.*

He gave me a look that said, *Well okay, but that doesn't mean we're good.*

I gave him a look that said, *Just take it already.*

If this detailed exchange using mere glances seems unlikely, bear in mind that Morris and I had been friends since we were five years old and we had a superior level of nonverbal communication.

He peeled off a thick section of rind. Blobs of reddish-brown fruit fell out. It smelled like raw hamburger.

In spite of the stink, Morris tasted a bit of it. Disgust pulled his front neck muscles taut. "It's raw-meat-flavored fruit. How revolting!"

I sagged with disappointment. There would be no sugary sweetness in my immediate future. I would have even preferred something as bland as raw zucchini over raw-meat-flavored fruit. "That must be what Lancelot fed us."

"At least we haven't been eating dead sloth." He hurled it away, and it lodged in a branch with a *thwick* sound.

If only Lilly were here now. She would find the humor in the raw-meat-flavored fruit. She would also point out the flowering vines and remind me that there are no garlands in hell. She would bring out my better self.

I resumed building the ladder on my own. I was standing on one of the rungs when Lancelot returned. His head feathers rose in anger, and he screeched so loudly my ears popped. He looked like he might shish-kebab me with that sharp beak of his.

I shot back up to the nest. He tore the ladder up, flicking the sticks away with wrathful jerks of his neck. That done, he perched nearby and began preening, thankfully ignoring me once more.

Morris looked wide-eyed, as if watching a tornado come his way. "We're stuck here. We're never going to leave."

"Au contraire," I said. "We're getting out of here. And we're going to do it together. We're going to find Lilly and the rest of humanity, and that's all there is to it."

Chapter Three

S hortly after Lancelot tore up the ladder, darkness fell and it began to rain. He sheltered us by sitting on us, which was awkward but surprisingly comfortable. We slept soundly, snuggled in with Dakota, breathing the smell of musty nest.

The next day was sunny once more. Lancelot left and we were at it again, breaking off branches, this time hiding them in the boughs above the nest so we could build the ladder down to the ground all at once during one of Lancelot's absences.

Dakota began squawking persistently. Returning to the nest, we found her beating her wings. Her leg was stuck between the sticks that formed the nest. We tried to get close enough to help, but she was panicked and kept thwacking us with her wings.

"Try to settle her down," I said.

Morris obliged, using his calming voice (a blend of Morgan Freeman and Christopher Walken), which always worked on his students. "Hocus-pocus, everybody focus. Macaroni and cheese, everybody freeze. All set. You bet."

She flapped less and less, and then was still except for the occasional head jut. He was so good with people and animals! Why didn't I have that kind of skill? I told myself to get over it. I was the one who'd asked for his help. I should be grateful.

I hunched down to assess the problem, which turned out to be complicated. I didn't know how she'd done it, but her leg was wedged between a crisscrossing of sticks, so that to move any one of them out of the way would put pressure on others and crush her leg bone.

I examined the trap as if it were a game of pick-up sticks. If I pushed this stick that way, it would move that stick that way, which would open up room over there, and so on. Each scenario I came up with would result in disaster, but I was determined to think it through. She'd gotten her leg in there somehow—surely there was a way to get it out.

In the meantime, Dakota made quiet chirrups of pain that wrenched my heart. Morris hummed the *Jeopardy!* game show theme that indicated your time was almost up and you'd better hurry to write your final answer or you'd lose.

"Eh," I said, a clipped, nasally exclamation indicating he should shut the hell up, which he did, saying, "Uh," to indicate his displeasure at being muzzled when he was only trying to help.

In the ensuing silence, I could hear my heartbeat. It sounded like a rhumba, a bit all over the place, but I refused to be distracted by it.

I finished calculating a plan of action. If I was correct, I'd identified two sticks I could move at the same time, which would have a cascading effect on the rest of the sticks, giving her an opening to pull herself free.

"Be ready," I said. Though she couldn't understand me, I hoped she would get my drift.

She squawked, which could have meant *Gotcha*, but could also have meant *Huh?*

I was nervous. If I failed, not only would it cripple Dakota, but it would draw Lancelot's ire. He treated us like his very own chicks, but I figured he would tear us to shreds if we hurt Dakota.

She gave a long, pained squawk. I had to do something. And do it now. The pressure on her leg was too much.

I moved the two sticks I'd identified. Other sticks shifted in response. A gap opened up around her leg. She yanked her leg out and clambered to the opposite side of the nest as fast as her harpy eagle talons could get her there, a mere a fraction of a second.

While she chirped at me—in thanks, I would imagine—Morris and I patched up the hole so she wouldn't get stuck again.

• • • •

A WEEK WENT BY. WE'D finally gathered and cached enough sticks and sap globules to build the ladder. Lancelot took off for his usual feeding run.

Our plan was to build the ladder during the next few hours and be gone by the time he returned. We had just gotten started when he paid us a surprise visit. With lightning speed he snatched our sticks and began tossing them away. I grabbed on to one, trying to stop him, but he beak-butted me into the bottom of the nest.

A loud cry tore through the jungle, making Morris scramble to join me. A second harpy eagle landed on the nest edge. It was twice the size of Lancelot. Morris and I clutched each other, panting, staring at the huge, red-eyed creature.

"The female," whispered Morris. "I name you Cordelia!"

Cordelia squawk-shrieked at us.

Morris looked joyful, like a sight-impaired toddler who gets special glasses and sees his mother for the first time. "I understand her! She's telling us hello and sorry she couldn't meet us sooner!"

His sudden comprehension of harpy eagle language made sense to me, honestly. He also spoke German and French, each of which he'd picked up in a ridiculously short time. Plus, he was good with words, which was why he was such a great poet. All he'd needed was enough exposure to harpy eagle language for comprehension to sink in.

I grabbed him by the lapels. "Ask her where the humans are!"

He looked down at his plaid shirt with its faux-leather lapel lining, crumpled in my grip, then back at me, implying that he would do no such thing until I treated him more respectfully.

I let him loose. "Come on. We can find Lilly! And your ancestors! And famous dead people you've wanted to meet. Just do it."

After pointedly adjusting his collar, he had an exchange with Cordelia that sounded something like, "*Squawk squawk? Reeeech arrrk.*"

"*Squawk shriek chik chik. Eeeek squawk rrrrrach eeech.*"

I nudged him. "What's she saying?"

"That she's never seen a human here, much less a woman with blue hair, but there are humans on the big plateau. That way." He pointed west.

The nest was too uneven for a celebratory dance. Instead I pumped my elbow. "Yes! How far?"

"Two days as the harpy eagle flies."

I scrunched my brow. It would take a lot longer than that to walk through a jungle, especially since the undergrowth was so thick, and there was no telling what additional obstacles lay below. "Ask her to carry us there."

"Are you kidding me? It was dangerous enough getting flown here."

"There could be rivers and ravines and wild animals between here and there. And poisonous things that bite. And plants with spikes that stick in your skin and make you itch, and—"

He knew me well enough to know I wasn't going to give up on this one. He threw his hands up. "Stop. I'll ask."

They had another exchange, a fairly long one. From Morris's finger fidgeting I knew it wasn't going well. Finally he turned to me and said, "They think we're birds. Cordelia didn't understand me when I tried to tell them we're human. She says there's no way she'd take us there, it's a bad place, and that we all have to promise to never go."

"You didn't promise, did you?"

"I said we'd never go to a bad place."

Dakota squawked adamantly.

Morris translated. "She said she'll never, ever go there."

The harpy eagles also explained something that I'd wondered about. The eggs that we'd seen when we arrived had been eaten by predators on Earth, and so they'd never had a chance to hatch. In the afterlife, chicks emerged and needed to be taken care of. Lancelot had seen us among the nests, assumed we had hatched there, and took us in because we were the right size, even though we looked a little strange.

Morris wasn't able to convince them to help us, so I stepped in with my business negotiation skills. He translated for me, but the harpy eagles got impatient with the cumbersome back-and-forth and said it was time for us young birds to be quiet.

That meant I needed to learn harpy eagle language well enough to talk to them directly. I hadn't been great with languages before, but I was motivated and could already pick out meaning here and there. I was going to learn, and I would do it fast.

• • • •

TWO DAYS PASSED. IT was morning, so Lancelot and Cordelia would be leaving soon. Morris and I had both learned harpy eagle language faster than we might have in life (just as we were stronger than in life), but I was still far behind him and still fleshing out my argument to convince the birds to carry us to the humans.

While talking with Dakota, we had learned how lonely she'd been before we arrived. Being an only bird was difficult. When she left the nest she would miss snuggling with us. She hoped that we would all be close as adults, and ride thermals together.

She too believed we were birds and couldn't be persuaded otherwise. "You shouldn't talk down about yourself," she admonished when Morris insisted we were humans. "Your feathers will grow in. You're just late bloomers."

Now, instead of flying off to find food, Lancelot bobbed his head in a manner that indicated resolve, authority, or an itch that was hard

to scratch. "It's getting really crowded around here. Time for you all to leave the nest."

"Yes," I began in harpy language, hoping to build on that idea.

Morris slapped his hand over my mouth. "Shut up. He's talking about us flying."

I pushed him away. "Of course not. He can see our feathers haven't grown in."

"He used a verb form that implies flight. He wants us to jump out of the nest."

My heart went pit-a-pat in all the wrong ways. All the harpy eagle words I'd learned flopped in my brainpan like beached fish, and I couldn't seem to snag any of them.

Dakota climbed to the edge of the nest. She launched herself. Her wings flapped expertly, as if she'd flown all her life. She circled around, then flew away.

Lancelot and Cordelia made the harpy eagle equivalent of clearing their throats. They expected us to follow suit.

"Quick," said Morris. "Look tired and weak."

We snuggled down and made fluffing-feathers-before-sleep movements.

"Time for you to leave the nest too," said Cordelia.

My heart pit-a-patted even faster in all the wrong ways. How could I make her understand that we would fall and hurt ourselves, and maybe even die a second death? "Morris and Leo no can swoop-swoop," I managed.

Morris made a better case. "You'd be super-duper lonely without us."

"Empty nest time," squick-squawked Cordelia gently but firmly.

"How about you put us on the ground and we start from there?" asked Morris.

"No," said Cordelia. "Go fly!"

As much as I hated being force-fed raw-meat-flavored fruit, I made the *I'm hungry* noise (as best I could). Morris joined in. I hoped it would trigger their instinct to feed us and that they wouldn't make us fly on full stomachs.

It didn't work. She lifted Morris with her talons and perched him on the edge of the nest. "You don't understand," he cried, facing her and high-stepping in a way that showed pleading in harpy eagle body language. "These aren't wings."

I climbed up and reached for his ankles, but she knocked me back down into the nest.

"You'll be fine." She placed her beak on his sternum and gave a single sharp nudge. Morris's arms windmilled. His feet shuffled. The nest creaked.

"Leo!" He tilted backward, limbs flailing, then tumbled out of sight.

I felt that bone-marrow-deep chill of sudden tragedy. My best friend was falling toward doom. His wail dwindled and faded away as he dropped. I pulled my shoulders to my ears and listened for a thud, but heard nothing. We were too high up.

Lancelot and Cordelia turned their attention to me. I was next. I tried to talk them out of it, something about the Wright brothers' many failures before their plane actually flew, but my harpy eagle language wasn't up to the task, and I might have actually told them that noodles were the best defense against pleurisy.

Abandoning verbal persuasion, I scrambled out of the nest and onto a branch one tree over. They inched their way toward me, wings raised, heads bobbing.

What to do, what to do? I spotted some blobs of pitch on the tree trunk. Several ideas spooled through my desperate mind. Stick myself onto the pitch so that the harpies couldn't push me off the tree? No—they might pick me apart in their attempt to yank me from it. Put the pitch on their wings? No, I wouldn't risk hurting them.

The two harpies would reach me in a single bound. I noticed that a couple of the pitch blobs were a lighter color, which typically meant they weren't as sticky as the others. Would they have exactly the right amount of stickiness to hold me to the tree, yet allow me to climb down its trunk like a gecko on a wall? I scrambled over, grasped onto the apple-size pitch lumps, and yanked them from the tree. I placed them lower on the trunk and found that they held my weight.

Down the trunk I went.

"What the hell is he doing?" asked Lancelot.

"He's a strange one, but you know what they say. There's one in every clutch."

I ignored my hurt feelings and continued downward. Morris was down there somewhere, and I had to help him.

I'd been a terrible friend, accusing him of being responsible for landing us in bird heaven. And now he might be a broken pile of a person. Paralyzed, or dead for the second time. And it was all my fault for wanting to go hiking. What would I find when I reached the ground?

Chapter Four

S caling my way down the tree was hard work and seemed to take forever because it was so tall. I was reminded of our first climb down to the ground when we'd looked all over for Lilly without finding her. Would this be the same? Would I look for Morris and never find him?

What if another large bird had come along and taken him away, like Lancelot had done with us to begin with? He would be all alone! And so would I. I imagined myself as a bent old former furniture designer in tattered red plaid, wandering the jungle floor for eternity, mumbling about armoires and early modernism.

Had I lost my best friend forever?

I passed through the mist to where I could see the undergrowth, which hid the jungle floor. When I reached the ground, I unstuck my hands from the pitch balls, calling, "Morris! Where are you? Come out, come out, wherever you are!"

Even though I was exhausted from the climb down, I bushwhacked through the undergrowth like King Kong looking for Ann Darrow (even though I'd always found the sexual tension between giant ape and small human to be a bit far-fetched). I might have pounded on my chest a few times and roared with overgrown gorilla ferocity to rev myself up. The plants were extra thick, up to my waist. I pushed aside tall fronds and dinner-plate-size leaves, calling for him over and over.

It was with a mixture of relief and renewed alarm that I finally spotted his boot. I dropped to my knees and pulled the plants aside. I'd found him, but he was out cold. Was he dead for a second time? Had he gone to the afterlife of the afterlife?

"Morris! Morris! Talk to me." I touched his shoulder, gingerly in case something was broken.

He began moaning like a foghorn with a weak battery.

"Morris! Are you okay?"

His eyes opened. He looked confused. He started to move, then yelped with pain. "Leo, help me. I broke my leg!"

I tried to sound strong, although I knew little about first aid. *Starve a fever; feed a cold* was also unhelpful—and inaccurate, from what I'd heard. "I've got you, bro."

His grimace made him look like a fashion model trying to achieve the perfect eye scrunch for the camera.

"Let me take a look." I unzipped the removable leg section of his hiking pants and lowered it, which made him hiss with pain. His leg was swollen.

"Why do you think it's broken?" I asked.

"I feel buzzy like the other times I broke a bone."

That meant it probably was broken. I bowed my head. This was a big setback. Not something he could just power through. "You're in shock."

On the ground was a mishmash of stuff that had fallen from the trees. Large and small branches. Lengths of vine. Bird down and feathers. Raw-meat-flavored fruit (ugh). I set to work fashioning him a splint using sticks and vines.

"You'll have to go look for people heaven without me."

I harrumphed. "Not gonna happen." Leave him here injured? Of course not.

"But I can't walk. It could take weeks—months..."

No! I couldn't wait months to see Lilly. Who knew what might happen to her in the meantime? "I'll carry you," I announced, admittedly without much confidence.

"If only we had a shopping cart."

We both smiled wanly, remembering a shopping cart race we once participated in. We'd come in last because we got the one with the bad wheel (which also happened to me in the stores, every time), but we still raised a big wad of money for charity, which was the point.

I stated the obvious. "No wheels would get far in this jungle." That was when inspiration hit. "No wheels." I jumped to my feet. "No wheels! I'm going to build you no wheels!"

"I'm the one who fell. Why are you the one not making sense?"

"I'm going to build you a travois! It doesn't have wheels."

"A what?" he asked.

"A travois. You know. Two long poles in a V-shape like the kind that a horse drags. It'll have a platform seat between the poles to carry you."

"Oh. I thought you said Quebecois."

"A person from Quebec? That makes no sense. I couldn't build a person."

"It makes as much sense as building a travois. You've never done that before."

His lack of confidence in me stung, making my own confidence waver. Sure, I was a competent designer. I'd spent years trying to elevate the common stool to minimalist yet gasp-rendering heights. One of my most ambitious stools featured twenty-four-karat gold entirely covered by stainless steel, with only a single notch in one of the legs to hint at the treasure beneath. It was a nod to nonostentatious wealth. I named it the Stealthy Wealthy Stool. It hadn't really caught on, not yet, and now it was too late.

But he had a point. I had no background in vehicle design. A travois would have to be light enough for me to pull for days, yet strong enough to be dragged over plentiful undergrowth. Could I make something that durable? And for that matter, would I have the strength to drag it? Would he be able to endure the pain of whatever I built? It wasn't going to be a smooth ride.

I could only try. I fell back on the essential: Function would drive form. Anatomy would dictate architecture. Precision would produce perfection.

I found two long branches that would serve as the basis of the structure. I wove clever vine spirals into the platform on which he would sit, to represent the twists and turns of our hopes and worries, but also to serve as springs to cushion the ride. I wove an extra-large, extra-thick combined seat cushion and backrest from long fronds, stuffing it with bird down. Then I wove straps to wrap around my shoulders so I could more easily pull the contraption.

If I'd had tools and more time I could have made a pattern inlay along the poles or created visually pleasing dovetail joints, but it wasn't bad, considering.

"Wow," said Morris. "That blows my mind."

"Limited materials force creative solutions," I said, repeating one of my design mantras while I wove harpy eagle feathers together to create a triple-level overhang to keep us dry.

I helped him onto the platform seat. The springs were a touch bouncy, but they helped to keep the travois from augmenting his pain. It seemed it was going to work!

As we started off in the direction of human heaven, he cleared his throat and recited a new poem.

"If God judges on a bell curve
He must wait
till all are dead.
If God judges on a bell curve
then even the saintly
may not be good enough.
What is the mean? The standard deviation?
How many will burn?
We wait in limbo

to find out
if God judges on a bell curve."

I clapped rapidly. Even death couldn't quell my friend's creative genius.

God judging on a bell curve. The ramifications were frightening. Could it be that I was separated from Lilly for that reason? What if I'd scored lower on the test of life than Lilly, maybe even just a point or two lower, and that was all it took to be dumped into a different category, and therefore into a different heaven?

Well then, I would just have to find her and fix that problem straightaway.

• • • •

TRAVELING IN THE ABUNDANT jungle growth wasn't easy. I had to pull the travois over the thick foliage and circle around obstacles such as trees, logs, and fern boles, all the while trying to get glimpses of the sun to make sure we were still going in the right direction. Plus, when I went over a particularly bad bump, Morris would howl like a Siberian husky accompanying a piano.

I was losing hope when we arrived at a grassland and could travel relatively unimpeded for a stretch. I dragged the travois more quickly now, and Morris no longer huffed like an aerobics student at a cardio workout.

We'd been at it for several hours when I took a break, sitting cross-legged, willing my body to recuperate so I could continue on.

"Whoa, what's that?" Morris was looking up in the sky, shading his eyes.

I jerked myself to my feet, on high alert, worried that another bird or something even more exotic (Pterodactyl? Giant shepherd's crook?) might drop down from the sky and whisk us away.

But what I saw about a hundred feet above us had no wings and was no animal. It was some kind of container with rounded corners, the size of a hot air balloon basket, but without the balloon and made of metal. As it descended, I could see details: red-and-gold decorative flames that looked almost real, as if fire was bursting from its sides.

I automatically looked for telltale wires holding the vehicle up and for signs of AI image discrepancies. Just habit after years of being a skeptic of all things online. But I didn't see any, and what was more, I began to feel a certain kind of presence. There was somebody in the vehicle, although I couldn't see them yet. That person had the aura of a supreme deity. I'd never before felt the word *mere* so strongly, as in mere human, mere mortal, mere Leo.

I grasped Morris's arm with both hands. "It's God! God has arrived! Look, he's going to land. Oh my god, I have so many questions. I'm so nervous."

I prayed, *please don't let me fuck this up*. Then I realized I was praying to God, who was right there, and it was totally weird that I was thinking that to his face, which meant I was already fucking this up.

Morris clutched me back, his fingers digging into my skin. "It's Zeus!"

I was confused. How did he know that? He couldn't. "No, it's God. Why would you think it's Zeus?"

"That's a chariot."

I looked at the vehicle in this new light. The size and shape was chariot-like, but I wasn't convinced. "No horses. No wheels."

"Then what is it?" he asked defiantly.

"It's... the thing that God is riding to come visit us."

"I'm telling you, that's a chariot, so it's Zeus. If it were God he'd be riding a cloud."

Over the edge of the vehicle, I could now see tousled curly hair and bright, inquisitive eyes. He was looking at us!

I didn't wave, since it was God, who knew everything, and therefore could hear me thinking, *Hey there!* He'd know that I would like to talk to him and get a few things straightened out. But what if it wasn't God? I began to have doubts, which was extremely bad timing, because God was right there and could read my mind. But what if Morris was right that it wasn't God, but Zeus or some other powerful being?

He was hovering as if he was considering whether or not to descend and meet us. I was terrified that he would find us uninteresting and ride away. I was also terrified that he wouldn't.

Morris took the bull by the horns, calling, "Hello, up there!"

The rider began to descend once more. All kinds of appropriate and inappropriate celebratory phrases jumped into my head. *Hallelujah, saints be praised! Goodness gracious, great balls of fire! Whoop-ditty-whoop-whoop!*

The closer he got, the more chariot-like the vehicle looked, but not quite like those I recalled from real life, or sort-of-real life, in the movies *Ben Hur*, *Gladiator*, and *Troy*. It was bigger, taller, and closed on the back end, which made sense to me, since it was flying in the sky and the OSHA-equivalent here would deem it unsafe otherwise. That probably wouldn't matter to a supreme being, but that was how my brain was working, trying to make sense of things with insufficient info.

God, or whatever powerful being he was, landed gently, opened a narrow door in the chariot like that of a walk-in bathtub, and stepped out.

He was perfect. So perfect he took my breath away.

A head taller than me, he was as beautifully proportioned as Leonardo da Vinci's Vitruvian Man, with similar tousled curly hair and flawlessly sized limbs. His facial features were finely chiseled into a beauty that surpassed any human's, male or female (apologies to my wife).

He wore cowboy garb, and wore it well, I might add, embodying lone masculinity much better than the Marlboro Man ever could. He turned slightly, and like a split-flap billboard, his aspect changed into something different. He was a resplendent king boasting a golden necklace and dark violet robes. He shifted again, and now he wore a crisply modern suit in a fabric that subtly expressed intelligence of a higher order.

I couldn't help myself. In spite of the pretentiousness of the quick-change artistry, I murmured, "You're perfect."

The corners of his lips raised in knowing satisfaction. "That is because I am Longtoe, the God of Perfection."

The implications spun me like a top. Not *the* God, but *a* god. That implied a pantheon! In life, myths were myths, mere stories. Fables. Not real. But in death, my worldview—no, deathview—was upended, and my head couldn't seem to wrap itself around yet another new normal.

Morris shifted on the travois as he looked Longtoe up and down. "Wow. Just wow."

Longtoe's smile faded into an authoritative pressing of lips. "You're in the wrong afterlife."

My breath caught. We'd gotten on his bad side already, but it wasn't our fault.

"We're here accidentally," said Morris. "We're just trying to find other people."

"Accidentally." Longtoe drew out the word, as if he didn't believe him. His eyes seemed odd, like insect-filled tree sap that would ultimately harden into amber but were now pools of golden liquid.

I spoke quickly to set things straight. "When we died, we arrived in bird heaven. If you could just tell us where to find people, we'll be gone in a jiffy." I winced at my word choice. I'd never used the word *jiffy* before, but then I'd never talked with a god before.

Longtoe pointed, stretching his muscular arm, reminiscent of God reaching out to Adam in the Sistine Chapel fresco. "That way. When you get to the river, follow it upstream. That will lead you directly to the plateau that holds the Afterlife of the Humans."

"Thank you!" I did something between a bow and a curtsy that felt wrong, so I put my palms together in gratitude.

"You've got a problem," he said. "It'll take you three days to get there, but the leafcutter ants will pass through here in two days, exactly at noon. All the leafcutter ants that have ever lived and died will be traveling along the jungle floor. Around twelve million years' worth of ants. That's a lot of ants."

"Leafcutter ants don't attack people unless they're threatened," ventured Morris.

"These ones will. They can't not cut." We must have looked confused because he added, "In other words, cutting is second nature to them. You'll be sliced to pieces, and those pieces will be carried far, far away." His tone was jaunty, making him seem oddly pleased to give us this bad news.

"So we should climb into the trees," said Morris.

"That wouldn't help. They'll come after you because you don't belong here. You won't escape them."

Morris grunted as if he'd just caught a cannonball in the chest.

I did too, as if that same cannonball had ricocheted onto me. I'd never seen a leafcutter ant, but since it was known for cutting things, I thought of garden shears. Many of them. Coming to cut me. *Snip snip*.

"Will you take us to the plateau?" I blurted. I'm not sure how I got the words out. Perhaps I was channeling my wife's moxie.

He raised one eyebrow and then the other, as if considering my request.

"And there's one more thing," I blurted while I still had moxie. "We're looking for my wife, Lilly. Lilly Cooper. She died with us, but she wasn't with us when we arrived here. Can you help us find her?"

Longtoe became very still, and I felt a chill in the air. Had I asked for too much? Maybe—unlike a genie in a bottle—you were supposed to ask a god for only one thing at a time.

"Lilly Cooper," he repeated. His eyes took on the squint of a card player who's just realized he's been cheated.

"My wife," I confirmed hesitantly.

"Lilly Cooper, dog trainer, influencer, and consultant?"

Ah. He knew of her. Had he seen her on social media? Did they have that here?

He rubbed his perfectly angled chin. "So then you are Leo Cooper?"

He didn't sound happy to discover who I was. In fact, he sounded so *not* happy that I felt like denying it and running away, but instead I nodded in a very small way in case I needed to gaslight my response away later.

He fished in his inner suit pocket, pulled something out, and threw it at us. I blinked, and suddenly we were enclosed in a golden net.

It was so pretty and sparkly, it seemed like it should have been a good thing, but we were contained, locked up. It surrounded me, Morris, and the travois and was somehow under our feet as well.

I clutched onto the net, but pulled my hand away immediately when he boomed, "Do not try to escape."

He gazed at me for a few moments as if I were a filthy, no-good, rotten something or other, and then he touched the net very purposefully with his index finger. Whatever he did made it glow red, and the fire where it touched me lightning-bolted from my skin to my insides. For the first time I knew exactly where each organ was positioned in my body, even the ones I considered more obscure, because each one was burning. I screamed and moaned and peddled my feet in place. Morris yowled and writhed and peddled the foot of his uninjured leg in place.

When the burning finally subsided, we puffed hard, trying to recover. When I could speak, I asked submissively, "Did I say something wrong?"

"If I ever see you again, I will ensure that you suffer unimaginable torment."

Unimaginable torment? I'd thought what we'd just experienced was bad, but apparently he had worse.

He flew off in his chariot with no further explanation, leaving us twitching.

Chapter Five

"**I**s he gone?" Morris kept angling his torso, trying to see the whole sky. "I think he's gone. He might be gone. I hope he's gone."

I craned my neck but didn't see Longtoe anywhere. My voice warbled, and I clutched myself like somebody emerging from warm water into cold air. "I don't get it. He was okay, and then he was really, really, really not okay. I made him mad, but I don't know what I did."

"He was fine until he learned who you were."

I hugged myself even more tightly. "He hates me. Why does he hate me? What did I ever do to him? I've never seen him before."

We kept looking into the blue depths of the sky, fearing he'd return and roast our innards some more. I tried to get hold of myself. A god hated me. So what? Not everybody has to like me.

"So. We only have two days to get to the plateau," said Morris.

"Let's get a move on." I pulled on the net, gingerly at first in case the motion would set it off again, but it didn't, so I pulled harder, then in different directions. Morris joined me, but to no avail. Nothing we did could get us free of it. I examined it more closely. I'd never seen anything like it. It looked as if it were woven of individual strands of metal, but it had the give of a braided silk rope.

We were quiet for a while, hoping for inspiration. I massaged my head to corral my ping-ponging thoughts.

Morris looked at his fingernails, then said, "I've got a hangnail." He had the frightened look of somebody who's choking, then began laughing giddily. I feared this had all been too much for him and his elevator no longer reached the top floor.

"A hangnail!" he repeated, as excited as if he'd won the lottery. "You've got hangnail clippers!"

It was true. They were on the lucky four-leaf clover keychain I'd almost thrown away. They were like fingernail clippers except in miniature form—about as long as an upholstery tack. Now I understood his enthusiasm, but I didn't share it. I tried to let him down gently. "They're too small to cut this net."

"Give them to me. I'm going to try!"

I handed them over, and he went to work. I expected to hear him grunt with exasperation, but after a few minutes he said, "It's working!"

"Are you kidding me?"

He showed me a hair-wide filament he'd clipped. We'd have to cut a hundred individual filaments to sever one strand of the golden net. And that would widen the one-inch opening to two inches. We'd need to do much more than that to actually get free. How much more?

I'd been through quite a lot in recent days, so I decided to forgo the hard math and estimate that we would get free "eventually," as long as the clippers didn't get blunt. That wasn't good enough, but I had no other ideas.

"Let me know when you want me to take a shift."

· · · ·

THREE HOURS LATER, our fingertips were sore from using the tiny clippers, but we were free. It had taken less time than I'd thought because the more we cut, the more the net seemed to lose its mojo. Its gold faded to beige and it became brittle, then splintered into fragments.

I pulled Morris and the travois across the rest of the clearing and back into the jungle.

Soon I was stumbling with fatigue (all that pain had sucked away my energy), so Morris talked with me to keep me going. "Remember when you were ready to give up furniture design, but Lilly wouldn't let you?"

"Yep," I grunted.

I'd worked at Looky Lou Furniture for five years when it was bought by another company and I was let go for being redundant. The new owner said I was no longer needed because they already had stool designers. They wouldn't listen to me when I explained that I could design a whole range of furniture and had been underutilized thus far.

At first I'd thought it was just as well—I'd find a better job at another company. I diligently updated my website portfolio and attended industry meetings to network with employers, but after half a year there were no bites. I was ready to give it all up.

Lilly gave me the pep talk that restored my initiative. We were drinking coffee at the kitchen counter, sitting on art deco stools I'd designed—brass with green pleather cushions.

"I'm worried about money," I said. "Maybe I should try another line of work."

She'd spoken lightly, as if the next step was obvious. "Start your own design business. Go luxury. Go big."

"I don't know. I don't run in those circles."

She rolled her eyes in that beautiful way she had where her irises traced the exact shape of a rainbow. In her most *duh* voice, she said, "Then I guess you'd better start."

"Well, there is a trade show coming up..."

"Take your stools, especially that steampunk one with all the gears and pipes."

"But I'm trying to get away from stool design!"

"Listen to Lilly. Bring the stools. People will pay attention."

As it turned out, they did. I got clients who wanted more than just stools, and my business was off and running.

Now I puffed out a response to Morris. "She told me my designs would change the world."

"They still can," said Morris.

Sure, I thought. *I just won't be there to see it.*

"You were good for Lilly too. You invented that dog hammock."

It was a good memory of a great challenge. The trick was to design it so Smiley, a three-legged French bulldog with a misaligned jaw, could get in and out of the hammock without falling. I'd used a mechanical gismo that kept it stable until it sensed the full weight of the dog in the exact center of the hammock.

Each time Smiley got into it, she made a *woof* of doggy happiness and her little misaligned jaw shifted back and forth. It made me want to jump with joy. A video of Smiley and Lilly went viral, and many people hired her to work with their dogs or tout their product.

I was proud, but the memory was sullied by regret. I should have won an award for that hammock design. Instead it went to somebody who designed a stress-minimizing cage for animal shelters. Which was commendable, I won't argue about that, but a cage isn't furniture and so shouldn't even have been considered for the award in the first place.

What it told me was that I needed to do even better. Design furniture so incredible it would sweep the awards and be celebrated even beyond the trade journals. When I was alive I'd hoped to do that, although at times I questioned whether I had enough talent.

I would never find out. My life on Earth was done, however hard it was to accept.

After a half hour, we arrived at the river that would lead us to the plateau. I took a quick drink from its frothing white water and carried some to Morris in a large leaf.

When I picked up the travois once more, something broke; Morris slipped sideways, giving a cry of pain. I helped him the rest of the way off the travois, then inspected it. A piece of vine had broken and needed to be replaced. I'd just finished when night fell and I could no longer see my hand in front of my face.

"Tomorrow we'll have one day to make a two-day journey," I said.

"Rest up," said Morris. "You're going to need every speck of energy you can muster."

Chapter Six

The river was noisy as all get out, so to fall asleep I pretended I was still alive, in my first apartment, which I'd shared with Morris. We couldn't afford a decent place, so we rented one right next to Interstate 5. Back then to fall asleep I pretended the freeway noise was from a river, and now I pretended the river noise was from a freeway. Go figure.

In the morning Morris seemed to be handling his pain better, and I started off once more with high spirits, but after an hour the jungle became too dense. I checked the riverbank for a way past, but mangrove-type trees with wildly splayed roots made it impassable, and the river itself had dangerous rapids with rocks like shark teeth.

We were at a total loss. How would we continue onward? I stared at the trees, willing them to part like the Red Sea, but I was no Moses, and trees are notoriously hard to move telepathically. However, my intense scrutiny allowed me to see something I otherwise would have missed: a face. A comically wide face with sensitive eyes and a winsome smile.

A sloth! Even just briefly looking into its eyes, I felt heartened, seeming to connect with the animal. We were two beings lost in a sea of trees, searching for the meaning of life and death. *I name you Darby*, I said, but not out loud. Unlike Morris, I'd never felt comfortable uttering random thoughts for all to hear. I had visions of me, Morris, and my sloth companion traveling among the trees—slowly, of course—as fast friends.

But my connection was either imagined or short-lived. It was Morris, once again, who was able to speak to him by learning sloth language.

Thankfully it took two hours rather than days. Morris managed to learn enough to convey our plight, and that we had to reach the plateau before the leafcutter ants came.

Darby (who was an adult male, it turned out), said that the sloths wouldn't show us how to get through their part of the jungle. They'd had trouble before from animals who messed the place up. Because sloths were so slow, by the time they got it clean, other animals would come through and mess it up again.

In fact, Darby only appeared to be serene and content. He and his compatriots were depressed about their sluggishness. For one thing, it was a constant source of embarrassment. Other creatures used the word *slothful* as derogatory, which pained them, but it was more than that. Sloths had the souls of extreme athletes. They especially envied birds and their ability to fly.

Not only that, but in the afterlife, they weren't supersized like the birds, so they were not only slow, but small. Even so, it was the sluggishness that bothered them the most.

I saw this as an opportunity. If we could somehow solve their problem, maybe they would show us a way through the jungle. But I had to think quickly, or we might never get to Lilly.

Lilly. If only she were here. She was so good with animals, she would have been able to convince them to guide us through. You have to be good to get a bulldog to do skateboard tricks.

Skateboards. Skateboards were fast. What if I built skateboards, which would make the sloths fast? I was on the right track, and skateboards were a good start, but they could only be used on paths or in clearings, not in the dense jungle. What could I build for them in addition to that? And how could I build it without tools?

I was getting ahead of myself. First we needed an agreement with the sloths. "Ask him if they'll guide us through if we help them to be faster."

Morris did so. "He's going to check with the others and get their approval. He'll probably be a while."

Darby left. We needed to be ready to go when he got back, so I set my mind on the problem. All I could think of was to change their metabolic processes to speed up their movement, and I had no way of doing that.

Morris came up with the answer. Well, not the actual answer, but a way to get to it. He pointed to a narrow waterfall at the edge of the river. Amid a bevy of rainbows, it poured down into a shallow pool. "Didn't you say that you always get your best ideas in the shower?"

It was true. There was something transformational about that sudden heat, that abrupt wetness, that transition from filthy to frothy. It often led to inspiration. However, I had my best bursts of creativity in medium-hot showers using a grade-three loofah and lilac-cucumber-aloe body wash, with the showerhead at a forty-one-degree angle. This was... well, not that.

I waded to it, unconvinced. Concerned that I was wasting time.

I needn't have worried. The moment I stepped under the waterfall, it poured onto my head in a nonstop noogie, and inspiration struck.

It's hard to describe what that's like for me, but I'll try. It's like the Grinch who stole Christmas, whose tiny heart expands several sizes, except it's my brain growing rather than my heart. Once my brain feels supersized, inspiration spills in, like a torrent of Captain Crunch cereal in 2 percent milk—please hold judgment on that, because while it sounds ridiculous, it's an apt analogy. The chunks are like creative nutrient, around which my neurons seem to coalesce, until everything binds together into one goopy mass of an idea.

The answer came to me as a combination of solutions. To un-sloth the sloths, I needed zip lines, skateboards, trampolines, and slingshots.

An hour later, Darby returned. The sloths agreed that if we came up with a solution, we had a deal, and they would guide us through the jungle. I described the items that we would need, and he took me (too slowly!) to various vines known for their strength and flexibility, to a type of tree whose sap resembled rubber, and to some fallen trees whose wood pieces were already the right size and shape for our purposes.

For the next hour, Morris and I fashioned prototypes for the sloths to replicate on their own. It wasn't easy without standard tools, but we did the best we could.

The sloths were satisfied, so Darby led us to a path that paralleled the river and would take us to the plateau where the humans were.

"Goodbye," said Darby. "Come back and see us soon."

"You might never see us again," I called to him, already pulling the travois away. "The leafcutter ants are on the way, and we only have until noon tomorrow to get to the plateau."

"You can make it if you travel all night," said Darby.

"But we can't see a thing."

"We'll help. We can see in the dark, and our sense of smell is awesome. We'll keep you on track." As it turned out, many sloths had homes in the trees along the way. Darby told the nearest sloths, and the word spread from family to family. *Help the humans travel in the dark.*

I hurried on. When night hit, I kept going. When it looked like I was in trouble, the sloths would shout in unison (so we could hear them over the sound of the river), "Veer left" or "Veer right" or "Careful, tree root ahead."

Morris kept up a chatter to keep me awake. "You know, there's something I still don't understand."

"What's that?"

"There was no snow on the slopes above us. How did it fall on us? I don't get it."

"Me neither," I said.

"And why does Longtoe hate you? You'd never met him before. Unless he was in disguise."

"No. I would know. You can't disguise perfection. Let's talk about something else."

We talked about more pleasant things for a while, then he fell asleep.

Think about something good, I told myself. I thought about my home workshop, a light-filled, tool-aplenty space that smelled like high-quality aftershave because of the various woods. Lilly often visited me there, and she smelled like roses (not like lilies) and sleepy dogs (not like wet dogs). I would never see the workshop again, but I hoped to set up a new workshop in the Afterlife of the Humans. We only had to get there.

When the sun rose I was still pulling Morris along the path. I don't know how I kept going, but I did, for another couple of hours, until we emerged abruptly from the jungle into an enormous open space.

The ground was clear except for some stands of tall bushes here and there. A hundred feet away, a cliff loomed. A family of sloths confirmed that the plateau we were looking for was at its top.

"We made it!" I shouted, but then I slumped. It's hard to slump while you're looking up, but I managed to do so when I saw our new challenge.

"Wow," said Morris despondently. "That's at least as high as the Burj Khalifa."

Which I'd heard was half a mile high. This cliff was every bit of that, maybe more. I had expected a steep grade and a bit of a climb, possibly as rugged as the hike we'd been on when we died. But this, this! I might as well try to climb to the moon.

Judging from the height of the sun, we had only a couple of hours until midday and the arrival of the ants, with no way to escape them.

Words bounced around in my brainpan. *Overpowering obstruction. Permanent setback.* Also, *Fail better*, a saying I'd never understood and which didn't help me now.

While I pulled him toward the base of the cliff, Morris asked miserably, "How are you at elevator design?"

I was too upset to appreciate his dark humor. All I could do was grunt my inadequacy.

In addition to being tall, the cliff was so wide that both ends disappeared in the distance miles away.

"We can't climb it," said Morris. "This is the end of the road."

If I believed him, then I would sink into a depression so deep I would never emerge from it. And get sliced up by ants. I had to think that we could overcome this obstacle.

I forced a cheerfulness I didn't feel. "Can't climb it? Just try and stop me!"

When we reached the base of the cliff, I listened in case I could hear people way up there. I knew it was too much to expect, but I also knew that things worked differently in the afterlife, so it was worth trying, but the top was much too far away. All I could hear was the breeze rustling the leaves around us.

But... we'd left the trees back there, and there was no wind in the nearby bushes. I got a sick feeling when I realized what the sound was. Looking off in the distance, along the treeless corridor next to the cliff, I spotted a thin brownish-red line on the horizon. My voice went hoarse. "The leafcutter ants. I think I see them."

Morris pushed himself onto his elbow and gazed at the horizon, then fell back. "We're done for."

"Maybe not. You can learn their language and tell them to back off."

He just grunted. We both knew there wouldn't be enough time. It had taken him two hours to learn sloth, and the ants would start slicing us the moment they got to us.

I held a stick up to the cliff face and began hammering it with a rock, hoping to make spikes that I could climb. I didn't think I was capable of carrying Morris that high, but I would try.

The dirt crumbled like cinnamon streusel. Grunting angrily, I threw the rock and stick down.

"Mmm." Morris seemed distracted. He poked his leg several times, the way you'd test rising bread dough to see if it was ready to bake. "Something's... different." Still wearing the splint, he pulled himself up to standing on his good leg.

"Stop!" I rushed to prop him up. "You'll hurt yourself."

He waved me away, not letting me support him. Then, arms out like a tightrope walker, he put his full weight on the broken leg. He looked at me with such joy that I cringed, because I knew in a moment or two the pain would hit and he would crumple to the ground. The broken bone would splinter and take even longer to heal. Maybe that wouldn't matter since the ants were going to get us, but still.

He limped in a circle like a peg-leg pirate. I followed behind, ready to catch him, sucking air through my teeth and wincing with every step he took.

He removed the splint and began to walk normally. I was still following right behind. How was he doing this? His leg was broken!

"I'm healed!" He did a leprechaun leap, heels together.

My jaw fell like the drop leaf of a dining room table. Not that long ago he'd been in serious pain. He had definitely done significant damage to his leg, yet now he seemed fine. I knelt at his feet, unzipped the removable leg section of his hiking pants, and checked his leg. The swelling was gone. I palpated his leg from ankle to knee. It seemed normal.

My probing didn't hurt him in the least. He shrugged. "I guess you heal faster in the afterlife."

Once it sunk in that he was fully mended, I realized that we were unhampered, so if we could just come up with a brilliant idea to get onto the plateau, we could execute it much more easily. I found some optimism. It had been squashed by our crisis, but now it plumped into shape.

I glanced at the sun. I estimated we had an hour and forty-five minutes until noon.

"All right." I circled my hands in a TED Talk opening gesture, one that implied that anything was achievable if we believed in ourselves to the fullest extent possible. "Brainstorming session. No idea is a bad one. I'll go first. Giant trampoline."

Morris's eyes went wide with enthusiasm, then his face fell. "That's a long way to fall if the bounce is too short."

"We can't really build one that'll get us a half a mile high. I'm just warming us up so the ideas will flow. Don't be discouraged already. Your turn. What have you got?"

"Ask the harpy eagles to fly us up."

Another impossible solution. We'd already tried that, plus they were too far away now. I countered with, "Jet pack."

Morris clutched his buttocks with his hands as if to protect them. "Been there, done that."

When we were teenagers, we made our own jet pack Halloween costumes. We had attachments that spit out sparks, and they caught our pants on fire. We each had small but painful burns. I probably shouldn't have brought it up, but I was trying not to censor myself.

"Escalator," blurted Morris.

We went on like this for a while without coming up with anything actionable, then fizzled out.

"We're running out of time," I said. "Let's walk along the base of the cliff. See what we can see."

"Hello!" said a husky yet feminine voice. "Do I hear people?"

Chapter Seven

T he voice startled me. I jumped.

Morris grabbed my arm, which made me jump again. Then he sprang up and down, pumping my arm like the cast-iron pump at a horse water trough. "Oh my god," he said. "Oh my god oh my god. It's a person!"

I loosened myself from his grip and spun around. "Hello? Over here!"

A woman burst out from behind some bushes. She was skinny, perhaps forty years old, with pointy facial features and spriggy hair. She wore cutoff jeans, black combat boots, and a black-and-white-striped referee jersey. She was a bit twitchy; her shoulder jerked, then the corner of her mouth. She reminded me of a roller derby skater I once knew whose elbows were her secret weapon.

She laughed somewhat hysterically. "Hello! I'm Ismenia. It's good to see you. I haven't seen any people for a long time."

"I'm Leo, and that's Morris," I gushed. "We're happy to see you too! But we don't have a lot of time." I pointed at the brownish-red line on the horizon. "Those are leafcutter ants. If we don't climb this cliff, we'll be snipped to pieces. How do we get up there?"

She looked at the ants, swore under her breath, then shook her head. "I've tried to climb up—to get a view of the territory—but I couldn't do it." She glanced around. "Is there anybody else with you?"

"Well—there should have been," I answered. "My wife, Lilly, died when we did, but we don't know where she is."

"You got here together, but then you lost her?"

"No, we didn't get here together," I said.

Her arm twitched, then her mouth. She looked pained. I appreciated her empathy.

54

Morris pointed upward. "We think she's up there."

She stopped twitching. "Really? How do you know?"

"The harpy eagles and the God of Perfection told us that's where the humans are."

"Wait, back up. You talked to eagles? And a god?" She seemed surprised, or perhaps doubtful.

"Come on," I said. "I'll tell you about it on the way. We're going over there to see if there's a way to get up."

She shook her head. "I've checked it out. There's a deep ravine. Can't go that way."

Disappointment pressed down on me like the weighted blanket Lilly got me for my birthday. What would we do now?

Morris's eyebrows knit together. Ismenia put her hand on his shoulder to comfort him. Why did he get comfort, while I was left to mourn on my own? Did she like him better than me?

I mentally kicked myself for putting thought energy into something so unimportant.

She began twitching again and rubbed her arms as if she had a chill. I'd guessed that she'd had a hard life, but it could have been that she'd had a hard death. Maybe that was why she was a bit odd. A few dirt stains marred the white stripes of her referee shirt. She'd been alone for who knew how long. At least I'd had Morris.

I noticed her eyes. So colorful. Not blue, but azure. Not green, but lime. Plus bits of toffee and onyx...

She caught me staring into them, but it was hard to look away. I feared she thought I desired her. *Don't worry, you're not my type*, I longed to say, but that was an insult, of sorts, and not completely true. I was drawn to her, but couldn't identify in what way. Not sexually, so what was it?

To cover my confusion, and to see whether she had any skills that could help us, I blurted, "Tell us about yourself."

She shrugged. Or was that a twitch? "Not much to say, really."

This concerned me, because it felt like she was hiding something. The more I considered her skinniness and her angular, hard-living appearance, the more I felt that she had the air of a small-time thief. But even if that were true—and I had no evidence it was—I had nothing she could steal. Plus there was also something fresh and enthusiastic about her that contradicted that impression.

"I'm a furniture designer, and Morris is a teacher," I offered. "What about you? What did you used to do? Anything that might help us out here?"

She was quiet, as if not sure what to tell us, then she seemed to find the right words. "I'm an artist."

At first I was disappointed. She wouldn't be able to watercolor us out of this predicament. But then again, a sculptor might have ideas for us. "What's your medium?"

"Everything." She chortled; the noise was a cross between a chicken and a hyena, yet not unpleasant. She plucked a six-foot-long, black-and-white-striped harpy feather from the travois overhang and held it up to her outstretched arm.

I figured she had clothing in mind, but the sight put an idea in my head. Bird wings! But could it really work? Sticks. Feathers. Pitch. We could get all those components from the travois. "Wings," I shouted. "We could make wings! Then we could fly to the top of the cliff and get to the Afterlife of the Humans!"

I felt like an inflatable holiday angel that had been confined in a storage box all year, then brought out and filled with fresh, glorious air. *Hallelujah!* I looked at the cliff above and imagined myself rising upward, upward, upward, bringing me closer to my true love.

"Brilliant!" She laughed, a strange chortle that became a guffaw that trailed off into a sigh.

I launched myself at the travois and began dismantling it to get sticks for the wings. Ismenia pulled the overhang off the travois and began unweaving feathers.

Morris sounded appalled. "You think you can fly? That's ridiculous!"

"It's a great idea! We're so much stronger in the afterlife, especially our arms. We'll be able to flap and hold ourselves aloft."

"We're too big. It won't work."

I huffed my dissent. "Harpy eagles are way bigger than we are, and they do it."

"They have hollow bones."

"It's worth trying."

"Nothing you can build will stand up to the strain."

I was floored. That hurt.

I already had self-doubt. In fact, I'd just been telling myself, *Bro, you're not an aeronautic specialist.* His skepticism made me want to prove myself, both to him and to me. "Look at the travois. It held up when I dragged you all over."

"It broke!"

"Just a little!" I had to get him to understand how different these two things were. Now that this idea had come, I felt like we were inches away from the Afterlife of the Humans rather than half a mile. "It broke because the ground was bumpy. The air isn't bumpy." I held out my arms to illustrate a glide, making wispy *shoop* noises to emphasize its softness.

"When wings break, you can't fix them midair. And then you'll fall and bust every bone in your body." He pressed my arms back down to my sides.

To be honest, I knew he had a point, but because he wouldn't give in a smidgen, I wouldn't either. With a petulant flourish, I held a feather aloft. "Not if we build the wings correctly."

"Don't you know the story of Icarus?"

I made a noise of exasperation. Must he always invoke literature? It contained so much truth, but not *necessarily* every time!

"Ah, Icarus," said Ismenia, still unweaving feathers from the overhang. "He flew too close to the sun, and the wax he built his wings with melted. And he fell and et cetera and so on. But that's just a myth. Leo, you're a professional. I bet you could design wings better than anybody!"

I felt myself standing taller. Yes, I certainly could. "And we're not going to fly close to the sun, which is, I don't know, a gazillion miles away."

Morris gestured *no*, palms down. "I don't want to fall and go through all that pain again. I don't want you or Ismenia to go through it either."

The leafcutter ant noise was getting louder. They sounded like a team of gardeners clipping box hedges.

"We've got no other choice. We'll build one set of wings. If they don't work, we can at least rule that out. Maybe we'll come up with an even better idea while we're working."

He looked at the line of ants and ran his hands through his hair.

It looked like he might be wavering, but just a little, and we didn't have time for any more back-and-forth. I laid a long stick on the ground. "I'm going to make wings, and you're the bird expert, so tell me, is this stick the right length?"

"You can't just use one stick per wing. You need at least an ulna and radius so you can bend the wing inwards during the upstroke and extend it during the downstroke."

I positioned two sticks end to end, then placed a mock-up row of feathers. "How would this be?"

He made a noise of exasperation. "You need more than just primary feathers. Shorter ones go here as secondaries. And then you need primary, secondary, and upper wing coverts. Here, here, and here."

Ismenia unwove more feathers from the overhang. Once we had the basic layout, I attached short sections of vine to the sticks to create a flexible elbow. Morris and I glued the feathers on using pitch. I might not have gotten his buy-in yet, but I was getting his help, which was a good start.

While we worked, Morris groused, "I shouldn't be dead. Who's going to watch *Masterpiece Theatre* with Mom and Dad now that I'm gone? I miss them."

Ismenia unwove vines from the travois so we could make loops for my arms and grips for my hands.

"I miss my dog." Sorrow shaped her mouth into a perfect upside-down half circle.

"What's your doggy's name?" I asked softly.

Ismenia paused, as if we would think it silly. "His name is Chaos."

I chuckled lightly. "So when you called him, the neighbors thought you were crazy. 'Chaos! Come, Chaos!' That's funny. What kind of dog?"

"Big." Her smile was sly.

No specifics—a mutt then? We'd learned something about her: She was a dog lover, perhaps a dog rescuer. That seemed like a positive.

"You said something about harpy eagles and a god," said Ismenia.

I summarized our time since we died, telling her about the harpy eagles, our encounter with Longtoe, and the help from the sloths.

When I finished my recap, we worked some more in silence, attaching the two wings together with a yoke made of vine.

Morris shook his head. "I can't believe you want to fly up there. Look how high it is."

Ismenia eyed the cliff. "It is pretty high up." She seemed to be having second thoughts, but I knew this was doable. The only thing between me and the top of that cliff was air. We didn't have to move mountains, we only had to get on top of one.

We finished. The long black feathers gave the wings an urban chic feel.

"You designed a masterpiece," said Ismenia.

This thrilled my heart. I craved her approval, although I wasn't sure why. I guess I was worried she would think Morris would make a better friend than I would. I mentally slapped myself on the wrist. Such thoughts were unhelpful.

The brownish-red line on the horizon was thicker now. The ants were getting closer and louder. I shrugged the yoke onto my shoulders, and they helped me tie it on, crisscrossing vines across my torso to secure it. I slipped my arms into the wing loops and clutched the hand grips.

"Careful careful careful," intoned Morris. He and Ismenia jumped out of the way. I took a running start, gave a single powerful flap, then lifted from the ground, feet dangling. I was flying! The wings worked! I flapped, getting a feel for upstrokes and downstrokes and when to pull inwards or outwards.

I rose to the level of the treetops. I couldn't celebrate this achievement or the feeling of freedom it imparted, because now I had a better view of the approaching leafcutter ants. The horde was massive, as if somebody had installed brownish-red wall-to-wall carpet that butted up against the cliff, reached into the jungle, and spread off to infinity. It was one thing to know that all the leafcutter ants that had ever lived and died were headed this way. It was quite another thing to see it.

I descended so quickly that I landed like a clumsy duck. "There are so, so many ants. A tsunami of them. Except not wet. And the sun is glinting off their cutters like they're really sharp."

"Schnell, schnell," said Morris. The danger—and the success of my flight—seemed to get him the rest of the way on board. Morris and I dove into making a second pair, with Ismenia acting as an assistant, handing us the materials. I was surprised she took a subservient role, but I didn't question it since it made the work more efficient.

"That cliff is pretty high," she said again.

"Don't worry," I said. "The wings work great. It'll be easier than you think."

We finished the next set more quickly, now that we were experienced wing crafters. We strapped Morris in, and he launched himself into the air. "I'm flying!" he cried. "I can't believe it!"

He looked over at the ants, then landed quickly. "Come on. We have just enough time to make Ismenia's wings."

She folded her arms. "Good luck to you both, but I'm not going after all." She put on a brave face, but I knew by the slump of her shoulders that she was crushed.

"What's wrong?" asked Morris. "Are you afraid of heights?"

Ismenia didn't answer, which seemed to confirm it. This was a disaster. We couldn't leave her behind to be attacked by the ants. "Try looking at it this way," I said. "You don't have a fear of heights. You have a fear of falling. And since you're not going to fall, there's no problem. Right?"

"It's not that simple."

"Just don't look down," offered Morris.

Ismenia grimaced. "I thought I could get past it, but... no, I can't do it. There's no way. Unless—" She turned away. "No, I can't ask you to do that."

"I know what you were going to say," I said excitedly. "One of us carries you, and you close your eyes. I'll do it. I'll carry you."

She shook her head, backing away. "I'll open them and panic and make you fall."

"We'll blindfold you," I said.

Ismenia backed away some more. "I'll tear it off and panic and make you fall."

"We'll tie your hands," said Morris.

"Absolutely not," she said. "I have merinthophobia."

Being a word guy, Morris was able to explain that to me. "Fear of being tied up."

What a terrible life she must have lived to have developed such a phobia!

She went to the travois and patted the seat cushion and backrest I'd woven. "I'll just sit here. At least I'll be comfortable until the end."

That's it! "We'll carry you in that, in the casing," I said. "That way there's no chance of you seeing anything that would make you panic, and you won't be tied up."

Ismenia protested weakly. I grasped her gently by the shoulders and looked right into her azure-lime-toffee-onyx eyes. Their depth surprised me. They had a certain kaleidoscopic beauty; I could have gazed into them for days. I blinked hard, saying firmly, "We're not leaving you behind."

She nodded. "Thank you. You're such a beautiful human being."

My heart soared. That meant good luck, because my wife often said that to me. Soon we would all go find her—and other beautiful human beings—together!

The leafcutter ants were now only a hundred feet away, making crisp, sharp *shik-shik* sounds that echoed ominously off the cliff wall.

I dove at the cushion and scooped the insides out, sending fluff flying every which way. Morris tied it to my back, and I kneeled to let Ismenia climb in.

She was much heavier than I thought she would be. I had predicted no more than a hundred and thirty pounds, but I could swear she was at least five hundred. I chalked it up to fatigue from dragging the travois and staying awake all night, but no matter. I would push through it and fly to the top, and then I would be able to rest.

By the time we were ready, the ants were only twenty feet away, and we could see them in excruciating detail. Like the birds, they were larger than life, about the length of my hand. Their reddish-brown color seemed unnatural. They were spiky with hairs all over their bulbous bodies, down to the tips of their lanky legs. They walked with preternatural precision on stilt legs.

The curved shears that came out of their faces were sharpened to a wicked edge. I wouldn't have been surprised if they could split a human hair lengthwise. I had plenty of sharp tools in my workshop, but none screamed *threat to life and limb* like these.

My only consolation was that they were so sharp I wouldn't suffer for too long. Or would I? This was eternity, after all, wasn't it? Once I was chopped up, would I continue to experience pain? Would my separate parts suffer separately? I had a sudden image of the leafcutter ants carrying my ears like boat sails.

"Go, go!" shouted Morris. We took our running starts and lifted off. Then we both flapped hard.

Morris continued upward.

I didn't.

Apparently Ismenia's weight was too much. I beat my wings frantically but remained only a foot off the ground.

The ants surged underneath me, step-stepping, clip-clipping, and snip-snipping. Some of them carried pieces of leaves, but most seemed available to cut and carry bits of me. I gulped hard. If I let up even for a second, I would fall into their midst. I would be chopped skin and chopped muscles and chopped lungs and chopped heart and chopped liver.

Chopped liver, I thought. *What am I, chopped liver?* That struck me as absolutely hilarious (you had to be there). I let out a guffaw.

I'm here to tell you, it's true that laughter makes you lighter. Because suddenly, I was. So I used it as a mantra, saying over and over, *What am I, chopped liver?* For good measure, I added *I can't hear you, I've got a banana in my ear* and *Who's on first?* Chortling, I flapped vigorously and rose higher, higher, higher! Below me the tree canopy fell away, and so did the carpet of ants.

I took a quick look around to make sure Longtoe wasn't anywhere nearby. He wasn't. That allowed me to concentrate on my goal, the cliff top, which was getting closer with each flap. I was already halfway there.

I looked forward to reuniting with Lilly, and also with my dead relatives and friends. What wild and cheerful reunions we would have!

But Ismenia's weight began to drag on me once more; she was as heavy as a bag of bowling balls. I returned to my mantras, combining them into a single powerful silent chant. *Chopped liver, banana, who's on?*

It worked, but about two-thirds of the way up, a feather dropped from one of my wings. Then another. Then a whole clump.

It didn't make sense. It wasn't warmer so nothing was melting. Was it something to do with the altitude? Or was I channeling Icarus? Surely my design wasn't faulty. No. Certainly not.

"My wings are falling apart!" I cried.

"Mine too!" cried Morris from above. "We should have heeded the tale of Icarus."

"Keep going," called Ismenia. "Stroke, stroke, stroke, stroke." I flapped with all my strength to keep up with her chant.

Now Morris's feathers were falling down on me, and fluff was circling in air eddies. It was like we were having a pillow fight, but with a big disconnect. Pillow fights were supposed to be fun, and this was excruciatingly not fun.

I saw Morris make it over the lip of the cliff. He was safe! Maybe I could be safe too! I pumped my arms hard, making I'm-going-to-succeed grunts. It was just that Ismenia felt so heavy. How could such a small person drag me down this much when I was stronger in the afterlife? What was she made of? Lead?

Morris called, "Come on, Leo, get up here! Understand the assignment! Get with the program! Execute the mission! Produce the goods! Forward the agenda!"

His encouragement helped. With each phrase I rose higher, then higher... and then I felt ground under my feet. "I made it!"

Morris and I celebrated like football players after a touchdown, except we were so tired our victory dances were more like victory squirms.

"What do you see?" asked Ismenia from the inside of the cushion casing.

"Nothing! I've got sweat in my eyes!" I didn't want to admit I was crying.

Morris answered instead. "We're in a park with flower arbors, a tiered fountain, and stone walkways. There are buildings in the distance. White spires. Gold and silver domes."

I wiped my eyes and blinked a few times. "I see two dozen people! They're coming our way. They're wearing iron codpieces, copper armor, and Brazilian dancer sleeves."

But as they got closer, I realized my error. What I'd taken as copper armor were scales. These were not people, even though they were bipedal and at least as tall as a person.

"Correction." Morris spoke breathlessly. "They're not people-people. They're reptile-people."

"They don't look happy to see us," I added. "And they've got spears."

"Retreat!" hissed Morris, an automatic reaction.

"Impossible," I hissed back. That would mean going back over the cliff. We would have to confront these creatures, whatever they were.

Chapter Eight

I held my winged arms up, fatigued as they were, to show the creatures that I was unarmed. Morris followed my lead.

The group stopped except for one who continued toward us. The leader, apparently. He looked like an upright lizard, with bulging eyes that operated independently of each other. He was such an odd mixture of Sunday morning cartoon and horror movie, I didn't know whether to chuckle or quake in fear, although it didn't matter because I had the energy for neither.

"I name you Thumbtack," whispered Morris. "He looks like he eats thumbtacks for breakfast."

Morris never explained his naming, so I knew he was discombobulated. But then, I was too. Where were the humans?

The reptilian stopped only a foot away. He examined me with one eye and Morris with the other, then scratched the edge of his codpiece and gave us a fierce, pointy-toothed scowl. "Why are you here?" His deep and sonorous voice reminded me of a cello.

"We were in the wrong heaven," I blurted.

"What's heaven?"

Morris and I exchanged looks that said we weren't getting off to a great start. I stuttered an answer. "The opposite of hell."

"What's hell?"

"The afterlife." I rubbed my neck, which was developing a crick from looking up at this reptilian being, who was taller than I was. "We were in the wrong afterlife. Meant for birds."

"You have wings." He shooed us away with a stubby taloned paw, then pointed at us with the business end of his spear. "Return to the Afterlife of the Birds."

"No, we're people." I whipped my arms out of the wing loops and waved hard, as if flagging down an Uber driver from the wrong end

66

of the block. "We made these so we could travel, but they're falling apart. We need to be with our own kind."

"Not that there's anything wrong with your kind," added Morris quickly.

He strode closer, looking me up and down; I fought the urge to sidestep, in case doing so would trigger a latent predator attack reaction. My heart was already pounding hard from the flight, but now it began skipping beats as if messaging me in Morse code to urge me to get out of danger.

With his taloned paw, he picked up my wrist, dangled my hand, then dropped it. He felt my upper arm with his smooth scaly palm; I suppressed a sudden urge to blurt excuses as to why I'd avoided my barbells for the last few years.

I feared he was going to push me off the ledge. I was so exhausted that even if I could get my hands back in the straps during the fall, I wasn't sure I would be able to fly anymore, and besides, my wings were in tatters, with feathers continuing to drop like fall foliage. And of course there was the tsunami (not wet) of ants to finish me off after my fall.

Thumbtack gestured at the Ismenia-filled casing tied to my back. "What's in there?"

I was going to answer when she struck me hard with her elbow. "Ouch!" I said.

"Oats. Yummy." He sneered again, revealing abalone-colored teeth. No wait—that wasn't a sneer, it was a smile! "Well then, you may pass alongside the Home of the Gods on your way to find other humans. That way." He pointed to a cobblestone walkway.

I could hardly believe it. We were free to move along? But yes, the creature was standing back, gesturing like an usher. All we had to do was put one foot in front of the other.

Morris had a silly half-smiling doofus expression of relief. I probably did too. Later we would tease each other about it, and I looked forward to that.

"How far?" I asked eagerly.

Thumbtack's black tongue snaked out and cleaned one eyeball. "Two or three hours."

"Thank you," I burbled. Our journey would be hours, not days. Soon I would see Lilly!

"Are you a god?" asked Morris.

The reptilian made a clucking noise more befitting a chicken than a lizard. The others joined in. I realized they were laughing. "No. Not a god. A sentry."

"How many gods are there?" asked Morris

"Three hundred thousand and twenty-seven."

"It's three hundred thousand and twenty-six now," corrected a reptilian wearing an orange sash. The one next to him hissed and poked him. It reminded me of my mother elbowing my father to get him to shut up. So had the orange-sash sentry said something he shouldn't have? Why was there one less god, and why was that a secret?

Maybe there wasn't one less, and it didn't matter anyway. What mattered was that we were only hours away from Lilly. I reminded myself to be watchful on the journey alongside the Home of the Gods, to avoid Longtoe, God of Perfection.

The creatures began to march away.

"Three hundred thousand and twenty-six gods," said Morris. "So many they have a hard time keeping track of the number. Wow."

"Help me get this off." I tugged at the vines that secured the casing to my back. Morris reached out to help.

"Carry me a little farther," whispered Ismenia.

"I can't. I'm exhausted." We kept untying.

"Morris, you carry me," pleaded Ismenia. "I've got anxiety."

"Not possible," he said. "You'll be fine."

She continued protesting, but we set her down. She didn't get out of the casing.

While we removed our wings, I said, "Buck up. Gather your courage." I felt like I needed to add one more imperative, since they're better in threes, and what came out was: "Put on your big girl panties." I winced, because it sounded sexist, but it was already out of my mouth.

Morris picked up one end of the casing and spilled her onto the stone ground. Ismenia's wild look made me think she'd taken umbrage at my thoughtless utterance, but I realized that wasn't the case after she looked over at the reptilians and took off running. My comment wasn't *that* bad. Something else was wrong.

"She must have herpetophobia," suggested Morris. "Fear of reptiles."

"Look at her go. I've never seen anybody run that fast."

Thumbtack made a throaty noise of alarm. "Catch her!"

The other sentries scurried off in her direction. Meanwhile, Thumbtack shot over to me, grasped the back of my neck, and held me in place.

"What's wrong?" I asked.

He made a harsh squeal that I interpreted as *Shut up or die.* When the others returned without having caught Ismenia, he lifted me by the nape of my neck. I writhed as uselessly as a worm on a fishhook. The skin on my neck burned. My feet tread bare air.

"You have brought the God of Trickery back into the Home of the Gods." He spoke the words as if spitting out spoiled fish.

Suddenly I understood. Ismenia wasn't who she appeared to be. She was a renegade god who had tricked us into sneaking her here.

I'd been so stupid. She'd led me by the nose, making me think it was my idea to build wings and carry her in a cushion casing, when in reality she just didn't want to be recognized by her god peers.

We were in deep trouble.

"You've got it all wrong. That's Ismenia." Morris leapt to my aid, pushing my buttocks upward to relieve the pressure on my neck, which caused me to slip out of Thumbtack's grasp. I fell back onto the ground, and the lizard-like creature clomped a warning foot onto my stomach—if I moved, a heavy stomp would squish out my innards like mustard from a bottle.

Up to then, Morris hadn't understood the problem. But then he pressed one palm against his forehead, holding up a finger as if requesting not to be disturbed while working out a complicated math problem. Finally he asked, "Is Ismenia the three hundred thousand and twenty-seventh god?"

Thumbtack paused before speaking, seeming to struggle with how much to tell us. "Yes. Banished for unleashing Chaos among us."

My gorge rose. Ismenia's dog was named Chaos. We had unwittingly attached ourselves to a god who had let a violent dog run free to hurt others! She hadn't seemed like the cruel type, but I was no judge of divine character.

"Come with me." The reptilian's cello-like voice resonated like a dirge. Surrounding us, the sentries force-marched us along a path through a park filled with oak and willow trees, old-fashioned streetlamps, petunia-filled flowerboxes, and benches hewn from cream-colored stone. It was cooler here than in the jungle below the plateau, like spring instead of summer. It would have been a nice stroll as nonprisoners.

Ismenia had betrayed us. I kept imagining stuffing her back into the cushion casing and tossing her off the plateau. It didn't make me feel better, but gave me the energy to keep moving in spite of having been awake all night pulling the travois. Morris, however, was having a hard time keeping up, and I worried that they might hurt him. I hooked my elbow in his to give him some support. He seemed grateful for it.

I tried to keep track of our route in case we managed to escape, but there were too many twists and turns, so I abandoned that idea, instead taking the opportunity to learn more about what we'd gotten ourselves into.

"Where are we going?" I asked in a tone intended to be inquisitive rather than demanding.

However, my puffing from exertion must have sounded seductive, because Thumbtack said suggestively, "Wouldn't you like to know?"

This gave me mixed feelings, as I was never one to lead somebody on, and I didn't want to find myself in a situation with the sentry that would be hard to extract myself from. I reminded myself that I was already in a difficult-to-extract-from situation, and besides, I was probably anthropomorphizing the creature. The look he now gave me was probably disgust, not lust.

"Yes, I really would like to know where we're going."

He rolled his eyes—disconcerting because one went clockwise and the other counterclockwise—and said with satisfaction. "I am bringing you to see Longtoe, God of Perfection. We are going to his palace."

I felt a frisson of fear. It frissoned the back of my neck, then frissoned me all over. Longtoe already hated me. Now he had even more reason to do so. This was bad news, bad news indeed. Longtoe's words echoed in my head. *If I ever see you again, I will ensure that you suffer unimaginable torment.*

Why did the god hate me so much? What had I ever done to him?

Morris piped up. "Can you take us to Zeus instead?"

The sentry grimaced. "What is Zeus?"

"How about Ra?" Morris puffed once between each name. "Loki? Shiva? Athena? Freya?"

Thumbtack waved him into silence with a clawed paw. "Stop talking gibberish."

I started to ask another question, but he growled wetly. "No more talking."

• • • •

WE AWAITED LONGTOE in front of his palace. Fittingly for the God of Perfection, the structure was perfect, its porticoes inlaid with jewel mosaics in symmetrical patterns. Seven arches were supported by Doric columns. In each opening, between the columns, hung drapery.

Oh, the drapery. Its perfection was beyond perfect, requiring a nonexistent word in place of mere *fabric*. It must have been spun by magical silkworms, for it seemed ethereal, barely there, and yet the detailed embroidery was thick and vibrant.

Its images came to life! How was that possible? Unicorns and fantastical beasts trotted across the curtains, yet somehow remained embedded in the threads.

And what lay behind the perfect drapery? We couldn't see, but it had the air of a theater on opening night, the anticipation of some great enactment. Fury and spectacle, sound and action, swords and daggers. Lovers reaching for one another. Comedians with perfect timing. Slapstick, operatic arias, violins and kettle drums, soliloquies and monologues. (What was the difference between a soliloquy and a monologue? In my enraptured state, I couldn't remember.)

I longed to know what furniture the God of Perfection lounged upon, although I feared that once I saw its flawlessness I would view my own work in a different light. Shoddy, a waste of a life's work, embarrassing.

And yet, I knew without being told that I would never see for myself. Because of the moat that barred physical entry to the structure, but also because a sense of isolation infused the place, telling me that no others were allowed inside. If an imperfect being such as myself ever entered that hallowed place, it would defile it and render it imperfect.

It was all too overwhelming, so I forced myself to look away. In the other direction stood a roller coaster, a Ferris wheel, and a large entry plaza paved with pinkish stone.

Longtoe lived right next to an amusement park. It had been my childhood dream to be able to bound across the street from my home and jump on rides (as long as they didn't turn me upside down). Other children wanted ponies. I wanted to live next to an amusement park. But I never did.

Don't get me wrong. I wasn't a spoiled brat—there were plenty of things I never had as a child, including sometimes a meal or a warm coat. Still, it can be hard to meet up with someone of privilege who is living out your secret dream without wondering petulantly, *Why him? What makes him so special that he gets an amusement park and I don't?* Heat started up at the level of my duodenum and grew to a hot coal.

I didn't see Longtoe emerge from his palace, but Thumbtack's sudden stiffening alerted me. I turned and saw the god in all his perfection. Clichés reeled through my head, but they were all true. He was as handsome as the day was long, as muscular as an ox, and as smart as a whip.

The coal in my duodenum became a lump of white-hot iron. Why did he get to be the God of Perfection? Why not me? Why had I been born an ordinary human?

Longtoe's eyes kaleidoscoped brilliant scarlet, neon eggplant, and midnight purple, then settled like a Vegas slot machine coming to a stop. "You!" he cried.

Both Morris and I jerked in fright, but then straightened. *Keep a level head*, I told myself. *Try to learn from this experience.*

Longtoe glared at us as if we were specks of filth sullying the polished black paving stones on which we stood. "Wicked humans, Leo Cooper and Morris Johnson. You smuggled Ismenia, God of Trickery, into the Home of the Gods. What do you have to say for your blasphemous actions?"

"She tricked me," I said. "She said she was afraid of heights." But even as I said it, I realized she had never spoken those words, only led me to believe them. "I thought she was human."

"Nonsense," said Longtoe. "You would have known from her eyes."

My heart sank. When looking into her kaleidoscope eyes, I'd known she was special, but I'd thought it was an unexplainable afterlife phenomenon. I couldn't have known she was an immortal being. How could I convince Longtoe of this when he seemed too angry to accept it?

"I swear we didn't know." I sounded a lot like a toddler denying scribbling on the bedroom wall even while clutching a magenta crayon in his tiny fist.

"Double swear," said Morris. "We just died, so we're new in town. We haven't been around the block. Newbies. Have a few things to learn still—"

Longtoe sneered. "Lies come so easily to humans. The only redeeming virtues of humans are cooking and poetry, and even then—"

Poetry. Was it that simple? Could it save us? "Morris is a poet," I said brightly.

Morris gave me a look of dismay that said I'd just thrown him under the bus.

I gave him a look that said I hadn't really, and that he would do us proud, I knew it.

Longtoe wheeled toward Morris, his tone that of a hopeful child. "He's a poet? Really?"

While I was more than a little shocked at the difference between the powerful god and the needy god, and how he could still exude such perfection after the transition, I had to move quickly to take advantage of this new development. "Yes," I wheedled to give Morris a little time to prepare. "But never mind. Your godly being doesn't need bolstering with beautiful words and iambic pentameter to retain your state of exact precision. You don't need an Ode to Longtoe. Not at all."

Looming over Morris, Longtoe reverted to the more powerful, more demanding, more alarming version of himself. "Recite an Ode to Longtoe, God of Perfection."

Morris cowered. I gave him a look that said, *Come on, you've got this. Remember that poetry slam where you were up against the best rhymesters of Walla Walla and you blew them all out of the water?*

"Now," boomed Longtoe.

My poor friend jumped, then blurted,

"There was an old God of Perfection..."

A limerick. Lordy, lordy, no! His fear was leading him astray. He was supposed to weave splendor out of words to tout Longtoe's perfection, but instead... this. My brilliant idea was working against us. We were doomed. Morris continued.

"Who couldn't get an erection."

Longtoe grunted. I uttered a groan that was a cross between utter agony and total terror.

Still cowering, Morris opened his mouth to continue. I grabbed his arm to get him to stop—couldn't he see he would only make it worse?

My deluded friend shook me away and kept on.

"He remembered his power
as the God of the hour
and from then on excelled at ejaculation."

He had failed. Putting aside the fact that there were too many syllables in the closing line, he'd insulted a god. I waited for a thunderbolt to strike him. When that didn't happen, oddly, I feared a falling piano. That didn't happen either.

Longtoe howled, "You will answer for this." It sounded like a proclamation. His words bounced off the palace structure and out to the amusement park, making the rides ring like tambourines. "I call a Meeting of the Gods to determine the fate of these humans!"

Chapter Nine

The Convention Center of the Gods was the most ornately decorated place I'd ever been, and that was saying something, because my career had brought me to many places that were trying too hard. This conglomeration of connected buildings would win first place in the category *overflowing with adornment*. Its halls featured gold-veined marble statues of divine beings in heroically anguished poses, sapphire-encrusted goblets, chandeliers with crystal pendants, and gilt-framed paintings of gods frolicking in pastoral pleasure.

I noted this all a bit distractedly because my anger at Ismenia was growing with each step. This was all her fault. She'd used us, and she'd used us badly. She was pond scum. No, lower than pond scum. She was the muck at the bottom of the pond. She was... much more cunning than I could ever be. Why wasn't I that crafty? I would have used my trickery for good, not to trod upon poor defenseless humans who had no understanding of the afterlife. I would have tricked billionaires into building low-income housing. I would have tricked corporations into stocking up food banks with healthy yet delectable groceries.

My thoughts continued in this vein while the sentries marched us through a narrow hall that seemed downright dingy after all that ostentatiousness, past many unmarked doors, to a dark place that smelled cloying, like the perfume-testing area of a large department store. I couldn't see my surroundings, but I could tell the room was sizable because I felt a draft moving about and... Was that the murmuring of many people?

My hopes rose. Had they taken us to other human beings? Perhaps a waiting area where we could talk with people who could advise us on how to extract ourselves from this nightmare—or at least instruct us on proper afterlife etiquette so as not to worsen it?

High above, banks of lights flashed on with a *floosh*, so bright I could feel their heat. I held my hands up against the glare, blinking hard to see past them.

We were in a stadium-size theater, with many, many faces staring at us from a massive ground floor, several tiers of balconies, and box seats. I had a sudden rush of stage fright (which makes me sweat like a pig), for we were on stage! It wouldn't have been so bad if I'd had time to prepare myself the way I did before speaking engagements, panels, and award ceremonies (at which I'd presented awards, but—as I've mentioned—never won). To be so suddenly in front of this many people was too startling. It was the difference between seeing a tarantula from across the room and finding it crawling on your shoulder.

Wiping sweat from my brow, I wondered who they were, many still seating themselves in blue velvet fold-down chairs. They were dressed in the kind of impractical clothing you'd see on a runway, with stiff taffetas, gossamer scarves, fuzzy capes, and metallic ponchos. They wore hats of all kinds: Herringbone pillbox. Polka-dot stovepipe. Striped sou'wester.

And their eyes... they were colorful, kaleidoscoping.

They weren't people. They were gods. I mentally palmed myself in the forehead. Longtoe had called a Meeting of the Gods, and this was it.

I began to sweat harder. We'd learned that there were three hundred thousand and twenty-six of them. What did one do in front of so many omnipotent beings? Kneel? Prostrate oneself? Sing praises? Sacrifice goats?

Morris looked stunned; I must have too. For both our sakes, I tried to embody confidence instead. I nodded at him. He swallowed hard, squared his shoulders, and nodded back.

Longtoe strode out beside us, looking perfectly comfortable onstage. My duodenum had calmed, but now it flared once more at his seeming lack of stage fright. I was sure he never had to prepare before a public event like I did. I doubt he'd just been backstage shaking out his limbs, performing quiet vocal exercises, and repeating the mantra, *I have a valuable message, and people want me to succeed.*

"The Meeting of the Gods will commence!" he boomed.

My legs shook. I twisted my fingers together. Morris cleared his throat and jerked his head toward my hands to tell me to stop. I did, but then started right back up again.

Thumbtack stomped forward and announced, "Ness, the God of Just Ness, will preside over this trial of justice." I was momentarily confused. *Just Ness* sounded like *justice,* but the sentry had enunciated clearly, so I knew that wasn't what he'd said. Did Ness have genuine skill as a judge, or was he here because of his name? My thoughts dove into a rabbit warren of meanings and wordplay, but I was getting too distracted, so I snapped myself back to attention.

Ness tread onto the stage. He had the demeanor of an upright meercat—alert and attentive. Although he was wearing a lavender tracksuit, he threw a black robe over himself and stood behind a lectern. *Good,* I thought, *he's taking this seriously.*

He raised a diamond-and-emerald-encrusted gavel and pounded it on the lectern. The thump resounded throughout the theater, causing everybody to fall quiet. An emerald fell from the gavel, and he took his time searching for something in the lectern—a tube of glue, as it turned out, which he applied to the jewel to stick it back on.

Finally he said in a nasally voice, "Let the trial of the treacherously deviant humans begin."

Morris and I gasped. Was this to be a sham trial? Had we been convicted before it could even take place?

"Deviant? No!" shouted a voice in the audience, which gave me hope that the gods had a sense of fairness, until the voice continued, "*Deviant* means departing from accepted sexual standards, which doesn't fit in the context of the charges." I saw now who was talking: a bespectacled being with padded shoulders. "Perhaps you mean *devious*, meaning skillfully underhanded."

"Thank you, Loofa, God of Semantics." Ness scowled. "Let me rephrase that. This trial of justice involving treacherously devious and possibly deviant humans."

The God of Semantics settled back with a grin of satisfaction.

I rubbed my sweaty hands on my pant legs and wiped my sleeve across my forehead. If I didn't nip this kind of lopsided thinking in the bud, we would be convicted for sure. "I object," I shouted loudly and clearly.

Morris gave me an appreciative fist bump.

I was about to explain my objection when Ness barked, "You shall not speak!" A wide beam shot from his gavel, surrounding me in ruby-colored light. My skin itched like crazy, yet I was frozen in place, unable to scratch. What torture! I couldn't say *stop with the light already, I won't speak*, because that would be speaking. Instead, I fought hard to lift my hand to my face, then mimed zipping my lips.

He lowered the gavel. The beam died off and the itching stopped. I sighed (soundlessly) in relief.

Brow furrowed, Morris poked me, I think to make sure I was still intact. I held up my hand to indicate that I was functional.

Functional, but not optimistic. We were in a trial that could damn us for all eternity, yet we would not be allowed to say a word in our defense. I wondered if they would allow additional mime instead. I had in fact learned quite a bit of theatrical movement from my uncle, who had studied under the greats in Paris in his youth, and I could portray the sequence of events that led to this moment with great clarity, without saying a single word or (horror of horrors) utilizing overdone tropes such as being locked in a box or walking into a wind. Using my body alone, without "mugging" (employing unnecessary facial expression), I could convey everything that led up to this point: the avalanche, the harpy eagles and sloths, the arrival of Ismenia, her hints that led to building the wings, the leafcutter ants, and so on. I could also portray the fall of Icarus in astounding, heart-clenching slow motion, which even this audience, I was sure, would appreciate under the right circumstances.

However, I could read the room, and I sensed that this wasn't the moment for such an offering. Plus, I worried that the gods, like many humans, had become prejudiced against mimes after seeing too many bad ones.

"We must first determine the fate of Ismenia," said Longtoe.

"She must be banished," called one of the gods.

A god in the front row stood up. I got the feeling he relished this opportunity to show off his dress, which resembled a giant badminton birdie with a scrumptious red bodice and white rectangle lace skirt. While he looked magnificent, his words were harsh. "She was already banished for unleashing Chaos. Fat lot of good that did. We need a new punishment. Something that will stick."

He emphasized the word *Chaos* as if it was a terrible scourge, and the gods gasped in horror at the mention, which told me it could be something more dangerous than a dog. So was it some other creature? Some kind of weapon? A disease?

"Thank you for the clarification, Wendex, God of Obvious Observations." Longtoe seemed genuinely pleased with his support, his smirk brimming with righteous pleasure. "When we find her, we will chain her to Leo and Morris, and she will endure an eternity of their fate."

I clenched my fists, which wasn't easy, given how sweaty they were. Why should we be chained to the god who'd betrayed us? It wasn't fair!

"What fate is that?" asked a god who wore leg-of-mutton sleeves that were so wide they took up the seats on either side.

"We haven't gotten to that yet, Noupla, God of Personal Space Bubbles," said Wendex.

"I know," she said pointedly. "My question was really a clever prompting that we needed to determine that fate."

"A little too clever. Nobody got it. You should have said, 'I wonder what that fate will be.'"

Noupla dismissed him with an exasperated wave that bubble-wobbled her sleeve.

There were various suggestions for our fate. "Itching powder." "Hang them upside down." "Draw and quarter them."

My mouth grew drier with each new proposal, and I kept swallowing to get my salivary glands started up again. I surreptitiously glanced around for a way out, and I saw Morris doing so too, but neither of us gave the other a *let's make a break for it* sign (three taps on the left nostril). I shifted my feet, testing the stage floor for a hollow-sounding spot and looking for the telltale outline of a trapdoor, without success. The rafters were too high above us, and I could see no catwalks to leap for. Besides, we wouldn't make it far. There were too many gods blocking the exits, and sentries lined the stage.

Longtoe raised a hand for silence. Everybody quieted. "We must also determine the fate of Earth, from whence these beings hail. You are all aware that so many humans die every day and then join us here that it's become an invasion. They're crowding us out."

Wait, I said to myself. *Back up a step.* The fate of Earth? Most of its inhabitants didn't need a worse fate. Their lives were pretty dicey already.

He raised his chin regally. "It used to be there were only a few of them, then more and more came. Now there are billions on Earth, which means there will be billions more here. Underfoot! Asking for godly favors and complaining that their afterlife is different than they thought it would be. If we don't do something drastic, the stinking planet will continue to spew out its refuse and send us more trouble. Therefore, I demand that all human beings spend the rest of eternity—or the perpetuality of time, whichever doesn't end first—in the Afterlife of Biting Insects."

I gasped, imagining monstrous horseflies, sharp-needled mosquitoes, and things that burrow under the skin on their way to rendezvous with one another. I'd complained that the afterlife should be even better than I could imagine, but it was the opposite. Everything was sure to be worse than I could imagine.

Morris gulped and gave me look that said, *Well, he goes big, doesn't he?*

I gave him a look that said, *We're doomed, but we have to try our best not to be.*

He gave me a look that said, *Not to be what?*

I gave him a look that said, *Doomed. Not to be doomed.*

He gave me a look that said, *Oh, I get it.*

Ness raised his gavel.

My wife was in jeopardy. My friends would suffer endlessly. Morris would never again eat avocado toast.

"Wait!" I called, in spite of the directive to keep silent. "You can't just sentence billions of people—"

Longtoe interrupted me. "Nothing you say is of any importance. You are merely a..." He sniffed derisively. "...furniture designer."

It rankled. And worse, it sidetracked me. Many people don't understand the importance of design, but a god? Gods know a lot. Maybe not everything, but the basics at least, plus knowledge and understanding beyond our ken. I would have thought that a god would get it, but this one didn't, and so I couldn't help myself. I had to school him.

Guessing my intentions, Morris clapped his hand over my mouth to stop me, but I pried his fingers loose, pushed them firmly aside, wiped some spittle away with a quick swipe of my forearm, and declared, "Design isn't just making pretty things. Design improves lives! It enriches us and improves our well-being; it makes things function better, thereby making people function better. Good design improves efficiency."

A few gods perked up, lifting their chins and murmuring with approval.

This heartened me. I continued with increasing fervor, my hands rising of their own accord into the pose of a preacher afire with holy spirit, my voice booming with expressive emphasis. "Design makes healing possible. Design saves the environment. Design is the pinnacle of the built object. In fact..." I paused for dramatic effect. "...you can't make anything without designing it!"

Wendex, God of Obvious Observations, cheerfully repeated my words. "You can't make anything without designing it! Exactly!"

Loofa, God of Semantics, nodded so furiously that his spectacles flew off, which made me whoop with delight (at his concurrence, not at his flying spectacles).

Longtoe's shoulders slumped ever so slightly; he looked contrite. "You say it improves lives?"

My chest swelled. What a turnaround! My logic had swayed the God of Perfection.

Before I died, I had been sketching out my ideas of how to improve our world through design. How to better incorporate nature, psychology, sensation, and well-being. I had hoped to impact the world with my green-roof beach chairs, which had actual flora planted on top of their built-in umbrellas. If I do say so myself, it was a smart combination: combating urban heat buildup by utilizing the pleasure of sunbathing.

But I'd wanted to do so much more. I'd hoped to collaborate with urban planners and architects to design whole communities, whole cities, and even (dare I admit it?) whole countries! Perhaps now that I was in the afterlife, I could somehow continue on with my dreams. I was overreaching in my thoughts, perhaps, and definitely getting ahead of myself, but I could start by...

Longtoe interrupted my musings with a barking laugh. "So what if it improves lives? You're dead."

Some of the gods chortled at the way he'd put me in my place. I saw too late that his faux turnaround was a ploy to lift me higher in order to make me fall harder. He was a bully, then. But how could that be? He was perfect.

Did that mean I deserved to be bullied?

No! I refused to believe it. I would only allow that I didn't understand this place yet, although it appeared I wouldn't be given the chance to.

"Ness, God of Just Ness," said a god.

"Yes, Olivenaught, God of Deterioration?"

A spotlight shone on a god in a balcony. Living up to his name, he was deteriorating everywhere. His face, his clothing, his body. Yet he should really have been the God of Deterioration and Restoration Then Deterioration Once Again, because his parts kept growing back like the forest floor mushrooms in time-lapse photography—I supposed in order to give him something that could deteriorate anew.

Morris made a little noise of disgust. I elbowed him to remind him not to do anything to get on the wrong side of another god. He elbowed me back to remind me he hated being elbowed.

Although Olivenaught's lips were a bit flappy, his words were clear. "We can't continue with the trial."

Longtoe's nostrils flared, but he seemed otherwise composed. "Why not?"

Olivenaught's ear dangled by a single strip of flesh. I was distracted. When would it fall? He pressed it back into the side of his head, allowing me to focus on his words. "The lawyer for the defense, Moonilla, God of Procrastination, has not arrived."

"The God of Procrastination has not arrived," repeated Longtoe with a peeved sigh. "Why am I not surprised?" He motioned to a sentry. "Get her."

Fifteen minutes later a metallic green chariot landed on the stage. Moonilla strutted out, clad in a well-cut charcoal suit that appeared versatile enough to wear in the boardroom or on a night on the town, paired with two-tone slingbacks that came to a nicely rounded point at the toe.

"What took you so long, Moonilla, God of *Procrastination*?" Longtoe spoke sarcastically, which seemed uncalled for. I presumed her tardiness was a direct result of her god title. But then, I was new here and unfamiliar with divine customs.

She responded breezily, "It takes time to be perfect, Longtoe, God of Perfection."

At that, even Longtoe had to concede, for she was perfect, from what I could tell. Completely composed, symmetrically beautiful, with an air of supreme knowledge.

I rolled my shoulders, easing the tension. With Moonilla as our lawyer, we would surely be exonerated.

Longtoe pivoted on his heel to address the gods once more. "As I was saying, humans are an infection, a boil on our home."

"Technically," began Loofa, God of Semantics, "a boil doesn't grow on an inanimate object—"

Longtoe spoke louder than the angle grinder in my workshop (for which I use ear protection). "And they have been persistent boils, overflowing with pus, treading their grime all about, debasing our domain. Over the years they've multiplied like yeast."

The God of Semantics nodded. He either approved of the wording or the sentiment of the statement. Perhaps both.

"They began as a trickle," said Longtoe, "and now they're overflowing into the corners and seams of the Home of the Gods."

Ness cleared his throat. "We will now vote on whether to sentence humans to the Afterlife of Biting Insects."

Morris and I gulped simultaneously. I motioned toward Moonilla. *Help us, please!*

Moonilla nodded at me. *Don't worry, I've got this.* She held her palm out to interrupt. "I request..."

My friend and I grasped each other's forearms. Our fate—and that of all humans—was in her godly yet procrastinatory hands. What would she say? *I request that the court of gods consider how these two humans have been duped by one of our own. I request that all charges be dismissed. I request that these humans be allowed to live out their afterlife in comfort and happiness.*

She said none of those things. Instead, she spoke coyly. "I request more time."

Longtoe put his hand to his forehead. "Of course you do, Moonilla, God of Procrastination."

"Request granted," said Ness. "You have four days. In the meantime, humans Leo and Morris will be detained in the Afterlife of Slime-Emitting Creatures."

For a split second I admired the efficiency of combining all slime-producing animals into one afterlife rather than having a separate location for each, but then the ramifications struck me. We would be confined with all the slugs that had lived and died, plus... What other creatures emitted slime? It seemed that, horrifically, I was soon to find out.

Morris made a peep of terror and mouthed the words, *I shouldn't be dead.*

It was my fault he was here in the afterlife. When my wife suggested hiking, I'd asked him along. It was also my fault we were being judged by the gods, because I had insisted on bringing Ismenia, whether she had tricked me into it or not.

"Please let Morris go," I wailed. "He hasn't done anything wrong."

"That's a big nope," said Ness in his nasally voice. He banged the gavel. A jewel fell off. While the other gods chattered and uttered declarations of *guilty* or *kind of guilty* (none spoke of innocence), he reached for his tube of glue.

Chapter Ten

Within the hour Morris and I were dumped unceremoniously into a block-wide pit that stretched as far as we could see and smelled like warm pickles. Its three-story sides slanted inward at the top, so we couldn't scale them, at least not freestyle.

We hurried forward, hoping to find a way out somewhere up ahead, where the cliff might not be as steep or where climbable tree roots stuck out of the dirt.

We began encountering puddles of water, then small pools here and there. Each featured something unappealing, such as a gray froth or smears of oily bubbles.

"Smarmy things live there," warned Morris. "I mean, lurk there."

I shuddered. Then I shuddered again. I kept shuddering, until I'd shuddered myself out, at least for the time being.

We reached an area where slime trails crisscrossed the dirt, some a hand's width and some two feet wide. They smelled like ammonia with a hint of used gym socks. We bounded over them at first, but after twenty more minutes of walking they were so numerous we were forced to slog right through them. White slime trailed from our hiking boots and wouldn't rub off.

"Hey, look," said Morris. "A hill!"

The mound of dirt in the middle of the pit was as tall as the cliff walls. I whooped. "We can build a ramp to freedom!"

Hoping it was loose enough to scoop with our bare hands, we hurried forward.

"A ramp to freedom. I feel a poem coming on!" He puffed with effort while he recited.

"I never knew
A ramp was all I needed.
A ramp to escape from the damp

Slime.
Yes, slime.
Cocooning our feet
Lovingly.
Like the cheese from a slice
of piping hot pizza."

My heart was near to bursting. Such beauty in the midst of abject horror! "Brilliant," I managed to say through my emotion.

Morris grabbed my shoulder, pulling me to a stop. "Wait! Hills aren't supposed to move."

"And hills don't have antennae."

The hill fell open, like a giant soft, gooey caramel muffin being pulled apart by a hungry consumer.

Morris scrunched his face. "Ewww. It's a mound of giant slugs."

I could have added that the not-a-hill contained banana slugs (yellow with thirty percent brown splotches, like a too-ripe banana), as well as brown slugs (the color of seventy percent dark chocolate, no splotches), but I didn't have time. They were faster than in life, and as big as sleeping bags. They *schoom-oop*ed like wet nylon as they sailed across the ground straight for us.

"How fast can you learn to speak slug?" I asked, knowing that it was impossible in the seconds we had before they'd be all over us.

He tried some human languages instead. "Wir sind sehr salzig! Nous sommes très salés! We're very salty!"

It was a good idea—salt being deadly to slugs—but they must not have understood because they kept advancing, skirts rippling.

A side note: If you've never looked closely at a slug, when I mentioned a "skirt" you might have pictured something cute and flouncy, perhaps made of gingham. However, a slug skirt is short, thick, and slimy and looks to be made of the same stuff as the rest of the slug. There's nothing cute about it. Just wanted to make sure you had the right image in your head.

The first one reached us. A banana slug, its face startlingly odd. The two upper tentacles sported eyes, while the lower ones formed a horseshoe mustache. Since the eyes were on the stalks, its actual face was blank, making it appear sinister. Yet I didn't get the feeling this was an attack. On the contrary, it seemed like they wanted to show us some brotherly and sisterly love.

But that didn't make this better. In no time we would be smothered by our newest family, crushed under a hill of slugs, breathing in slime that would coat the insides of our lungs more thoroughly than a ten-second squirt of nonstick cooking spray.

The first one reached us, and we pushed it away. It was like tossing a soggy sleeping bag. Another came right after, and we pushed it away too. Then another, and another.

"They're surrounding us," I wailed.

What was worse, now jumbo worms, snails, salamanders, and lizards of various colors and complexions were headed our way. I didn't know what they planned to do when they got to us, except that I could be sure it would involve more slime.

"To the water!" Morris held an imaginary sword aloft, as if leading a calvary charge. We sloshed into a pool, and soon the slimy creatures were behind us.

The pool grew wider as we progressed, until there was no dry land at all, but there was no going back. Soon we were knee-deep in water that looked and smelled like old dishwater.

A few feet away, something fat, lumpy, and gray broke the surface, then disappeared as quickly as it had appeared.

I backed away. "What was that?"

"Slime monster," offered Morris disgustedly, also backing away.

"We'll be okay," I said with as much confidence as I could dredge up, no pun intended. "Let's keep going. We'll find a way out."

An eellike creature approached my shins. In the murky water I made out pointy protuberances on its head and gray skin like the crumpled velvet of a love seat that's seen too much love. I whooped in fear and sloshed to the side.

"I recognize it!" said Morris. "That's a hagfish."

"Is it poisonous?" I stumbled around, but it was quicker than I was, darting here and there, now in front of me, now behind. "It's toying with me!"

"Don't worry." Morris swiveled nervously. "I think they mostly eat dead things."

"We're dead!"

"Right. We should worry then. Assume the defense position."

We positioned ourselves back to back, the way we did as kids, so that our enemy could only come at us from the sides and front. Kicking like cancan dancers, we managed to fend it off, but more hagfish appeared, swirling and curling and weaving among our legs.

Hagfish produce scads of mucus, and abruptly, they did. The water was filled with white goop. We tried to loosen ourselves from the threads, but they wrapped around our ankles. "Why's it so stringy?" I asked.

"Plain old mucus would disperse in water, so it's thready. Makes it harder to get loose from."

The hagfish were making a smacking sound underwater that sounded suspiciously like a person about to enjoy a good meal. They began nipping at us. "Crabwalk!" I called. We shifted from side to side, churning the water. It now resembled egg whites whipped to soft peaks (but not stiff peaks). That reminded me of cooking meringue pies with Lilly.

Poor Lilly, not knowing where her husband was! Poor me, about to be scarfed down by hagfish for lunch! Or was it dinnertime? I didn't have enough bandwidth in my mind to know.

"Grapevine step," directed Morris. Dutifully, I crossed one foot in front of the other, then one foot in back, over and over as I went side to side. It did seem to confuse the hagfish, who didn't nip at us as much, but eventually we had to change it up.

"Waltz," commanded Morris.

I thanked my lucky stars that I'd taken that ballroom dancing class with Lilly, but soon the waltz stopped working and we switched to other dances. Square dancing, tango, ballet, contemporary, Russian folk dancing (without the squatting, which could have been disastrous for our low-hanging fruit).

"Hokey pokey," said Morris. In perfect sync, we put our left feet in and our left feet out, then turned ourselves about. That kept the hagfish at bay once more, but for how long?

We heard a loud squawk. A giant bird swooped overhead. I glimpsed a black hooked beak, white head and belly feathers, and striped wings.

Dakota, our sister harpy eagle! I hollered with happiness. She plucked Morris up by his shoulders, giving him an instant shrug. Stringy hagfish slime trailed from his legs, turning him into a sickly jellyfish.

They flew off. Still putting my left foot in and my left foot out, I watched them disappear beyond the edge of the pit.

Why hadn't she taken us both at once? And why had she chosen to save him first? She *did* like him more!

I feared that she was taking him back to the Afterlife of the Birds, which would take a long time. It could be hours before she returned for me.

To stave the hagfish off, I had to do something akin to a grand finale's worth of dance, so I channeled my inner Rockette and kicked as high as I possibly could, over and over. The Rockettes are tall and flexible, and so am I, so that was less of a challenge than it could have been. I added interludes of fake yet energetic tap dancing, salsa, and last but not least, any step I could recall from the movie *Singing in the Rain*.

I was exhausted and grateful when only a half hour had passed before Dakota returned to snatch me away from the Afterlife of the Slime-Emitting Creatures. She grasped me by my shoulders, and we rose into the air.

"Thank you, Dakota!" I said. "May the wind carry you to excellent paint blobs!"

It was an in-joke about how bad my harpy eagle language was. She responded happily with another of my bloopers: "Be sure to stretch your elephants before frying six kumquats."

However, she had picked me up backward, which was disconcerting. I never sat in the backward-facing train seat because it tended to make me carsick. She hadn't picked Morris up backward—why would she be so neglectful with me? Still, I was out of that pit, which was shrinking in the distance.

My relief was short-lived. Something was headed our way. Something in a chariot of red and gold. Something tall and handsome and determined and perfect.

Longtoe, the God of Perfection, was coming to take me down.

Chapter Eleven

While hanging backward from Dakota's talons, I had a clear view of Longtoe's approach. The way the sun hit the red-and-gold decorative flames on his chariot, they looked real, as if fire was bursting from its sides.

"Evil god, coming in hot!" I warned Dakota. "The one who dumped us in the pit."

"Hold on tight."

I gulped. The way she gripped me by my shoulders, I couldn't reach up and hold on to her at all, much less do so tightly. And she was about to do some wild flying. However, I couldn't tell her to take it easy, because we had to get away.

We rose suddenly. My feet cramped from clenching them so hard.

Longtoe adjusted easily, swooping up to follow us. I could now see his perfectly chiseled facial features, his perfectly curved nose hairs, and his perfectly pouting mouth, slightly open like an indie singer about to launch into his signature song.

He seemed so perfectly righteous that I questioned myself. Should I submit to him? He was the God of Perfection, after all. That was hard to argue with.

He raised something that looked like a crossbow. Its gut-piercingly sharp arrow gleamed with a yellow substance that was surely a damage-inducing poison.

I shook myself out of whatever folly I was under. "Dive!"

Dakota reacted instantaneously. We dropped like an elevator car cut loose from whatever holds up an elevator car. I wailed, and continued wailing, with two or three key changes within the next few seconds.

Dakota circled back, then rocketed down into the pit of slime-emitting creatures. The slime on the water's surface now resembled my most unsuccessful attempts at foam art on my morning latte.

I feared she was planning a *Star Wars* maneuver, where she would head for a cliff and pull up at the last moment, leaving Longtoe to crash into it. I didn't trust that she would be able to rise in time while carrying my weight, not at this speed. After all, she'd only just learned to fly.

For better or worse, she didn't get the chance to try. Longtoe created a perfect (of course) arc in the air to head us off, and she had to abort, pulling out of the pit. However, we were still above it, with Longtoe aiming his crossbow directly at my belly button. If it hit me, I would be knocked back into the pit, injured and unable to protect myself.

Dakota went into full evasion mode. In life I'd viewed videos from a drone's point of view that made me feel as if I was the one flying, dipping, rising, and banking. This was just like that except the wind was flapping a loose feather in my face, ropes of hagfish slime hung from my feet, and a terrifyingly powerful god was in hot pursuit. Plus I was flying backward, which was making me nauseated.

Finally she straightened out, with Longtoe still only a short distance away. In my peripheral vision, I saw that she was aiming at series of stone arches that resembled the orange-red ones in Utah's Arches National Park, where I'd planned to take my wife one day, but alas, that would never happen. I would have admired the beauty of these afterlife arches, but I was too busy fearing their rock-hardness.

It seemed that Dakota intended to perform a modified version of the *Star Wars* cliff maneuver that she'd aborted earlier, using one of these arches instead of a cliff. She would fly straight for it, then abruptly change direction, leaving Longtoe to crash into it.

However, she seemed to forget I was dangling beneath her. I was about to hit the first stone arch full on! I couldn't see exactly, but guessed when to lift my knees to my chest. The bottoms of my shoes missed the top of the arch by a mere centimeter. However, the equal and opposite reaction of my knee lift propelled Dakota into a loop-de-loop, and my back slammed on a different stone arch.

The blow wrenched me out of Dakota's talons. I flopped over and was now clutching onto the arch, helpless as a turtle on its back. (But don't let that confuse you—I was belly down. I just mean that I was a sitting duck. Don't let that confuse you either. I wasn't sitting.) My back ached from the blow, and my shoulders burned from the cuts Dakota's talons had made.

Longtoe dipped and headed for me. Dakota zoomed toward him, reaching for him with her talons. *Get him, Dakota*, I thought to myself, but I didn't say it aloud because my voice was occupied with groaning.

At the last moment, Longtoe swerved, and Dakota overshot him.

He cried with triumph. It was such a perfect cry of jubilation and beauty that it made my groaning seem even more ridiculous than it already was, and my voice trailed off to a guttering stop.

Longtoe rocketed toward me. I held on to the stone arch with one arm; with the other I yanked hagfish slime from my shin and wielded it like a lasso. (That cowboy workshop during a vacation in Laramie finally came in handy!) I used a tried-and-true over-the-shoulder toss. I would have attempted a Houlihan, just for fun, but there wasn't time to get fancy. The toss landed on the first try, pinning his arms to his torso. That made him lose control of the chariot, and he veered off, struggling to untangle himself.

I experienced only a moment of triumph before Dakota grabbed me by an ankle (yikes, upside down) and whisked me away.

We entered a forest—although confused by my upside-down state, I could tell by the many branches slapping against me. After what seemed an interminable amount of time, she carried me to a clearing and set me on the grass. It was an awkward landing, as I was head down, but I quickly righted myself. Dakota landed beside me.

Morris was standing there! I was on the ground, out of Longtoe's clutches, reunited with my best friend. My whoops were weak but heartfelt.

"What took you so long?" asked Morris in English, not harpy language, implying that any delay was my fault.

I was indignant until I realized that he was joking because he'd been sick with worry. "I stopped off for a beer."

We did our version of a bro hug (handshake with hug, slow-motion punch in the jaw). Morris never sang, but he poetry-chanted the words to that old 1970s hit "In Heaven There Is No Beer" while I wiped the slime off myself and onto the grass as best I could.

Dakota rested for a bit from the exertion of the flight. "You two are way too much trouble," she said kindly. I realized that she hadn't carried us both at the same time like Lancelot had because she wasn't as big yet.

With a respectful fluttering of my "wings," I said, "Thank you, Dakota!"

"What happened to you two anyway? After my first flight I came back to the nest and you'd disappeared."

We told her about Morris's fall and recovery, our run-in with Longtoe, our deal with the sloths, and so on.

When we'd finished our tale, she told hers. After she couldn't find us, she decided to go see the Afterlife of the Humans. Her parents' warning against it made her intensely curious to see what the fuss was about. Once she got there, she saw other humans and realized that Morris and I were humans too, not featherless birds whose poop was the wrong color.

I described Lilly and asked if she'd seen her.

"No, but there are endless flocks of humans here. I wouldn't know where to start."

"How did you know we needed help?" asked Morris.

She tilted her head in a way that passed for a smile on a harpy eagle. "A certain someone told me."

I heard a familiar voice. "Hey, guys!"

I wheeled around and saw Ismenia striding toward us. I hunched into a gorilla stance to make it perfectly clear she wasn't welcome, since sometimes people mistake my mad face for my confused face. I didn't want there to be any doubt.

She wore army fatigues in a camouflage pattern of gold, silver, hot pink, and neon green. I thought how ridiculous it was because a camouflage pattern was supposed to make you blend in. Then I realized that in the flamboyant Home of the Gods, that might be exactly the right combination.

She was smiling like somebody handing out lollipops to children, and I wasn't having it. "You lying, cheating, evil, nasty—"

"She's a god," whispered Morris. "Don't anger her." He tried to push my forehead up to ease me out of gorilla pose. I didn't budge.

Ismenia tut-tutted. "I'm only here to help."

"We're done with you," I said, still summoning my inner silverback.

She shook her head. "I can't leave you hanging. They're going to sentence all humanity to the Afterlife of Biting Insects."

I straightened, lifting my chin haughtily. "We don't need your kind of help."

Morris nudged me. "What's your plan then?"

Ismenia gave Morris a smile of appreciation. She *did* like him better!

I threw my hands up. "I don't know!"

Her shoulder twitched. "I'm sorry I got you in trouble, but if you'd just carried me a little farther—"

"Um," I said, "it's not an apology if a *but* comes with it."

Ismenia blinked a couple of times, then nodded. "Okay, okay. I apologize. No *buts*. And I'm here to make it right."

It was true that we really needed help. I didn't like it, but there it was. "All right then. Fix this."

"First things first," she said. "We have to keep moving. Thanks for your help, Dakota."

"Anytime."

Morris and I rubbed her beak goodbye. She flew off.

Morris squinted one eye as if he'd just figured out something important. "Hey Ismenia, why didn't you just get a bird to carry you back to the Home of the Gods?"

"Partly because I weigh so much," she responded.

So it hadn't been my fatigue that made her seem so heavy. She really was much heavier than she looked. Maybe five hundred pounds. Maybe more. I didn't understand why when she was so skinny, but perhaps it had something to do with bone density.

"You could have made your own wings," he said.

"No, banishment takes away that ability. Remember how I just handed you the materials? Also, somebody had to bring me here. You'll learn how things work here eventually. Anyway, we should get going."

"Where?" I asked.

"To my house."

I shook my head. "You're a fugitive. That's the first place they'll look for you."

"No problem. It's a mobile home."

That wasn't better. *Mobile* home was a misnomer because they didn't typically move, much less move quickly. I pictured a large double-wide with built-in porches and mature but overgrown landscaping. Perhaps a lawn gnome or two and a rusty swing set.

She produced something that looked like a TV remote, except that it was gold with black buttons. After pressing a house icon, she returned it to her pocket. "It'll be here in a minute or so."

"A self-driving mobile home," said Morris. "Interesting."

Perhaps she was talking about an RV then. I got hopeful, imagining a shower and kitchenette. I didn't know when I might see Lilly, but I didn't want to be this stinky and messy for our reunion.

There was a low rumbling, like thunder in the distance.

"Here it comes," said Ismenia.

I glanced over and saw a metallic sphere the size of a split-level house rolling toward us at a high speed. It was going to hit us!

"Incoming!" Morris rushed away.

I automatically grabbed Ismenia by her wrist, dragging her toward the edge of the clearing. My heart was pounding. The sphere stopped with a screech a few feet away from where we'd been standing. We wouldn't have been hurt after all, but I couldn't have known that.

She spoke warmly. "Once again you put yourself at risk on my behalf. I won't forget that. Thank you."

I realized that she could probably have gotten loose from my grasp, but instead she had let me "save" her. Was it a test? Was she trying to embarrass me? What was I missing?

Again, I needed to remember that she was a god—of trickery, no less. Her resemblance to a wiry, skinny human was all show. Yet I couldn't help speaking irritably. "You're welcome, I think."

The sphere's surface was opaque, with no windows or doors. It looked like it was made of stainless steel, burnished with a pleasing crosshatch design.

I wasn't sure how it was possible, but it seemed to exude emotion: a feeling of adventure with a touch of something that I can only describe as insanity. The emotion seemed familiar, but I couldn't pinpoint why.

"You live in a ball?" asked Morris.

"Not a ball," said Ismenia. "A mobile home."

He shrugged. "I guess it doesn't get much more mobile than that. How do we get in?"

"Hands." Ismenia placed her own on the sphere.

I was hesitant to get close to that giant emotion-spitting orb, but there wasn't much choice. Timorously, I followed suit. Its surface felt—I'm not sure how else to describe it—buzzy. How I imagine a force field would feel, but without the pain. Or maybe just a little pain.

My body felt suddenly compressed, as if being squeezed through a didgeridoo. It was happening too slowly, my body squirming to pass through. It felt both physically achy and psychologically wrong; the human body wasn't meant for that kind of compaction. I heard Morris yowling in a constrained manner; perhaps I was too.

I champagne-cork-popped into a five-by-ten-foot room, landing on my butt, puffing hard.

Ismenia was already there, standing normally. "You made it," she said perkily. I scowled. A little sympathy for human discomfort would have been welcome right then.

Morris landed next to me. He grunted a few times. "Helluva way to get in."

Bolted to the wall were padded seats much like you'd find on an inversion roller coaster. "Strap up," ordered Ismenia, sliding into one.

The seats implied that the ride would be rough, and since the sphere rolled, we were certain to be upside down at regular intervals. My body was shaking, urging me to exit the sphere with all due haste. However, I didn't want to digeridoo myself again, and I had no alternate plan, so I crawled to a chair and buckled myself in.

Morris buckled in as well. "Is there any way to move this thing without rolling? Let's think about this. There must be a better—"

We rolled. Fast. But not consistently. There were jerks and turns and reversals—it was like being a yo-yo in the hands of a world champion.

My muscles stiffened and I screamed like a baby, while Morris sounded like a wildcat. Our two sounds entwined to make an unnerving discordant music, if you could call it that, which periodically harmonized into a chord that was almost pleasant to the ears.

Ismenia whooped. "I love traveling! Just lean into it. Go with it. Get loose."

I didn't think I could, but I had to try, since I felt like my mind would unravel if I didn't get control over myself. I concentrated, using the mantra, *I am flopsy and loosey-goosey.*

It didn't go well. I was too stressed-out from misplacing my wife and also being responsible for the fate of humanity. Plus my mantra was completely ineffective.

Yet I couldn't give up. I massaged the mantra by adding more words. *I am flopsy and loosey-goosey, like a stuffed bunny, and I am calm and coordinated but still ready for action.*

It got to where I was so distracted by constructing a successful mantra (Was it too long? Did it hit the right psychological buttons?) that I forgot to be terrified, and everything felt smoother, easier. Exhilarating, even.

By the time we stopped, I was almost disappointed that it didn't go on longer.

"Let's not do that again anytime soon," moaned Morris. I made a mental note to share my mantra with him at an appropriate time.

We unstrapped and staggered through a bright red door. I was shocked to be in a roomy hallway the length of a city block. Apparently this place was much bigger on the inside than it looked from the outside. Its floor was tiled in a metallic purple-and-orange

checkerboard pattern. Not a choice I would have made, but then I'm
not a god.

Ismenia shooed us along. "You can clean up in the guest
bathroom."

Yes! I thought, striding forward with hopes of a grade-three
loofah and lilac-cucumber-aloe body wash, or the equivalent. Maybe
there would be something even better, since this was the home of a
god.

On the way we passed a garage-size iron door covered in strange
round symbols. I sensed something emanating from it: power
combined with madness. The same as I'd sensed before I'd entered
the spherical home, only stronger. Every single hair on my body
stood on end: on my head, my torso, my legs, even the straggly few
on the tops of my feet.

"What's in there?" Morris gave the door such a wide berth that
he pressed me against the opposite wall.

"My dog, Chaos." Her face relaxed into sweetness, like a mother
watching her baby sleep. "He can be trouble, but I love the little guy,
you know?"

Little guy. Probably not so little. Given the size of the door and
the strength of the emotion emanating from it, it was monstrously
huge. What was I doing here? Could I trust Ismenia? Was she luring
us with promises of cleanliness, only to turn us into food for her pet?

She flung open a pink lacquer door and ushered us into a
bathroom that had a grotto-of-the-gods feel, with a pleasant mix of
spotted philodendrons and purple ivy. Calm music chimed softly.
Although I didn't recognize the instruments or the musical
signature, it seemed like something a monk would meditate to.

There were a dozen teardrop-shaped tubs, since, as Ismenia
explained, bathing is a social activity for gods. Water ran continually
from their lily-shaped faucets. (Lilly! I missed her so. What was

she doing right now?) A minimalist Scandinavian bar cart held a smorgasbord of cheese, crackers, and grapes.

"How did this all stay put when your house rolled?" asked Morris.

"Stabilizers. Works on objects, but not on beings." Ismenia gestured toward an archway. "When you're done, you can sleep in the adjoining room. There's clothing in the dresser. In the morning, go back out into the hall and look for me behind the yellow door." She left.

After shedding my slime-infused duds, I climbed into one of the tubs. The gunk on my body floated to the surface, then was taken away by continual water replenishment. The hot, comforting water did more than just cleanse me; it sped up the healing of the nicks, bruises, scratches, and bites I'd gotten so far.

While I soaked and scarfed down the food, my worries and misgivings faded, at least for a time. This made up for a lot.

"Ahhhh," said Morris from the tub next to me. "This is the life."

I didn't correct him, as "This is the death" seemed totally unsuitable to the moment.

By the time we were done with our baths, fatigue had caught up with us. We dragged ourselves to the adjoining room. There were several beds whose four posts were shaped like intertwined trees, complete with wrought iron leaves. I appreciated the superior handiwork, but, as Morris said, it was "too soon," reminding us too much of the jungle treetops we'd recently inhabited. Still, we slept hard and well.

· · · ·

IN THE MORNING, WE found tunics, harem pants, and embroidered slippers in a highboy dresser. They were odd, but fit us well. I was glad for deep pockets that would easily hold my cell phone, but then remembered I no longer had one.

No matter. I felt overdressed yet courageous. Ready to face the next challenge. Ready to suss out the nuances and betrayals of gods. Ready to pivot from talk to action and back again.

Morris performed a quick Hammer dance, that slick sideways move that MC Hammer popularized in the 1980s, obligatory for anybody wearing floppy pants such as ours.

Back in the hallway, I sensed that feeling of power combined with madness, and my courage flagged. Ismenia had told us her dog was big. I was probably the size of its chew toy. I tried not to think about my limbs being torn asunder and my bones, organs, and connective tissue being gnawed and strewn about.

As Ismenia had instructed, we opened the yellow door. Spread out before us was the most comfortable-looking living room I'd ever seen. A low built-in couch lined three of the walls, piled with throw pillows of blue, purple, and at least one other color I couldn't name because it didn't exist on Earth. On a black-and-white zebra-pattern rug, poofy sitting cushions surrounded low tea tables of carved mahogany. If I had to give the style a name, I would have called it Neo-Moroccan Pillow. I walked in, taking in arched alcoves featuring intricate brass lamps and woven baskets.

I stopped so suddenly that Morris ran into me. At the far end was a home bar with a counter. That counter was lined with stools. Not just any stools. The ones I'd designed when I was alive.

My steampunk stool was there, with its gears and pipes. Also the art deco green pleather one. But most surprisingly, Ismenia had a Stealthy Wealthy Stool, the one made of twenty-four-karat gold covered by stainless steel. Only one of those had ever sold; apparently she had been the anonymous buyer. I didn't know what to think about that.

"You have my stools." I rubbed my chin. This meant something, but what?

Morris slipped around me and scooped up a book from a tea table. It was one of the three poetry books he'd written, the one featuring avocado toast on the cover. "You're trying to make us feel at home."

"That's not why I have those," she explained brusquely. "I'm a god. I like quality."

It was validating, but disquieting. Ismenia had clearly known about us before we ever met her, yet she'd never mentioned it. Our relationship, or whatever you'd call it, was lopsided, even discounting the differences between gods and humans.

We sat at the counter on my stools, and she fed us bowls of something that looked like fruit-studded oatmeal but tasted much better. Out of five stars, I would have given it a thousand. Ismenia had none, saying she'd already eaten.

I felt I should learn more about her, and about the gods in general, so we could plan our next steps, but before I could formulate a question, Morris asked, "Why do you call yourself a god rather than a goddess?"

It seemed like a waste of time, since it was obvious to me that it was a feminist stance, but Ismenia's answer was more practical. "Dispensing with the extra syllable was the idea of Ubel, God of Brevity. During the course of our existence, we've saved twenty-two years by not voicing the extra syllable."

"Wow!" said Morris. "What other syllables have you dispensed with?"

His question seemed to endear him to her. How did he always manage to come up with the right thing to say?

"We say *postpone* instead of *postpone until later* and *confrontation* instead of *direct confrontation.*"

Morris got a sly look. "Even so, I bet you still say, 'tiny little baby kitten.'"

She beamed. "That's exactly right! Of course we still say, 'tiny little baby kitten!'"

This fun fact wasn't the type of insight into the gods that we needed. I was still formulating better questions when a gong rang, rich and somber. It sounded like something you'd hear in a fabled kingdom before an announcement of great portent.

Morris and I glanced around expectantly.

"That's the doorbell. A god is arriving." Ismenia pressed a button on her remote control.

The god materialized in front of us. She wore a lumpy cream-colored outfit that looked as if it had once been part of a padded cell. That might sound drab and unflattering, but it was quite becoming, as was she, with her white lipstick, white hair, and white veil, but what really attracted me was that blossoming smile behind the veil, as if she had a secret to impart, only for me.

My knees went weak. Even though Ismenia was a god, she didn't glow with celebrity brilliance. This god, however, had that certain something that made you stare and mumble something vaguely close to "Your Highness."

"This is Hahahaha, God of Laughter."

Hahahaha spoke, and I didn't know what she was saying, her words were so rapturous. I lost myself in the presence of such elegance, such novelty, such beauty.

Ismenia sighed. "Tone it down, Hahahaha. Remember they're humans."

The God of Laughter's brilliance dimmed. "All right then. This better?"

It felt as if I'd been released from a spell. Morris and I blinked a few times as we got our bearings once more.

"Later I'll train you on how to be in a god's immediate presence without drooling," said Ismenia, a bit sarcastically I thought, given the circumstances.

"As I understand it," said Hahahaha, "we need to stop Longtoe from dooming humanity to the Afterlife of Biting Insects."

My full stomach gave me the enthusiasm to jump right in as if I were in a design group planning meeting. "Right, then. Let's start with other gods. What kind of manpower can we count on?"

"Person power," corrected Morris.

"Deity power," corrected Hahahaha.

Using my typical meeting leadership style, I nodded my appreciation of their discussion input and tweaked accordingly. "Deity power. Yes. So who are your allies?"

There was an awkward silence. Ismenia scrunched her mouth like somebody trying to remember what was for lunch the other day. I began to feel something heavy in the pit of my stomach, and it wasn't the food I'd just eaten. That wasn't a hard question. Why was she having such difficulty answering?

"Don't tell us you don't have any allies." Morris had the eyes-wide expression of a skydiver whose parachute won't open. "Out of hundreds of thousands of gods?"

Ismenia said offhandedly, "My affiliations are ever shifting. To tell you the truth, I can't be certain at the moment, aside from Hahahaha."

This seemed nearly insurmountable. How were we going to counter a god who was by definition perfect without at least a battalion of gods to help us?

"Is there, like, a god of weapons we could lure to our side?" asked Morris.

Ismenia frowned. "That would be a weird name for a god."

"But all the god names are weird," I said.

Hahahaha pursed her lips and gave me side-eye.

Ismenia rolled her eyes. *Foolish human.*

I backpedaled. "What I mean is, the names aren't what I would have expected. I'm more familiar with gods of love, war, harvest, fertility. Things like that."

Ismenia shook her head. "Those qualities are important to humans, not gods. In your myths, the gods are named for how they help you. The reality is that most gods pay more attention to each other than to humans. Our names mean something to us, not to you."

"How about a god of sharp implements?" asked Morris.

Ismenia sighed as if her patience was being sorely tested. "It doesn't work like that here. On Earth you can clobber each other to get your way, but gods are complex. You have to remember that each one of us has been around since... since... let's call it the dawn of time, and we've gotten smarter along the way."

"How did you get smarter?" asked Morris, who read a lot of self-help books and was always looking to improve his mind.

"It just happened. Around three million years ago, give or take. Before that, we were..." Her face clouded, as if she couldn't remember. "Well, not as smart."

Three million years, give or take. What was the significance of that number? Not for the first time, I wished I could search the internet. But then, like most people, I was prone to rabbit-holing once I got going (Really? Platypuses sweat milk?), so I supposed it was just as well. I didn't need random distractions.

"But what triggered you to get smarter?" pressed Morris.

Ismenia shrugged. "I don't remember. I suppose we just reached a tipping point, that's all."

"Hold on, I have an itch on my nose." Hahahaha lifted her veil and scratched.

It was the funniest thing I'd ever seen. I began chortling. So did Morris.

In response to our merriment, Hahahaha giggled. Her giggles grew and grew and grew, and circled and spiraled around us, a sweet miasma; I could almost see ribbons of gold and silver. We were enchanted and entertained, and life was suddenly worth living... I mean, death was suddenly worth deathing.

Now her laughter was a low screech that built to a roar like a jet taking off, then it became something like champagne bubbles popping but much louder.

Morris and I fell onto floor pillows and lay there pounding on the tufted carpet as we screamed with gaiety. Ismenia was laughing too, but in a controlled way, and more at us than at Hahahaha.

Finally, when I felt myself about to burst and my stomach muscles throbbed, she replaced the veil. I held my gut, trying to contain myself as my chuckles faded like the last few bursts of popcorn in a microwave.

I saw where Ismenia had gotten her odd laughter, but hers was mere imitation. This, *this* was laughing greatness. The Nanna Ditzel of laughter! (For those of you not familiar with furniture history, she was known for designing the Hanging Egg Chair.)

We dragged ourselves onto the couch, which was the softest I'd ever experienced. I realized that Ismenia liked comfort because she was so bony. That seemed important, but I didn't know why.

She brought us glasses of water to help us recover. It tasted fresher than a mountain spring.

"Can't we use laughter to get the gods to back off?" I asked after I'd drunk mine down.

"Laughter is a good tool," said Ismenia, "but it's not enough by itself. Some gods wear laughter-canceling earbuds. Others have no sense of humor. And I've spent enough time with Hahahaha that my reaction is manageable."

A thought occurred to me. "Hahahaha, I don't want to seem ungrateful, but why are you on our side when most gods oppose us?

It would help to know why, so we can change the minds of those gods."

"Hold up," said Ismenia, "It's not that the other gods oppose us, per se. It's just that some of them have gotten into the rut of following Longtoe's lead because they like the idea of perfection. The idea of it—not the actuality of it. As for the others, they don't care about perfection or about humans, and so they'll just go along with things to get the trial over with so they can get back to their own interests."

"The fact is," added Hahahaha, "there are gods who appreciate humans, though it's not in fashion to admit it. I myself love humans because they laugh so much. They laugh when things are funny, when they're embarrassed, and at nothing at all. They don't always realize it, but they'll laugh just because they finished saying something. They laugh a lot more than they think—about five laughs for each ten minutes of conversation." She looked wistful. "And so many different laughs! Get people together, and it's like a bouquet of laughter!"

"I guess that makes sense," I said.

Hahahaha pointed at me. "You see? You just did it."

I looked down at myself, confused. "Did what?"

"You laughed at nothing," said Ismenia.

Now that she'd pointed it out, I realized I had given a little chuckle after saying that she made sense. I hadn't noticed it at the time.

"Your laugh was a lovely rumble," said Hahahaha, "like a bullfrog choking on a duckling."

I didn't know whether to be offended or pleased by that odd description. I chose pleased, since she seemed to mean it kindly, and anyway we needed to be on good terms to work together to save humanity.

"To be honest," said Hahahaha, "I'm not loving the company of most gods lately. They're dour. Brooding. Bored. After three million years, give or take, it's hard to find good entertainment."

Again, three million years, give or take, seemed important, but I didn't know why.

"We'll need more support," I said. "Especially during the trial."

"It doesn't matter how much support we have," said Hahahaha. "You'll be found guilty, and humanity will be doomed to the Afterlife of Biting Insects."

"No," I said. "The God of Procrastination asked for more time so she could put our case together and defend us. In fact, we should meet with her as soon as possible."

"Nothing she can do in the trial will save you," said Hahahaha.

"Right," said Ismenia. "It's a sham trial. Some gods love ritual and procedures. Some gods love shows. It's just entertainment, and it's more fun if you're found guilty. So you'll be found guilty, on all six million seventy-two counts."

Morris clapped his hands to his head. "Six million... We're screwed."

"Not necessarily," said Ismenia. "As the initiator, Longtoe's presence is required. If we can stop him from getting there, then it will be dropped. Or if we can get him to drop the charges."

"How do we do that?" I asked.

There was silence.

Ismenia gazed upward and pulled her lips to the side, as if searching for the best way to impart bad news. "Our problem is that after so long together, we gods know each other too well. We've tried everything on one another. Longtoe will anticipate anything we can come up with. And so you two have to come up with a plan, something that will blindside him."

Talk about blindsiding. We were the ones who were blindsided. From the look on Morris's face, I could tell he was thinking the same thing I was: They had all that godly power, knowledge, and ability, and yet we were the ones who had to overcome him?

"Let me think a minute." I breathed deeply, trying to induce a state of flow. A state where ideas would surface like bubbles in soda pop.

I felt blocked. I was a creator, not a fighter. How were we going to incapacitate a perfect god? "I don't know what to do. Morris, what have you got?"

He shrugged. "I'm a poet, not a fighter."

Hahahaha brightened suddenly. "I know! You should ask the Oracle."

Ismenia, who had just taken a sip of water, coughed after getting it down the wrong way. She slapped her chest, then waved, indicating she was fine.

"What's the Oracle?" I asked.

"A human," said the God of Laughter. "She's relatively new among the dead—she's only been here a few years—but I hear she's full of wisdom and answers and predictions."

Morris jumped up. "Let's go! Where is she?"

"In New York New York," she answered.

I wondered why she repeated the name, but of course was more interested in how to get there. She wouldn't have brought it up if it was impossible. Breathlessly I asked, "Can you send us back to Earth?"

Hahahaha fluttered her hand *no, silly human*. "It's not *New York*. It's *New York New York*."

"Oh," said Morris. "Like Baden-Baden and Bora Bora?"

"Right," she answered. "It's at the edge of the Afterlife of the Humans, right next to the Home of the Gods. It's one of the places humans arrive after they die."

"So Lilly could be there!" I jumped up, imagining our joyful reunion in the New York New York equivalent of Central Park.

Hahahaha shrugged. "Hard to say. There are other arrival points. And it's huge, bigger than the other New York, and more sprawling."

"Why do they call it New York New York?" asked Morris.

"Ask the humans," said Ismenia. "They're the ones who named it."

"It's a funny name," said Hahahaha, who must have meant funny-strange, because she wasn't laughing.

"Right, then," said Ismenia. "Hahahaha and I will go roust up support from other gods. Leo and Morris, we'll drop you off near New York New York and meet you back there in eight hours."

"Watch out for dragonflies," said Hahahaha.

I waited for a punchline from the God of Laughter, but it wasn't a joke. She added, "Longtoe sends dragonflies out as scouts, searchers, and information gatherers. They're his eyes, ears, and tasters."

"Tasters?" I shifted uneasily, imagining long insectile tongues reaching out to lick me.

"Dragonflies have a convoluted sense of honesty," said Hahahaha, "and so Longtoe would require them to take a little sample of your skin as proof they found you."

"And how much of a"—I used air quotes—"*sample* would they take?"

"Small," said Ismenia. "Like a punch biopsy. You've had one of those."

I narrowed my eyes at her. "How do you know that?"

"Don't all humans get them?"

"No."

She shrugged. A twitch turned it into a double shrug. "Anyway, it's small. Only around four millimeters wide."

"Sure," I said, "but it's not just the surface skin. It's down into the fat."

Morris covered his arms protectively. "And lots of bites could add up."

"Don't worry." She waved away our concern. "It grows back." She paused, then added, "Eventually."

"Avoid the biting dragonflies." Morris sighed. "Got it."

I couldn't picture a dragonfly mouth and therefore couldn't picture being bitten by one, which was probably just as well. Still, there was so much about this place I didn't know, and I had a nagging feeling these two gods were leaving something out, intentionally or otherwise.

However, we were finally going to the Afterlife of the Humans. We would be consulting the Oracle about Longtoe, but maybe I would find Lilly there too!

Chapter Twelve

Right after our meeting, Ismenia drove us (well, rolled us) to a hill overlooking New York New York. From its summit, the city and its winding streets seemed endless, disappearing into a vanishing point on the horizon. Here and there a hill interrupted the flatness. The buildings themselves were like battered cigar boxes, squat and scuffed. There were no skyscrapers, no brick buildings, no signature structures, no parks. The only resemblance to the original New York was its enormous size.

The city nudged up against the Home of the Gods, which featured wide avenues, green parks, blue canals spanned by arched bridges, and tall gleaming buildings. The contrast between the two was startling. One side was like a sepia photograph, the other a full-color magazine spread.

Fingers of New York New York extended into the Home of the Gods. I could see why Longtoe felt they were being encroached upon and suspected that humans often "invaded" the Home of the Gods to experience its beauty. And why not? What made the gods so special that they could live in luxury while humans had to scrape by?

Ismenia gave us watches that were basically just little sundials and said she'd meet us back there at three o'clock.

"You're not coming with us?" I asked.

"Humans and gods don't get along that well, especially here, close to the border. Besides, I have to drum up more support."

"This place is mega-normous," said Morris. "How do we find the Oracle in all that?"

"And what if the Oracle only oracles on alternate Wednesdays?" I added.

"Ask around," she suggested, then left.

"Onward and upward," said Morris, a phrase that always encouraged me, except that this time it was onward and *downward*.

We skidded down the steep switchbacks toward the city's edge. I buzzed with nervous energy. We were about to reach the Afterlife of the Humans, but would we find what we needed or get lost in its shuffle? What would other dead people be like? Helpful? Indifferent? Vindictive?

After an hour we reached an overlook and saw that the streets teemed with people: thousands of them in a wide range of clothing styles. Taffeta dresses with bows and bustles. Knickerbockers and knee socks. Tribal capes and beaded necklaces. Silk tunics and conical hats. Everybody was on foot; there were no vehicles.

"It's like a Hollywood lot down there," I said.

"This is supposed to be an arrival point for newly dead people, but I don't see anybody wearing modern clothes."

"Then it might be hard to communicate with them."

"I'm not good with *dead* languages," joked Morris.

"Too soon," I said lightheartedly, though I actually meant it.

We descended to the city's edge. The gutter water shone like beef gristle. The buildings appeared thrown together, boards leaning against one another like playing cards and fabric serving as doors. They were built of refuse that had once been colorful and ornate, but was now dull and stained. It stunk of body odor and rotten cabbage.

People called and shouted and cried and wailed, creating a strident cacophony. Now that we were closer, I saw that their outfits were tattered and grimy, presumably from wearing them for so long in death.

I automatically scanned for Lilly among the throngs of people, but I saw no cherry-red windbreaker, teal-dyed hair, orange shape-sculpting leggings, or engaging smile. Not yet, anyway.

We marched into their midst. I couldn't read their faces. What were their agendas in the afterlife? Were there muggings here? Random violence? Did we stand out as gullible newcomers with our fresh, bright clothing?

Morris, too, looked stiff and wary, his eyes darting from person to person. Even so, he spotted a man in jeans and a T-shirt and asked him about the Oracle; however, the man didn't speak English, French, or German. My mime skills didn't help us either. We tried another person, and another, without success.

"We'll find that darn oracle," I said encouragingly, for both of our benefits. "Won't be long now."

In the interest of efficiency, I shouted, "Oracle? Oracle?" and "Lilly Cooper?" I felt like a town crier. Morris called out as well. Nobody spoke up.

As we pressed forward among the multitude, the stink and the noise began to get to me, and I felt myself drooping. Our shouts for help became rote and haggard. I felt as if nobody would answer, and why should they? Plenty of others were making just as much noise as we were.

After another half hour a woman told us haughtily, "The Oracle is up there," as if we should have known all along. She pointed to a hill that was much higher than the one we'd climbed down. Near its top we could see a building facade hewn from a rock face, much like those of the ancient city Petra on Earth. It had Corinthian-styled columns, narrow and fluted, which I'd always found to be elegant.

Elated, we thanked her profusely. I wanted to ask her questions about the Oracle and the afterlife, but she left, clearly wanting nothing more to do with us. That didn't dampen my enthusiasm, because the structure looked so promising. Surely a wise and intuitive person would occupy such a regal place. With renewed vigor, we navigated through the crowds, along the winding streets, and to the hill.

Happy to be free from sharp elbows, we started upward, tromping on sickly patches of weeds, sidestepping past rocks, and puffing with the effort of the climb.

"What do you think the Oracle will be like?" I asked.

"She'll be a mysterious young woman with a connection to an unseen font of wisdom. Also, beautiful, wearing flowing folds of aqua-colored silk trimmed with gold and faux ermine, silver-embossed huarache sandals, and a super high-quality wig."

I nodded, this image now seared into my thoughts, adding, "With a velvet voice that embraces five octaves, but only during a performance and never in casual conversation. In spite of her superior wisdom, she'll be kind and welcoming, and leave us with a sense of having had a really great day."

While we climbed we watched out for the dragonflies we'd been warned about, and also for Longtoe himself. Happily, we didn't see them.

We reached the building. It was ancient and timeworn, in contrast to a sandwich board sign that read *Ask the Oracle* in colored chalk, like a menu in an artsy coffee shop. It featured an expertly rendered cartoon of a confused person with question marks exploding from his head. The fee was listed as negotiable, and the hours of opening were nine a.m. to noon and two p.m. to four p.m. Our sundial watches showed ten a.m., so the place was open.

Morris and I gave each other looks of concern. It seemed much too whimsical and, frankly, downright capitalistic.

"Looks kind of scammy," I said.

"Well, we're here." Morris clomped up the majestically wide stairs. Sighing, I followed him, and we pushed open a wooden door carved with geometric panels.

Inside the air was cool and smelled of ancient dust, much like my unfinished basement at home. Narrow-necked clay amphorae lined one stone wall, the kind that might contain wine or olive oil. There was a bed-size malachite platform, with intricate forest-green swirls and patterns—an altar perhaps?

A woman sashayed into the room. Her face was full, like a finger-pressed snippet of dough, with deep-set eyes and even deeper-set dimples. She was dressed in overalls and a pink checkered shirt.

When she spotted us, she hurled herself in our direction, screaming like a goat being squeezed by a corset. "Morleo!"

"Grandma!" I cried happily.

Grandma Tiboni "T-Bone" Johnson had passed away five years ago, leaving a big hole in my life. But now here she was! That domineering yet devoted woman who ruled my childhood while my parents worked long hours.

She enfolded us in a great bear hug. "Morleo!" she repeated, which was her portmanteau version of our names. In life, even as kids, we were always together, so she had shortened *Morris* to *Mor* and tacked *Leo* on at the end. It was quicker when calling us to dinner or calling us out on some mischief we'd gotten into. It also kept the wrong Leo and Morris from answering her call, which happened more than you'd think.

Grandma held us both by our chins, tightly, as if to make sure we didn't escape her questioning. "Well, I'll be dipped and rolled in cracker crumbs! Why are you dead so young?"

"A fluke avalanche got us," I said.

"An avalanche? That sounds like one of your famous excuses. Figures it would be something ridiculous. But anyway, you're here now, bless your hearts." She let go of our chins, leaving red marks that would last at least a half hour.

"Grandma, it's so good to see you, and I want to catch up, but we're in a bind and we need to talk to the Oracle."

"That's me." She jabbed her thumb toward her clavicle. "I'm the Oracle."

Morris's jaw relaxed in that way it does when you can't hold it up because all your energy is going into being confused. My jaw fell too, along with my heart. Grandma T-Bone, the Oracle? A mistake had surely been made. She was an unlikely candidate for such a thing. Don't get me wrong, she was a smart woman, but she was a regular human being, and a quirky one at that. I had a hard time believing that somebody who used to drive a Volkswagen Beetle with eyelashes on the headlights would have access to the god-fighting type of knowledge we needed.

Or would she? She'd always seemed a bit crazy around the edges. What if that meant she had some sort of deeper understanding? Plus, she could often predict when I was going to do something wrong. Had that been mere grandmotherly foresight or oracle foresight?

And then there was her ability to find lost things. Keys, toys, virginity. That last item I was always a little confused about, but such was her reputation.

A side note: You might think it a coincidence that the Oracle would turn out to be one of my grandparents, but the chances were higher than for the typical person. What with the divorces, remarriages, and polyamorous situations, I actually had fifty-seven grandparents in the afterlife (one hundred eighty-five were still alive).

Another side note: I'd never seen her eat a T-bone steak. She had a penchant for barbeque ribs, but didn't truly live up to her bony moniker. Either her parents had hoped she would grow up to embrace expensive cuts of beef or they hadn't talked through the possible nicknames when they named her Tiboni.

A third side note: She was born in Seattle, but her vocabulary, attitude, and mode of dress didn't spring from there. For whatever reason, she embraced a more Southern sensibility, so that I always imagined her as having been born in a cabin on a bayou.

We sat on chairs whose backs were wooden cobras with their hoods spread wide. We told her our situation, and she slapped her thighs angrily, hissing, "What are you doing getting involved with gods? That's the doggone worst thing you can do, and you've only just gotten here. And what's worse, you've gotten yourself on the wrong side of Longtoe, God of Perfection! How do you always get yourself in these situations?"

"That doesn't matter now," I said. "We've got to stop Longtoe from condemning humanity to the Afterlife of Biting Insects. And find Lilly. Can you help us figure out what to do?"

Grandma T-Bone sighed, a great long sigh full of grandmotherly annoyance and resignation that went on for ten seconds, which might not seem like a long time unless you're receiving the brunt of that annoyance. Morris winced as if he might get slapped, and my insides went a little watery. I suppose she'd been a bit godlike to us when we were kids, and her ability to make us feel small had never waned.

"First of all, I can only work on one major issue at a time. You can try to find Lilly or you can try to stop Longtoe. Sounds like you have to deal with him first, then come back next week to ask about Lilly."

I took an anguished breath in, then let it out slowly, trying to think of a good reason to find Lilly first, but I couldn't. If I didn't stop Longtoe, all humans would suffer, including Lilly.

"She's right, Leo. We'll get this other mess fixed, then come back." He held out his fist for me to bump.

"I guess so." I bumped it back, but not vigorously.

Grandma clapped her hands together. "All right, then. I'll ask how to stop Longtoe, but you can't expect miracles. I don't get full answers when I consult the Doobie."

"The Doobie?" I asked. Was she going to smoke weed?

"Yes, the Doobie. That's what I named the ethereal universe that I consult to get answers to questions. As in Doobie Brothers, not pot." Seeing our blank expressions, she added, "They were a rock band in the 1960s. They were visionaries too. Anyway, when I consult the Doobie I get snatches of words that need interpretation. Sometimes I see a vision, but that's not guaranteed."

"Anything will help," said Morris. "Even Ismenia and Hahahaha don't know what to do. It's on us."

"All right. I need to prepare."

We stood, assuming we would need to leave.

"Sit your asses down."

We did. A little hard. My tailbone complained.

Grandma explained, "The ones who ask the question have to be present." She produced a green glass liquor bottle and took a swig, made an "aaah" noise, then handed it to me. I obediently took my own swig. For a moment I could taste it—some kind of liquor with a side note of anise, and then it hit. It was like I had drunk fire. I gasped, choked, and rubbed my throat.

She gave a full-hearted laugh, slapping her thighs, then snatched the bottle away and thrust it at Morris.

He batted it away with both hands, but Grandma was not to be deterred. Holding it to his lips, she growled, "Bottoms up!" He drank.

She stepped back, admiring the result of her effort: Morris coughing and choking while doing a tiptoe dance, which took him in a circle around me. I was still coughing and choking too. Together we sounded like the Little Train That Couldn't trying to get up a hill. We staggered around and then ended up leaning against the malachite altar, foreheads on forearms.

"Lightweights," said Grandma with actual glee.

When we'd recovered, we watched her warily. What else were we expected to endure? But she waved us back to the cobra-back chairs, where we sat, wiping tears from our eyes.

She climbed wooden steps onto the malachite platform, rolled up her sleeves, raised her arms, and closed her eyes. It didn't look promising. Maybe it was the overalls that made me dubious. *Or should I say Doobie-us?* I giggled, feeling a little disoriented. Had the drink done something to me?

"Doobie-doobie-doobie," she said in a reverent tone. I kept expecting her to add the syllable *doo*, until I realized that I was thinking of Scooby-Doo. But then, wasn't there a song with the words *doobie-doo*? Probably several.

"Oh Doobie-doo," she said. There it was! The *doo*! In my altered state I was jubilant I'd been right.

"Tell us how to keep the gods from dooming humanity to the Afterlife of Biting Insects," she chanted, then was still, listening. She nodded, lips pursed in a decidedly displeased manner. Finally she said, "Uh huh... yup... Got it... Is that everything?"

She descended from the platform and planted herself in front of us. "There is one thing you can do, and you're not going to like it."

Chapter Thirteen

Within ten minutes we had recovered from the mystery beverage. Grandma T-Bone flung open the double doors to her walk-in closet. It held mostly overalls and riotously patterned shirts, but also a wall of shelves crammed with platform shoes of all types, with red glitter, black-and-white zebra stripes, bright orange swirls, and much more. One pair even had transparent heels filled with water, in which telescope-eye goldfish swam.

She spoke with satisfaction, chin held high. "I knew these would come in handy one day."

"Are we going to have a fashion show?" asked Morris uncertainly.

I imagined clunking down a runway in these loathsome monstrosities, playing air guitar, something by KISS, though no specific song came to mind. The thought made me shudder. I have nothing against KISS or old-school glitter rock in general, but they're not my brand.

"We're going to barter them for patronage, right?" I asked hopefully. The gods seemed partial to gaudy outfits. It might only be a question of whether we had enough pairs to trade for the salvation of humanity.

"There are a lot of gods to win over. We'll have to get several hundred thousand more," said Morris. "We have three days. It'll be tight."

"No, we're not going to barter them. We're going to wear them." Grandma seized a pair of six-inch-high shiny gold platform boots and dumped them into my arms.

"I'm tall enough already."

"That's not why we need them," she said.

"I'm not putting these on." I shoved them back onto the shelf, partly because I could twist an ankle in them, but mostly because

I couldn't see how debasing myself would save humanity. Had she faked the whole oracle bit? Maybe she was getting back at us for all the trouble we'd caused her when we were young. If so, she clearly didn't understand the gravity of the situation.

I tried to think of how to get things back on track—first ditch Grandma, then get advice from a lawyer. There must be plenty of those in New York New York.

But then, maybe she hadn't faked it. She didn't cotton to liars, after all. In that case, what could the Doobie possibly have told her to make platform boots the means to save the day?

"You're saying you're not putting these on?" she asked sarcastically. "You'd rather humanity suffer for all eternity? Sounds pretty selfish, if you ask me."

She gave me the Grandma T-Bone glare. It was like being in a police spotlight at midnight at the end of a dead-end alley, with police dogs barking and a dozen cops aiming at me with fully loaded weapons.

Trembling, I reached for a pair of four-inch-high platform sandals that would allow my skin to breathe. They weren't so bad if you ignored the red tassels and the diamond-like rhinestones.

She snatched them away from me. "Wear the ones I gave you. You'll need steel toes."

Steel toes? Were we going to a construction site? Platform shoes would be highly impractical at such a place. Nevertheless, I shoved my feet into the metallic-gold monstrosities. Luckily—or not so luckily—they fit me. Grandma had huge feet, and so I could get them on, though they were a touch narrow.

For Morris, she chose psychedelic boots with the colors of the rainbow. His feet were a couple of sizes smaller than hers. There being no tissue paper in the afterlife, or at least none handy, he had to stuff the toes with pairs of Grandma's G-string underwear. "They're clean," she assured him, but still he handled them gingerly between thumb and forefinger.

Grandma donned a pair of pink platform hip boots and admired herself in a full-length mirror. "Eat your heart out, Elton John."

I had to admit they did her bulging calves and ample thighs proud. She moved confidently in them, as if she'd been born wearing them—*don't think too hard about that*—while Morris and I stumbled awkwardly, like drunk stilt walkers.

"Come on, you two, put some gumption into it and stomp like nobody's watching. Pretend like you're chasing the chickens into the hutch, the rabbits into their hidey-holes, and the blues into the back forty. You need a lot of practice."

"Why?" asked Morris.

Grandma held up her palms as if he'd asked her the stupidest question ever. "Would you ask a stegosaurus, 'Why the back plates and tail horns?' Would you ask a porcupine, 'Why the sharp quills?'"

Morris didn't answer. Just waited.

"All right, then," she said. "Too dense to connect the dots. I'll tell you then. Protection."

"Against what?"

"Trickle-trackles."

I searched my memory for the term. I'd never heard her say it before.

"You mean rats?" asked Morris.

I imagined hordes of fat, afterlife-size rats. I hid my retching by shifting my weight to the side.

"Rats?" She let out a *whoomph* of annoyance. "Not rats. I'd have said rats if I meant rats. It's trickle-trackles you need protection from!"

"What's a trickle-trackle?" I asked.

"I saw them in my vision. Little animals with big teeth. They like to bite toes, *nom-nom*. Wiggle your toes. Be glad you have them. For now." She belly-laughed.

Where were we going that would have such creatures? After that unsettling news, I felt glad for those clunky yet protective steel-toed platform shoes. No trickle-trackles were going to bite my toes today.

"Stomp some more. Get used to them."

We tread steadily, like grape stompers with a large harvest in the vat.

"No, no, no. Stomp. Stomp! When I say stomp, you say, 'how hard?'"

We put more effort into it. She made a *pfff* noise at our underperformance. "Like this." She stomped while turning in a circle, elbows up, portraying the frantic finale of a clog dance.

We did our best to imitate her, going all in, stomping faster and faster.

"You're getting the idea!" She gave us a thumbs-up, which gave me a warm feeling. "Okay, that's enough. Come on, y'all. No dillydallying. No rest for the wicked."

She handed me a metal flask, the kind kept in a breast pocket for an occasional nip. I remembered her drinking from one when we were young and telling us it was medicinal barley juice and that we wouldn't like it. I later realized she'd been talking about whiskey, and so that's what I expected now, but the flask was empty.

"What's this for?" I asked.

"The Doobie told me to bring it. Empty. And that you'll know without question what to do with it when the time comes. That's all I know about it."

Having no coat and therefore no breast pocket, I stashed it in the pocket of my harem pants.

"Now we have to go to a long darkness near the teeth of three million—give or take—years," said Grandma.

"Where's that?" I asked.

"We have to figure it out," she said. "Sometimes the Doobie speaks in riddles."

"Three million years, give or take," I mused. "Ismenia and Hahahaha had said the gods had gotten smart around three million years ago. And she also said 'give or take.' What's the connection?"

"Don't know," she said. "Got any ideas where the place might be?"

"The Arctic Circle?" asked Morris. "It gets dark for a long time there. And mountains look like teeth."

Grandma tapped a finger on her plump cheek while she thought. "The Doobie wouldn't send us somewhere unprepared. It didn't mention snowsuits, husky dogs, or ice picks. And platform shoes would be impossible in snow and ice. Naw, that's not it."

"Catacombs are long and dark," I said. "And they have actual teeth."

"Yeah, well, catacombs aren't a thing in the afterlife. Everybody wears their skulls and bones." It was an odd way of putting it, but it made a certain sense. We still had ours.

Morris spoke solemnly. "I've got it. Depression. That can be seen as a long darkness."

"Oh, sure," said Grandma in her most derogatory tone, "I'll slip back into my postpartum depression, then you two tell each other sob stories until you're just as miserable as me."

Morris sagged. I clenched my teeth. He was truly hurt, plus the future of humanity was at stake. "Don't shut him down, Grandma. We need his creativity, otherwise we might not come up with the right answer."

Grandma gestured lamely, showing that maybe, possibly, she was in the wrong, but there was no apology, and I hadn't expected one. "Whatever. My point is that we need real places that are dark, not figurative ones, because we have to actually go there. In person."

Morris bounced back more quickly than I thought he would, saying evenly, "It's dark in the ocean. The abyssal zone."

"Again," she said with a huff, "the Doobie would prepare us. Platform shoes do not prepare us to go deep into the ocean."

"They prepare us for costume parties..." I trailed off when Grandma looked annoyed. "Look, Grandma, I know that's not the right answer, but in brainstorming you have to let it all out to get to the right answer."

As if to prove me right, Morris continued my train of thought. "Costume parties have dancing. Some people won't dance without a drink. Maybe they'll drink a margarita with salt on the glass. You can get salt from salt mines." He jumped up and did a hip-circle touchdown dance. "Salt mines are dark!"

I jumped up as well, punching a victorious fist in the air. "Brilliant! As are coal mines, gold mines, uranium mines—"

"There aren't any mines at all in the afterlife," said Grandma. "The gods do their hocus-pocus and they have metal without digging."

"Maybe they don't dig mines, but they could dig tunnels," I said. "Hey, that's it! A tunnel. That's a long darkness."

"Oh!" cried Morris. "Tunnels are definitely long darknesses. Nicely done. We just need to find a tunnel near some really, really, really old teeth."

"Well, I'll be hornswoggled," said Grandma T-Bone. "I know just the place."

• • • •

AN HOUR LATER WE MARCHED into the midst of giant teeth. Well, not really. They were stone monoliths, twenty feet tall, that sort of looked like teeth from a distance if you squinted. They needed fillings and a root canal or two, perhaps some braces to align them properly.

"Stonehenge on steroids," said Morris.

"Except not in a circle," I said. Most of them stood in a double row. Others were placed randomly, which messed with my sense of order.

This area just outside of New York New York was as dry and hot as the Sahara Desert. I could understand why the city hadn't expanded here. Aside from the heat, it seemed infused with bad energy, as if being here for very long would do irreversible damage to your neurons. We had just arrived and I was already itching to leave.

The ground was flat, with no sign of a tunnel, so we headed for some hills about a quarter mile away.

On the way, Morris said dully, "If you'd told me a few months ago that we'd be walking around a Stonehenge-ish place, and wearing harem pants and embroidered slippers, and Grandma T-Bone would be with us, and we'd be lugging glitter backpacks full of lanterns and psychedelic platform boots, and something called the Doobie would have us looking for a tunnel near three-million-year-old teeth, give or take, I'd have said you were crazy."

"True that." I knew what he meant. I was continually astonished to be here in the afterlife. I'd think, *I need to tell Lilly about this crazy dream when I wake up*, but then remember it wasn't a dream.

"You'll get used to it soon enough," said Grandma, but Morris tilted his head as if to say he doubted it.

We scoured the hillside, pulling aside thorn-studded vines and peering into craggy holes. After an hour of searching, my throat was as dry as the parched hillside. I wished I'd put water in the empty flask I was carrying.

We sat down to rest on the top of a hill. "You said the tunnel was near the teeth," I said. "We've scoured the place. Maybe these aren't the teeth after all."

Grandma scowled. "Are you questioning Grandma T-Bone?"

Internally I quailed, but I told myself I was an adult now, and humanity was on the line. "I'm questioning the Doobie," I said as evenly as I could. "Why does it have to be so obscure? Why can't it just tell us where to go and what to do in no uncertain terms? How do we know it's the Doobie speaking to you and not some god toying with you?"

Grandma rose, hands up in slapping position, dimples nonexistent. I sprang into a defensive posture: forearms up, side stance, eyebrows raised as if to say, *You sure you want to start something with me?*

Morris cried, "Hey, look!"

He was pointing at the monoliths. At first I thought he was trying to distract Grandma from lighting into me, but then I saw something from this perspective that I couldn't have seen from below. The double lines of monoliths formed the stick part of an arrow, and the rest were its arrowhead. We'd been unable to discern it because several stones were missing, but from above we could see depressions in the ground where they should have been.

"It's an arrow!" I jumped like a kid. "It's pointing to where we need to go. That way."

Grandma's animosity vanished. "Well, butter my backside and call me a biscuit."

"Except that there's nothing where it's pointing to," said Morris.

He was right. It was an empty field with a bit of grass and some scrubby bushes.

"Ah, what the hell," said Grandma. "Might as well go see. The day's already effed up. Might as well eff it up some more."

Soon we discovered that there *was* something there: a narrow ravine. We descended into it, and there it was: the opening to a tunnel. After all this searching, I hardly believed what I saw. "Wow," I said.

"Double wow," said Morris.

"Well, cut off my legs and call me shorty." She turned to me and said threateningly, "Never question the Doobie again."

I raised my palms. *Peace.*

She backed off. Opening her backpack, she pulled out her pink platform hip boots and wiggled into them with a quickness that made me suspect she'd done it many times before. Morris and I donned our platform boots as well, stashing our embroidered slippers—which had taken a beating during the trip—into our backpacks.

Cool, dead air flowed like labored breaths from the tunnel, giving me goosebumps. The thought of entering that midnight-black hole made me fumble while trying to light my lantern, which I tried to play off as the fault of the stick matches, but after three failed tries, Morris discreetly lit it for me.

We shuffled in. The dirt tunnel was barely taller than me in my platform shoes. It had no beams. The uneven walls bore dents, as if the diggers had used crude tools. An oily sheen coated the walls.

"Is this safe?" I asked.

"Oh lordy," said Grandma T-Bone. "Depends on what you consider safe, I guess."

I meant whether the ceiling would collapse or not, but she could have been talking about the tunnel or the trickle-trackles, or about our whole endeavor. She had a habit of leaving important information out and then dumping it on us when it was too late, such as "There's a pig's head in the fridge" or "Grandpa Buzzy is practicing being a nudist." What hadn't she told us yet? But there was no point in asking; she'd tell us when she felt like it.

The more we walked, the more it seemed like the tunnel itself was displeased at our presence, because I kept feeling resistance, yet nothing was touching me. A few times I stumbled in the platform shoes and was lucky I didn't fall, because I refused to touch the greasy tunnel walls to right myself.

Morris said quietly, "Something doesn't want us here."

Even Grandma seemed apprehensive. "The sooner we get in and out, the better. The first thing we need to do is cross the water that's up ahead somewhere."

Water? A sewer that originated in New York New York, perhaps? I hoped not, because aside from noxious gases, it would be slippery. I hoped for a shallow underground stream instead.

The eeriness of the place grew stronger. Our shadows played across the rough tunnel walls, jerking from spot to spot. More than once I drew back with a gasp, thinking a trickle-trackle was leaping out at me. Each time Grandma whooped at my insecurity, which was cruel but made me vow to be strong just to spite her.

The air was getting even warmer. "We're not going to hell, are we?" asked Morris. "I'm not okay with that. Hell isn't on my bucket list."

"Don't worry," I said jauntily. "A bucket list is pre-death."

"Oh yeah," said Morris uncertainly. His neck straightened, and his eyes focused ahead. "Hey, we're almost there!"

As a matter of fact, I could see the outline of the tunnel opening. I halted to better prepare myself for whatever was to come, but Grandma gave me such a hostile look that I decided I preferred the unknown over her famous swat on the nape of the neck. I was tall, but she had the arm reach of a gorilla, plus we were all stronger in the afterlife. The term *heads will roll* came to mind. I gathered my courage and kept going.

When we reached the end, the tunnel seemed to spit us out like a mouthful of past-date bologna, making us stumble forward into an enormous cavern. We could only see so far in the lantern light, but it was enough to make out the edge of a lake, black and smooth as a layer of heavy-duty three-mil garbage bags fresh from the box.

"Probably don't want to touch the water," said Grandma.

"Why?" I asked. "What would happen?"

"Our hair will fall out," suggested Morris, "and drift to the ground like little birds. Then our toenails will rear up and dislodge from our toes like tiny Titanics. Then our skin will flake into little snowstorms of human dermis, until we're nothing but heaps of human crud."

I always appreciated Morris's creativity, but this wasn't his usual uplifting output. Clearly this place had affected him negatively. "I was asking Grandma."

She snarled, "How would I know what'll happen if you touch the water? I'm an oracle, not a hydrologist."

Unfortunately, we were going to have to touch it. There was a dock, which indicated that the water wasn't shallow. We would have to swim to get to the other side.

I sensed something emanating from the lake—something cold yet burning. Something evil. This was a mistake.

"Let's bail," I said.

"Eyes." Morris's voice warbled. "I see eyes."

Chapter Fourteen

I followed Morris's gaze. The eyes were a couple of bright spots low to the ground. They blinked three different ways: horizontally, then vertically, then diagonally. This made my skin crawl, but even worse was their red color. Not cherry red, not fire-engine red, not tomato red. Not even blood red, but something much worse: the red of damnation and destruction, the red of evil and torture, the red of the end of all hope.

I heard a ribbit. Frog-like in tone yet malevolent in intention. The noise intensified as it bounced off the cavern wall.

Another set of eyes appeared, blinking at three different angles and looking just as evil as evil could be. Then another set, then another.

The eyes zoomed toward us. "Here they come!" shouted Grandma with a maniacal laugh, very mad scientist.

I braced myself. We should have brought weapons or shields. If they could bite off toes, then certainly they could bite off fingers. Why stop there? They would bite chunks of flesh from our limbs, like land-based piranhas, congregating and feasting until only our bones remained. I almost would have preferred the slime creatures pit, which in a practical sense wasn't better but at that moment seemed like a step up.

The closest trickle-trackle was now a foot away from me. It had hairless, battleship-gray skin. Its body was only as big as a hamster, but its thick neck held up a baseball-size head. Those teeth! They were slanted, forming the shape of a guillotine blade—perfect for slicing off toes. It bit the bottom of my platform boot; the sound was sharp, clean, and metallic.

I scrabbled backward. It drooled; the black glob hung for a moment, then hit the dirt with a sizzle. A thin trail of noxious-looking smoke spiraled upward.

The creatures climbed onto one another, perching expertly like little rodent cheerleading squads in spite of their bulky heads. Within seconds my kneecaps would be in harm's way. I needed those kneecaps; they weren't optional equipment, even in death.

I braced for retreat, hoping the trickle-trackles wouldn't follow us back into the tunnel, but Grandma trilled, "Onward!" She rushed ahead.

We trailed her, shrieking. I'd like to think I followed because of a sense of honor (can't leave Grandma behind!), but it was more of an automatic response. You did what Grandma T-Bone said, or else.

I was ready to plunge into the lake to escape those guillotine teeth, but I also feared the water. Its sense of evil strengthened the closer I got, making the hairs on my neck stand up, as well as the ones on the back of my hands and those in my ears.

A sudden thought made my gut twist. What if trickle-trackles could swim? I pictured them dog-paddling after me on the surface of the water, those guillotine teeth approaching my nose, slicing it off. My best feature, disappearing into the gullet of a trickle-trackle!

Grandma stopped and set down her lantern next to a row of mounds that were as high as my shoulders. She dug into one, and I joined her. The dirt was so dry that dust filled the air, making us cough so that I couldn't ask what we were uncovering, but at least it kept the trickle-trackles away for the time being.

Soon I saw we were digging out an upside-down canoe. We didn't have to swim after all, and it was large enough for all of us to ride together! We flipped it and set our lanterns inside. I lifted one end while Morris hoisted the other; Grandma positioned herself in the middle. We trudged toward the lake.

The trickle-trackles resumed their attack. This was where the stomping practice was useful. While we trudged, we stomped and kicked; the trickle-trackles grunt-growled as they bounced away, seeming to promise retribution for the indignity.

Grandma helped by singing the phrase "kick off your Sunday shoes" in a continuous loop while Morris and I chanted the word *footloose*. I silently thanked Kenny Loggins and Dean Pitchford for the lyrics and music. Despite the weight of the canoe, my feet were flying and so were the trickle-trackles, launched by our kicks. We were dancing our way to safety! Still, I was careful not to fall, lest the creatures slice me like deli pastrami.

Between stomping, kicking, and carrying the heavy load, my muscles shook with fatigue; I wasn't sure we would make it to the lake. I dug in, telling myself this was not the time to wimp out. We needed to accomplish... whatever it was we were here for.

We clambered onto the small wooden dock. It was quite the feat to lower the canoe into the lake while kicking away the awful creatures. When it landed, the splash drenched several trickle-trackles and they yelped. En masse, the creatures fled from the dock. I was relieved but also concerned. Why were they afraid of the water? Were they like cats, finding it distasteful? Was it toxic?

Grandma whooped. "Get your butts in there 'cause we're going for a joyride."

As we piled in—awkwardly because of the platform shoes—she warned, "It also might be best if you don't look directly into the water."

"Why?" I asked. "What's in it?"

"Kraken," suggested Morris. "Wife of Kraken. Son of Kraken." He pulled his hands off the canoe rails and held them close to his torso.

I imagined tentacles encircling my waist and brandishing me like a prize trophy. I leaned away from the water on one side, which brought me closer to the water on the other, which made me lean back the other way.

"Stop freaking out," said Grandma. "I don't know what's in there, I'm just being cautious. Get the paddles."

Morris and I each detached one from a holder inside the canoe and set to work, while Grandma positioned herself at the prow with a lantern, looking like a plump and powerful yet surprisingly angelic ship figurehead.

While paddling, I accidentally splashed myself. The water felt—I don't know how to describe it—dull, perhaps. Unpleasant, for sure. I held the paddle at a better angle so it wouldn't happen again.

A half hour later we reached a stone quay running lengthwise along a bank. Our approach made the water lap at the quay, like a starving man pawing at spoiled food, knowing he shouldn't touch it but too hungry to stop himself.

We climbed out, tied the canoe to a bollard, and gathered the lanterns. The water was smooth once more, now that we weren't disturbing it with our oars. Dark and still. But wait... what was that?

"Come on, Leo, she said not to look in the water."

"I saw something."

"Sweet sassafras, what's that?" asked Grandma.

"Reflections of people," I said. "But not us."

"But there's nobody else here," said Morris.

I shuddered, hunching my shoulders. I didn't want to keep looking at the images, but the mystery drew me. They were gray as smoke and just as vague, though I could make out wispy silhouettes and facial features. They moved limply and seemed to sigh. There was no interaction between them.

"Hey, I recognize one," I said. "Well, almost."

"Me too," said Morris. "But I can't think of who it is. It's not my students. It's not any of the teachers at my school. Is it Benedict Cumberbatch?"

I squinted, though that didn't help. Why had I thought it would? "I don't know. Maybe they only look like people we know."

"It's like looking at clouds," said Grandma. "You think something's there, but it's just your brain playing tricks on you. Time's a-wasting. Let's git while the gittin's good."

We peered into the darkness beyond the lantern light. Oddly, I sensed that something was there but not there at the same time. Something empty and yearning.

Morris's shiver made his voice quaver. "It's like there are ghosts here, but they're taking a coffee break."

I imagined a ghost drinking coffee, the liquid falling straight through him and splashing onto the dirt. The comical image did nothing to raise my spirits. This place felt stiflingly claustrophobic and frighteningly limitless at the same time.

"Everything is so... so... gray," I said.

"It's beyond gray," said Morris. "It's like an absence. An absence of color, of life, and even an absence of death. There's a shitload of nothingness here."

"I think that describes it best," I said. "Shitload of nothingness."

"We'll have a shitload of failure if we don't get moving," said Grandma. "Stop getting distracted. The Doobie wants us to find a chain."

This was new and interesting information. I pictured Jacob Marley, the ghost in *A Christmas Carol*, wrapped in his chains of regret. Was that how we would subdue Longtoe? With a heavy iron chain?

"What kind?" asked Morris. "Industrial chain? Bicycle chain?"

Grandma gave an annoyed grunt. "I told you how it works. I get words, not a novella. We're supposed to find a chain. That's all I got."

We tramped around, kicking up dust that somehow smelled tired and ancient. There were urns and empty pedestals. Stone benches. We discovered we were on an island the size of a city block. Soon we'd traversed it entirely, finding nothing useful, especially not a chain.

"I see something," said Morris. He scurried over the ground astonishingly quickly in his platform boots, kicking up a trail of dust.

About time. I followed, ready to help carry it if it was heavy, but his lucky find was just a lone paper clip, nestled in the dirt. I exhaled loudly. "Oh good. Now maybe we can find a nice set of binder clips. Maybe a desk organizer or two."

Morris narrowed his eyes at me. I should have been kinder, but this comatose place was penetrating my pores like foul ash from a long-dead fire. I just wanted to find what we came for and get out.

"It's an anomaly," said Grandma. "Out of place. Means something. Pick it up."

You pick it up, I wanted to say. I pinched it between my thumb and forefinger. As I raised it, other paper clips, previously covered by dust, came up with it.

"It's a chain!" cried Morris. "A paper clip chain. We were supposed to find a chain."

"What are we supposed to do with that?" I asked. "I mean, they're very handy, and I got a lot of use out of them in life, but still. This can't be it."

Grandma took it from me and examined it from end to end, shaking her head.

"We've looked everywhere," said Morris. "This is the only chain we've found."

"Whether it's right or not, it's time to leave," said Grandma. "The weirdness is marinating my brain." She fastened it around her neck. I wondered why she didn't just put it in her pocket, then I saw that her overalls had fake pockets, with double rows of stitching in their place.

"I can't believe that's it," I said. "Let's just have one last look around."

"Whatever you say," said Grandma.

Morris and I both froze in place. Never in our lives had we heard that phrase come out of her mouth, and yet she didn't sound as if she was joking. That agreeable lilt was new as well.

"Are you all right?" asked Morris.

Grandma seemed to glow with congeniality. "Leo is such a smart cookie. If he says we should stay, I'm all for it."

Morris and I turned to each other, mouthing, *the paper clip chain*.

Grandma just stood there smiling, her dimples deeper than ever.

"Let's test it," I said.

Morris took a step back, I assume to stay out of harm's way if Grandma decided to whack him.

I spoke clearly. "Grandma, touch your finger to your nose."

She did so. Oddly, she chose her pinky instead of her index finger. She looked down at it cross-eyed, then at us, then back at the pinky, cross-eyed once more.

I didn't like complacent Grandma T-Bone. It threatened to upend my view of life as well as death. I had been forced to accept and absorb the idea that there were many gods, as well as separate afterlives for different species, but this was taking it too far. A complacent Grandma T-Bone? No, thank you. I removed the chain from her neck.

Grandma seized my ear. "Never, *ever* tell me to touch my nose again. Got it?"

The pain of her grip was like fire. "I won't," I squeaked.

She let go, suddenly merry. "Hot damn. I was downright obedient. Just put that paper clip chain around Longtoe's neck, and all your problems will be solved."

• • • •

A HALF HOUR LATER WE'D paddled the canoe across the lake and had almost reached the dock when I remembered the flask in my pocket. "Hold on." I stopped paddling and pulled it out.

"You're not going to fill that here, are you?" Morris kept his voice steady, but I could sense his underlying alarm.

I unscrewed the lid. "The Doobie said to bring the flask. Why else would we need it?"

"Air sample?" He sighed. He knew better.

"Be careful." Grandma's tone was so low and ominous that I nearly reconsidered.

I leaned over the water. I could see the ghostly reflections but not my own. I gripped the flask firmly, telling myself to go ahead. But that would mean touching that dreadful water.

"We haven't got all day," goaded Grandma. "Do you want me to do it?"

I submerged the flask. It began to glug, air bubbles escaping as it filled.

My hand was fully submerged. A chill traveled up my arm, and I imagined my blood vessels freezing solid, becoming an icicle tree, like a winter holiday decoration, white with a hint of iceberg blue. I shivered hard. For such a small flask, it seemed to take a long time to fill.

Everything blurred. I was no longer in the boat. Instead I was in a dream world. I wasn't me—I was some other person who was physically very different.

Somebody needed help, and I was digging a tunnel, trying to get to them. A torch burned nearby; I felt its heat on my shoulder. It smelled like scorched coconut oil.

Others were with me, also digging. A dog accompanied us; it jumped and twirled, full of energy.

The dream world shifted. I was on the island in the middle of the lake, the island we'd just left, reaching out to other beings. When we touched, I felt my soul pour into them, and something poured back. Together, we were a single mixing zone. Heat folded into cold, strength blended with weakness, awareness washed over ignorance.

The dog went wild, leaping and panting.

The vision faded, and I was back in the canoe with Grandma T-Bone and Morris. I pulled the flask out of the water. It took some time to collect myself, but when I did, I described what I'd seen.

"Scorched coconut oil?" mused Morris. "I didn't know you could smell in a vision. Can you smell in your dreams, too?"

"The important thing," I responded, "is that I was this other person. He felt so real. I could feel everything he touched. I knew everything he knew. I knew his wants and his needs. But it felt... I don't know... primitive."

They waited for me to say more, but it was fading. The feeling of being in my own body was overpowering the memory.

"Time to skedaddle," said Grandma T-Bone.

While repositioning myself in the canoe, concentrating on not spilling the flask, I dropped the lid. It bounced on the canoe rail, plonked into the lake, and sank.

Of all the stupid things to do! I was a known lid dropper. No lid had ever been safe in my hands. Lids from peanut butter jars, paint cans, pill bottles—I'd dropped all of those and more. Even a manhole cover once, which is kind of a lid.

It wasn't that I was normally fumble-fingered—far from it. I used screws and nails, washers, and other small items all the time without dropping them. Even tiny beads and straight pins were safe in my grasp. But put a lid in my hands and it would end up on the floor every time. So I always either set the lid down until I needed it or handed it to somebody else.

This time, however, I hadn't done that. I'd been too distracted coming out of the overpowering vision.

I felt queasy, as if I'd downed a full cup of peanut oil.

Morris put our quandary into words. "You have a flask full of potentially perilous water with no way to plug it."

Grandma T-Bone put it even more concisely. "Now you've done it."

Chapter Fifteen

I n the canoe I held the water flask levelly so as not to spill it on myself and glanced at the nearby shore. Trickle-trackles scuffled about, their red eyes blinking up, down, and sideways. Their malevolent ribbits bounced off the cavern walls.

Morris gave me a pair of Grandma's G-string underwear from the toe of his platform shoes and I stuffed it into the flask's opening. It wasn't much of a fix, but it would have to do for the time being.

Luckily there were no trickle-trackles on the dock. Morris and Grandma paddled the canoe alongside, then leapt out and tied it up. They readied themselves to protect me on the way to the tunnel, since I wouldn't be able to stomp and kick without spilling.

When I stepped onto the dock the ribbits stopped abruptly. A pair of eyes winked out, and there was the sound of feet scratching in the dirt as a critter rushed away. Then another pair of eyes winked out. Then the rest.

"They're leaving," said Morris.

Grandma T-Bone looked sideways at him. "Oh good. If they need a replacement for Wendex, God of Obvious Observations, I know just where to find one."

I nodded toward the flask. "They're afraid of this water."

"Two contenders," she said. "I'll inform Wendex that he's got serious competition."

I would have bristled at her, but she was just being Grandma, and I was too busy worrying about the flask and its contents, as well as wondering what in the heckfire (a Grandma T-Bone word long seared into my brain) I was supposed to do with it.

· · · ·

WE HAD A SHORT TIME to kill before our rendezvous with Ismenia so we returned to the oracle building and gathered in the kitchen, which was much like Grandma's kitchen when she was alive, with cozy nook benches covered in mustard-colored vinyl. Copper pots and pans hung on the wall, and white crockery perched on shelves.

It gave me such nostalgia that I didn't want to leave. For the first time since I'd gotten to the afterlife, I felt at home in my surroundings.

"First things first." Grandma searched through her cupboard and found a lid to replace the one I'd dropped. It wasn't a perfect fit for the flask, but a strip of oilcloth around the threads made it snug. I no longer needed to worry about spilling the water.

Next we had the first normal meal we'd eaten since we'd arrived: grilled cheese sandwiches with tomato soup. It reminded me of Saturdays when Morris and I would hang out and play video games, especially the zombie ones Grandma preferred.

While we ate, I pondered the dream world I'd experienced while my hand was in the lake. "I wonder what that vision meant."

"Describe it again," said Grandma.

"I was digging a tunnel, the same tunnel we went through today. But I wasn't me; I was somebody else. Somebody who was... How do I say this? Closer to nature. Plants meant a lot to me, and I knew a lot about them. I knew things that I—as Leo—I wouldn't know."

"Like what?" asked Morris.

I tried to call up bits of knowledge. Something to do with—sunshine on soft earth? Moonshine on... what? "No, it's gone. But... there were other people with me, and we all helped dig the tunnel. And a dog was with us. My body felt bizarre. My head was big, my arms were long. I felt... not quite human."

"Were you an alien?" asked Morris.

I considered that, but it seemed wrong. "No. Pretty sure I wasn't. Anyway, in my vision, when we got to the lake, we saw people on the island. Well, not really people. I don't know what you'd call them—they were insubstantial. They were more like the forms of people before being filled in."

"Phantoms," suggested Morris. "Shades."

I mulled this over. "Yes, shades. That's a good description. And there was something about them that told me they were suffering. Maybe it was the way they moved. Maybe I could feel it. Anyway, I and my people all agreed to help them."

"And?" asked Morris.

"And... I think we did. But it's all so hazy. We all reached out and touched them, and it was like we were sharing ourselves with them. Comforting them. And they shared themselves with us. It was difficult. I felt like I do when I'm upside down."

"Discombobulated," said Morris.

"Yes! But we were all stronger because of it. I know that's vague but..." I trailed off.

"It was a flashback from the drink I gave you before I checked in with the Doobie," said Grandma. "That's some powerful stuff. The recipe was carved into the altar. Don't ask what's in it."

Just thinking about it, my throat burned and I choked a little. Grandma gave me some water, and I quickly drank it down. Maybe she was right, and the vision meant nothing. Except that it felt so genuine. Not the result of liquor or a drug.

"Tell us more about the gods," I said. "How do we deal with them?"

Grandma shrugged. "We don't interact with them all that much. Mostly they keep their distance because they think they're better than us, but they're not. From the little I've seen, they're just like us. Some are nice, some are mean, some are smart, and some are so stupid they couldn't pour piss out of a boot even if the instructions were written on the heel."

"Just like people," observed Morris. "They're all over the board too."

"What do you know about Ismenia and Hahahaha?" I asked.

After a beat or two, Grandma took a big bite of her sandwich, as if she needed time to come up with an answer. She squirmed. I was quiet, patiently waiting. Finally she patted the corners of her mouth with a chicken-patterned pot holder, still delaying.

"Well?" I asked.

She set her sandwich down. "I've got a good feeling about Ismenia, and that's why I don't trust her."

"Wait, what?" asked Morris.

"It's all in the name," she said conspiratorially. "God of Trickery, so not trustable."

I'm not sure why, but I felt compelled to play devil's advocate. "Just because that's her name doesn't mean she spends all her time tricking people."

"Look what she did to you," said Grandma. "You play with snakes, you get bit."

This last part she said quietly, as if to herself. She wandered to the counter, lifted the lid on a porcelain cookie jar shaped like a crowing rooster, then replaced it.

Grandma knew me inside and out, and could tell when I was hiding something. The reverse was also true. I knew something was off with her.

"What are you not telling me?" I asked.

"Nothing," she said, twisting the tip of her fluffy slippers on the linoleum floor.

"Grandma, out with it," I ordered as intimidatingly as I dared.

She faced me, arms crossed. "All right, I'll tell you. She tricked me into thinking she's good people."

"How did she do that?" I asked.

"She brought me all this." Grandma motioned around the kitchen and at the food we were eating. "Soon after I got here, I was living in a cardboard box. She said my talent was being wasted. Brought me here and set me up as an oracle. She had food delivered here. You're eating the last of it, and now I know why it stopped coming. Because she was banished and couldn't continue getting it to me."

I felt a pang of anxiety. I thought I'd made it to solid ground, but now I realized a sinkhole lay below. Ismenia had known my grandmother but hadn't seen fit to tell me. Plus, she was the one who'd set Grandma up, and yet it was Hahahaha who suggested we come here, not Ismenia.

Morris gripped the table in a show of realization. "Ismenia choked on her water when Hahahaha mentioned the Oracle! Ismenia knew Grandma was the Oracle. Wow. The plot thickens."

I felt betrayed. "Why didn't you tell me all this earlier?"

"I'm sworn to secrecy. Telling you is a big risk. You know how dangerous gods are. I don't know what she'll do to me if she finds out, so keep it under your hat." She jabbed two fingers at us. "Both of you."

Morris held a pretend hat tightly onto his head, indicating he would. "But you're telling us now."

"Right. Because you need a full deck to work with. I don't want to end up in the Afterlife of Biting Insects any more than you do. I'm allergic to itching."

I inserted this card of knowledge into my admittedly thin deck and shuffled it in my mind. Way before she got banished, Ismenia had made trips to Earth, where she not only obtained my furniture and Morris's poetry books and learned about my punch biopsy, but also observed Grandma's house enough to know how it was decorated and what she ate for meals. What exactly was Ismenia's interest in us?

"What about Hahahaha?" asked Morris.

"I haven't met her, but again, it's all in the name. God of Laughter. Watch yourselves or you'll end up being the punch line."

"Tell us about the rest of the Afterlife of the Humans," I said. "How will I find Lilly here?"

She flipped her hand disparagingly. "This place is a giant mess. It'll be hard, no bones about it. There's no registry, no organization. Sometimes that's why people come to me, but the Doobie doesn't always help them." She became reflective, like talking about an old foe. "The Doobie has a mind of its own."

I must have looked miserable because she said, "She's out there somewhere. You'll find her. I'll help you as much as I can." She got a sly smile. "Tell me that story again of how you met."

It was my turn for a sly smile. We had one of the best first meeting stories ever. "She was a dog skateboarding instructor doing a video shoot with a famous bulldog."

"Named Poochie-Pie," added Morris, who'd heard the story many times.

"Named Poochie-Pie," I confirmed. "I happened upon the set, in a skate park, and that's when I saw her for the first time."

"You mean Lilly, not Poochie-Pie," said Morris, proud to make sure the point was clear.

I nodded. "That's when I saw Lilly for the first time."

She was beautiful, of course. She reminded me of the *Birth of Venus* painting by Botticelli, except she was wearing clothes and wasn't standing on a scallop shell.

Her frown was so heart-wrenching that I wanted to do something, anything, to make her life better. And when she saw me, her smile was so genuinely warm, I knew I needed her in my life.

"I asked her what was wrong. Her first words to me were..." I paused for dramatic impact, even though Grandma and Morris knew what was coming. They sucked in expectant breaths and got dreamy, romantic looks in their eyes. "'We're waiting for Poochie-Pie's stand-in.'"

As it turned out, Poochie-Pie was so famous that she didn't come on set before the lighting and props were ready. She had a stand-in for that. However, today that stand-in hadn't arrived, causing a delay.

I was taken with Lilly's beauty, but there was something more to her, something I'd never seen in anybody else. Morris repeated it for me. "She had joie de vivre!"

I nodded furiously. "I said, 'I'll be the stand-in for Poochie-Pie.' I jumped right up on the skateboard. I crouched down to bulldog height—as close as I could get to it, anyway—and put my mouth in an overbite position."

Grandma fist-bumped the air. "And that's when she knew you were the one for her! She called you a beautiful human being."

"She's the beautiful human being," I said. "I hope she's not hurt. You know, when she was young, she had an imaginary friend: a fairy godmother. I wish she really had one. She could use one now."

Grandma T-Bone could be fearsome, but I loved her. I wanted with all my heart to stay. But there would be no more contentedness of this kind unless we stopped Longtoe from condemning humanity. Soon it was time to go.

Chapter Sixteen

An hour after saying goodbye to Grandma T-Bone, Morris and I were waiting for Ismenia on top of the hill. I glanced at my sundial watch. We'd arrived before the appointed hour, because in my book, being fifteen minutes early is being on time.

The hilltop was bare dry dirt with a few waist-high rock outcroppings, but not much else of note.

I already felt nostalgic about New York New York, spread out below us. Would we see it again, or were we doomed to an eternity of biting insects? Was Lilly there in the city, or in a different city far away? How big was the afterlife? Would I have to continent-hop to find her?

It's not easy to be envious of billions of people at the same time, but somehow I managed it. I wished I could be one of them, moving on with death instead of trying to achieve an impossible task. But then, there would be nobody to envy if I didn't succeed. Everybody would suffer, including Lilly, wherever she was.

Even so, it felt wrong to be leaving when I could be searching for Lilly.

Morris, too, seemed unhappy to go, saying softly, "If I can make it there, I'll make it anywhere."

I tried to think of an inspirational proverb to keep me motivated. All that came to mind was that one about not taking life too seriously because you'll never get out of it alive. That didn't apply anymore.

A *floop* sound made me whirl around. At first I thought it was a bird, but then I saw the leathery wings of a bat, a pastel green one with a tubby body. "I've never seen a bat like that before!" I said.

Morris spoke with awe. "It's not a bat. It's an itty-bitty dragon!"

A dragon? I looked at it anew. It had scales, a pointy tail, and a stubby little snout with bulging nostrils at the end. It *was* a dragon!

Its tail curled and uncurled impishly while it hovered in front of me. I was enamored.

More arrived, a dozen of them. My worries flew out of my head while we admired them, oohing and aahing.

Abruptly, with no provocation, one swooped toward Morris, mouth wide open.

He jerked his arm away just in time. "What the hell! Dragons aren't supposed to bite. They're supposed to breathe fire!"

One flew at my arm and tried to bite me too. Suddenly I remembered Ismenia's warning. While dashing and swerving to avoid more bites, I said, "These are the dragonflies Ismenia warned us about! They're trying to take skin samples of us for Longtoe."

"Dragonflies!" repeated Morris. "That's misleading. They should be called dragons that fly, not dragonflies."

We kept moving, running and waving our arms to keep them away. They were persistent. I no longer considered them cute.

"Let's get out of here!" said Morris.

"We can't leave—she'll be here in ten minutes. Talk to them. Tell them to stop!"

Morris tried to talk to them in German, French, sloth, and harpy eagle, with no result. I felt a sudden sharp pain in my arm, and I yowled. A few seconds later, so did Morris. Each of our arms had a tiny round spot with blood welling up.

Abruptly, they left. "Guess they got what they wanted," complained Morris. "Ismenia better get here soon because now they've gone off to alert Longtoe."

"If he does come, I'll try to put the paper clip chain on him, but it'd be a lot easier with the element of surprise."

"How long do you think it'll take for Mr. Perfect to get here?" he asked.

"Hmm. Ten minutes for the dragonflies to reach him. Ten minutes back. Twenty minutes? Wild guess. We have seven minutes until the rendezvous time. If she's not late we're golden."

"We should have synchronized our watches with Ismenia's." He had a point, although I wasn't sure how you would synchronize sundial watches, and anyway it was too late now.

A shadow fell on my watch, making it impossible to read. I looked up. "Silly me." I meant that I'd been stupid to think that we had any leeway at all, when things worked so differently here in the afterlife. Longtoe was already above us in his chariot, carrying a huge net on a stick, as if for giant butterflies.

Again, I was struck by his perfect beauty, as well as the brilliance of his silver-trimmed white cloak. My duodenum began to heat up. I could never wear white without spilling coffee on myself. Plus, why wasn't I that godlike? I imagined myself in his place, cruising the sky in a chariot, the whole afterlife spread out below me. Everybody would admire my steady driving skill and my expert parade wave.

"Ha!" exclaimed the god in anticipatory triumph, the hunter hot on the trail of rare and elusive prey.

"Divide and scatter!" said Morris. It was our childhood method of escape, because the enemy wouldn't be sure which of us to chase, and the precious few moments it took to come to a decision usually gave us enough of a lead for both of us to save ourselves. I say usually, because it never worked on Grandma T-Bone.

Longtoe came at me. Instinctively, I flung myself below a rock outcropping. He swung his net and it snagged on the rock, making his chariot swerve awkwardly.

"Drat," he said, actually snarling. It was such an archnemesis reaction that I suddenly felt like a superhero, so invincible that during his next attack, I reached up and grabbed the net.

The handle slipped from his grasp, and suddenly I held the net end of the tool in my hands. The sensation of invincibility had passed, and I was confused beyond all measure. How could I possibly wield such a huge and ungainly item? I found myself wishing once more that Lilly's imaginary fairy godmother was real.

I had no fairy godmother, but I had a creative friend. "What do I do?" I cried.

"Flip it! Flip it good."

His allusion to the energetic 1980s punk song "Whip it" by Devo inspired the perfect rhythm to flip the net expertly around. I did just that and brandished it just as Longtoe was making another flyby.

Longtoe himself was out of reach, but I was able to hook one of the sculptural flames on his chariot. The net flew out of my hands and dropped into a ravine, but it had done the trick. The chariot overturned, flipping Longtoe out. It crashed to the ground, wedged against a rock outcropping.

Longtoe himself rolled awkwardly down the hill like an errant bowling pin. His cloak encased him, so that when a rock finally stopped him, he lay struggling to get his head and arms free.

This was my chance to put the paper clip chain on him! I scooted toward him, kicking up dirt as I went. I just needed to get to him before he unwrapped himself.

Although his shouting was muffled, I could make it out well enough. It was a continuous stream of variations on, "You will die a thousand deaths every day, and humanity will join you in your suffering." I thought it a bit harsh, even for this situation, but I resisted trying to think of an appropriate rejoinder. I needed all my focus. I had to get that paper clip chain on him before he got loose. The fate of humanity depended on me!

So it figured that when I reached him and tried to get the chain out of my pocket, the zipper stuck.

"Hurry," shouted Morris, arriving at my side.

"The zipper's stuck."

"Pull on the little piece of material that it's stuck on."

"I know, I know! Do something about him."

Longtoe's flopping had gotten the crown of his head free; his luxuriant curls spilled out. Morris yanked the cloak back over him.

I got the zipper open and pulled out the chain. My hands were shaking. I was about to tame a great god! I would go down in afterlife history as the Savior of Humanity. I would humbly refuse the title, I decided, and ask that instead, people go forth and treat each other with respect and kindness. Somebody would say solemnly, "We can do both. We can call you the Savior of Humanity *and* treat each other with kindness and respect."

But first I had to accomplish this simple yet delicate task. I couldn't put the paper clip chain around Longtoe's neck because it was covered by his cloak, so I wrapped it around his ankle, admiring the perfection of his Achilles tendon as I did so and reminding myself that the Greek hero for which it was named was still just a character in a myth.

I clipped the paper clips together and stood back. "Drop the trial against us," I said.

"And take back everything you said about humanity," added Morris for good measure.

Longtoe kicked his leg furiously.

"Stop kicking," I ordered, worried that the chain would come off.

He didn't obey me. In fact, he kicked harder and ramped up his threats—we would die a million deaths every day instead of a thousand.

"It's not working," said Morris.

"I see that." Perhaps it being around his ankle meant it took longer for the magic to rise to the rest of his body. "Let's give it a minute to soak in."

"Roger that." Morris continued to wrestle with Longtoe and his cloak, while I examined the paper clip chain for problems. There were no kinks, and all the clips were attached. It was a little loose, but he was clearly wearing it by any stretch of the definition, so it should have made him docile.

Longtoe gave a great heave of his body. The paper clip chain flew off his ankle.

What a fiasco! I rushed to get it, scooping it up and holding it tightly in both hands. What now? Try to get it back on him? But it hadn't worked!

By the time I turned around, Longtoe had gotten free and was holding Morris up by the neck using just one hand, as if he weighed nothing. I quickly considered how to attack. I had no weapon. I could punch, kick, or bite him, but I could see that even combined we'd be no match for him. He was too strong, too powerful, too perfect.

I wanted to be that perfect. I wanted to be him.

I mentally slapped myself for losing focus while Morris was choking, turning red, clearly in immense pain. Longtoe was going to squeeze my friend's head right off. That would take a long time to recover from, if it was possible at all. I had to act immediately. *No more dillydallying. Time's a-wasting.*

Shoving the chain into my pocket, I shouted, "You're not perfect!"

Longtoe's eyes kaleidoscoped black, red, and orange. I'd clearly touched a nerve. He dropped Morris, growled, and strode in my direction, just as I'd hoped he would.

For a mere millisecond I considered a little ruse: coyly confessing that I had been attracted to him since the moment we met, going in for a kiss, and sneaking the paper clip chain around his neck.

Ridiculous. And besides, the chain's magic didn't work on him.

Instead, I bolted. But it didn't take too long for him to catch up to me and pick me up by the neck. The pain was sharp, and my mouth tasted like iron. I couldn't breathe, and my attempt to draw air into my lungs sounded like chicken clucks. I pounded uselessly on his arms.

"You're not the God of Perfection," shouted Morris. "You're the God of Flaw." He must have thought that didn't sound right, because he tried other versions. "God of Flawness. Flawdom. Flawtitude."

Stop! I thought. *I was trying to keep him away from you!*

Longtoe dropped me and went after him.

I ran a little farther away and readied myself to continue this back-and-forth of attracting the god's ire until Ismenia arrived, but it wasn't sustainable. Our necks wouldn't take much more.

Longtoe's chariot was close to me, lying on its side. What if...? I scampered over. *This is a stupid idea. It probably works on god power or has super complicated controls.* Still, I righted it and vaulted in.

Although the outside was ornate, the inside was as smooth as a bathtub. I'd expected a panel of controls similar to an airplane cockpit, but there was only a single rod with a knob on its end, like the stick shift of a classic sports car.

"Stop!" Longtoe loped toward me.

I'm a firm believer in using a seat belt, but there was none, and no time to use one anyway. With both hands, I pushed on the knobbed stick.

Too hard. I shot way up in the air, making my stomach lurch. I pulled back, and the chariot dropped so fast it almost left me behind. Now I pushed the stick to one side, again going too far, too fast, exactly to where I didn't want to be: next to Longtoe.

He leapt for me.

My shriek sounded like a possum defending its territory (scratchy yet fearsome). I pushed the stick the other way, this time shooting past Morris too fast for him to get in. By moderating my touch on the stick, I managed to turn and go past him again, but still too fast.

Morris waved at me like an overcaffeinated traffic cop. "Slow down!"

"It doesn't go slowly!" I cringed inwardly at my recent fantasy that people would admire my steady driving skill. Ridiculous. My dexterity was totally inadequate for this task.

On my next pass, my friend leapt for me. His timing was perfect, but now he was hanging half in and half out. I grabbed his pants and yanked him into the chariot, which wobbled dangerously. I tapped the stick, ever so gently, and we rose upward.

Now I seemed to have a rough feel for driving the chariot, at least enough to get us out of harm's way. Just a little push on the stick and we would fly off. We were going to escape!

But a little push did nothing. Neither did another little push. Or a bigger push. The vehicle was frozen in midair, hovering in place. "I've lost control," I said, yanking the rod every which way without results.

Morris elbowed me aside and tried it himself. It didn't have any effect.

The chariot began to float backward. Gripping its edge, Morris and I peered down. Longtoe was about thirty feet below and thirty feet over, pulling hand over hand as if there was an invisible rope attached to the chariot. His biceps bulged and his face contorted as he marshaled his strength to the task.

We reached over the side, trying to feel for the invisible rope, but there was nothing physical attached to the chariot. I mimed pulling the invisible rope back our way, just in case, but of course that didn't work because he was using some godly magic that I didn't possess. We had to find another way to regain control.

The chariot kept moving steadily in Longtoe's direction. Bit by bit the god pulled us closer.

"Where's Ismenia?" I glanced around, but there was no sign of her.

"The flask of water," said Morris. "Use it now."

The Doobie had told Grandma that I'd know when the time came to use it. It didn't feel like that time. "No, not yet."

He grabbed my shirt to show he meant business. "Pour. It. On. Him."

I extracted myself from his grasp. "It doesn't feel right. Besides, he might have to drink it."

Morris looked like an idea had struck. He grabbed my shirt again. "Maybe *we're* supposed to drink it. Maybe it'll give us superpowers!"

The thought of drinking that stuff horrified me to the depths of my soul. Once again I pulled my shirt out of his grasp. "The Doobie said I would know, and I don't. I don't know what to do with the water." But was I interpreting the words correctly? Should I use logic, as I'd done when filling the flask in the first place? Or should I wait for knowledge to hit me, and would it do so like a thunderbolt or a nudge? How sure of any action did I need to be, on a scale of one to ten?

We were now twenty feet away and twenty feet over from Longtoe, getting closer by the second.

There was a sound like thunder in the distance. Ismenia's mobile home! The sphere screeched to a stop below, its height bringing it to within five feet of us.

I shouted with relief, but we had a quandary. "How do we get in from here?"

"I guess we jump."

However, there was no landing surface on the sphere. It was essentially a giant slide that would *sloop* us onto the ground, a two-story fall. We would break our legs. I winced, imagining my femur poking out of my skin like a toothpick in a club sandwich.

"Jump," said Ismenia's voice, which seemed to come from inside. So she thought it was a good idea. Did she know something we didn't? Or was she forgetting that human hands didn't come with suction cups? Either way, we had a choice: jump onto the sphere or allow Longtoe to pull us into his clutches.

"I will tear you limb from limb," shouted the God of Perfection. "And tear your limbs into little bits! And tear those bits into even smaller bits!"

That decided it. We jumped.

Chapter Seventeen

Morris and I landed on the sphere close to what I'll call its north pole. I hoped that the pleasing crosshatch design would provide enough friction to hold us there. For a precious moment we stayed put, limbs splayed like rain forest frogs.

It was not to be. The surface was ultra slick. We began sliding.

Time seemed to stand still. Inconveniently, I found myself imagining all kinds of furniture based on spheres. Spherical ottomans, spherical cupboards, spherical bookshelves. Such great ideas, but I would never be able to design and make them, and therefore none would lead to a prestigious award.

Why could I not get past this? I was dead. It no longer mattered. But while time was frozen, I obsessed. I'd especially coveted the World Side Table Award, which my design should have won. It was ergonomic, meaning it had different levels, so that nobody would injure themselves placing a drink on it. It was made of bamboo, a sustainable material. It was slightly off-center, representing our slightly off-center lives.

Instead, the winning entry was an ostrich burying its head in the floor. Such a literal depiction should never have been considered for an award in the first place. Plus, what kind of workmanship was that, where you didn't have to craft the head, the hardest part? Also, the legend says ostriches bury their heads in the sand, not the floor, and in fact they don't really do either, so the design perpetuated a fallacy.

Why was I spending this critical time on regret and envy rather than finding a solution to my literal downward trend? And why hadn't I used the water in the flask while I'd had the chance? Once my bones were splintered on the ground below, I wouldn't be able to move, even to lift the flask to anybody's mouth, including my own.

When I reached what I'll call the equator of Ismenia's mobile home, I felt that odd force-field-like buzzing pain, and suddenly my body was traveling via didgeridoo.

We plopped into the room with the padded seats, then scrambled to strap ourselves right in.

• • • •

TEN MINUTES AFTER OUR escape, the sphere was far away from Longtoe. Morris and I were sprawled on the pillow-filled couch in the living room with Ismenia and Hahahaha, having just described the paper clip chain failure.

Hahahaha put her hand to her forehead. *Ignorant human.* "Of *course* a chain of submission wouldn't work on his ankle. It has to be put around his neck."

We'd been so close to success but had missed out. *Damn the Doobie and its vague instructions.* "How were we supposed to know that? On Earth they don't have magic chains."

"Of course they do." She looked at Ismenia. "Don't they?"

The God of Trickery shrugged. "It's so basic. It's like knowing water is wet."

"We can try again." Morris rubbed the red marks that Longtoe had left on his neck. "But we need to test it first."

I saw what my smart friend was getting at. "Yes. On a god."

Ismenia's eyes kaleidescoped yellow and pink, and so did Hahahaha's. I got the feeling they were nervous about the idea rather than angry, but I wasn't sure.

"The gods are not test subjects," said Ismenia flatly.

"We won't make you do anything bad." Morris put on his pleading, it'll-be-fun expression, the one that had gotten us into so much trouble when we were young. He held out a hand for the chain, which I gave to him.

He leaned toward Ismenia as you might a cornered cat, slowly and calmly. "Come on. Just for a second."

She turned sideways, pulling her chin in and raising her shoulder protectively.

"You owe this to us," I said. "If you hadn't tricked us, we wouldn't be in this mess."

"I don't owe you anything," said Ismenia. "In fact, I taught you a valuable lesson."

I laughed mirthlessly. "Not to trust a god."

"No, no. It's about getting others to do things you want them to do. You thought wings were your idea, didn't you?"

I didn't answer. She was right, I had learned from her. If you get others to think something is their idea, they'll embrace it wholeheartedly. I'd known that, but I felt it viscerally now. I'd finally and truly learned it.

Still, that didn't make us even. And this whole conversation reinforced the fact that even though my gut told me she cared about us, I shouldn't trust the God of Trickery so completely.

It was at that moment I decided not to tell her about the flask of water in my pocket. I needed to make sure it was used in the right way at the right time.

I gave Morris a look that said, *Don't mention the flask or the vision I had.*

He gave me one back that said, *But they might know how to use the flask or interpret the vision.*

I gave him a look that said, *We need a card in our pocket.*

He gave me a look back that said, *Okay, if you really think that's best.*

"The chain will work if you get it around his neck," said Hahahaha. "I swear it."

How much could I trust that statement? I sighed. It seemed I would have to. "Did you get any support from the other gods?"

Ismenia perked up. "Did we ever!"

. . . .

A SHORT TIME LATER we picked up Nugatt, God of Fireworks. He bore an uncanny resemblance to Orville Redenbacher of popcorn fame. So much so that I wondered if his look was an homage to that businessman, with his tightly cropped wavy hair parted in the middle, thick black glasses, wide-lapel suit, and bow tie. But no, a god wouldn't pay homage to a human. It was just a coincidence.

"You should be the god of fireworks *and* popcorn," said Morris. "They both explode."

So he'd seen the resemblance too, but I hoped he wouldn't voice it. Nugatt might be offended by a comparison to a meek, unassuming consumer-obsessed food scientist.

Nugatt fidgeted. "What is popcorn?"

"Let's focus on the task at hand," I said quickly. "Can you create a fireworks diversion that will grab Longtoe's attention so well that somebody could sneak up behind him and put the paper clip chain around his neck?"

"Hmm. Well. Are you sure you want to do that? I mean, Longtoe can get pretty feisty about things."

"Once the chain is around his neck, it'll keep him from being feisty, at least while he's wearing it," said Ismenia.

Nugatt fiddled with his bow tie. "Hmm. Well. That's true, that's true." He seemed to brighten. "A nonfeisty Longtoe. That would be something, wouldn't it?"

"What can you do?" I asked.

Nugatt's indecisive frown pulled his neck muscles taut. "Hmm. Well, sparklers are always popular. And those snake things—you have to look down at the ground to watch them. He *might* not see you coming. Can you walk quietly?"

"Sparklers and snakes won't be enough," said Ismenia firmly.

"It'll be daytime, won't it?" I asked. "So it has to be loud."

"We need big booms," said Morris. "Stuff blowing up in the sky, so that when somebody goes to put the chain on him... Who would like to volunteer for that?"

I stiffened. His common classroom request implied that it wouldn't be him.

Both Ismenia and Hahahaha pushed their palms outward. *Not us.* "He'll sense us coming," said Ismenia. "One of you humans has to do it."

That left me. I supposed that since Longtoe was so tall, I was the obvious choice. I thought of his kaleidoscoping eyes, the burning pain of his golden net, and his promise of unimaginable torment. And then I thought of insects biting Lilly for the rest of her days. "I'll do it. But the fireworks will have to be staggeringly amazing."

"Hmm. Well," said Nugatt. "Maybe you should get somebody else. It's been a long time since I did a fireworks show."

"That's exactly why we need you," said Ismenia. "We need something novel to distract Longtoe."

"I'll do something small then, but I'm a little rusty on the big stuff."

"But the big stuff is what we need," said Morris. He cleared his throat and launched into a poem.

> "Pow pow. The fireworks are bigger than I thought.
> Up there in the sky.
> Pow pow, wow wow.
> And then, a big boom."

I clapped, nearly overcome with emotion. That simple poem packed such power. "Bravo!"

"Well done!" exclaimed Ismenia.

"Super!" cried Hahahaha.

Nugatt, however, seemed to brood, as if offended. Then he suddenly lost his meekness. His eyes kaleidoscoped into black and silver, which seemed to identify him as a particularly powerful and multifaceted god. He seemed much larger than his physical presence.

The room smelled like sulfur. His voice lost its hesitancy and deepened, as if backed up by taiko drums. "I'll turn the sky to darkness, make the sun and moon cower, and force the stars to burn out and fall away from the heavens."

Morris's mouth formed a little oval of surprise.

I blinked a few times. This was a reminder to be wary, because even this timid god who seemed a bit slow on the uptake held superior powers.

"My fireworks will fill the sky with color and awe. More awe than color. Yes, really high in awe."

Morris and I were already awed without the fireworks. If he could produce a show to match his new bearing, then it would be the huge distraction we needed.

Hahahaha and Ismenia gave each other a look that said, *the confident fireworks god is back!*

Nugatt smoothed his middle-parted hair with both hands, a gesture of efficient supremacy. "All the gods will have reverence for my handiwork, which no other god can do. They will bow down to my superiority in pyrotechnics and rue the day they ever derided me."

His enthusiasm filled me, in turn, with passion. I pumped my fists. "All right," I said. "When the fireworks start to go off, I'll sneak up behind him and get that chain on him. I'll do it!"

"You'll need disguises," said Ismenia.

"Great idea," said Morris. "Can I be the God of Race Car Driving?"

"There's no God of Race Car Driving." Ismenia grimaced as if the idea were ludicrous. "Besides, since we gods can sense each other, he would know right away that you're not a deity. I've got something better. He uses automaton servants, so I've made you some disguises that resemble them." She waved and a closet opened, revealing two metal costumes hanging from hooks.

They resembled Robby the Robot in the movie *Forbidden Planet*. Dome heads shaped like upside-down laundry baskets. Barrel chests. Various red and green tube lights. Legs like a series of bulbs sitting on top of one another. And the pièce de résistance: hands that were merely tongs, rounded like a blacksmith's tool.

"Oh," I said, meaning *What kind of fresh hell have I gotten myself into?*

Morris whistled in appreciation. "Cool costumes."

"Disguises, not costumes," said Ismenia touchily.

In some respects, they weren't horrible. They would have made fantastic Halloween costumes, albeit the type you'd remove during the course of a party because of their sheer impracticality. You'd take off the helmet to drink something, the bottom part to sit, and the upper torso with its built-in arms to do anything at all, because of the useless tong appendages.

Ismenia opened a little hatch in the torso of the taller disguise. At first I thought it was a poorly placed pee opening, set at belly-button level and too far to the side. Did gods have different equipment than humans?

Morris's exclamation set me straight. "Wow, a velvet-lined secret compartment!"

"For the paper clip chain," said Ismenia.

I fingered the mechanism that held the hatch shut. "How am I supposed get the chain out of there and put it on Longtoe using those tong hands?"

"Practice," said Hahahaha, tittering, seeming pleased with herself.

To my dismay, Nugatt nodded, and Ismenia also agreed with her. "Yes, practice. Humanity's fate depends on how quickly you can attach the two paper clips to one another. The tong hands have magnetic properties, which will help."

I sighed heavily in a passive-aggressive sort of way that was meant to inspire her to come up with a more workable disguise, but I doubted she would, and I had no alternate plan.

Morris and I donned the suits; the others helped us fasten twenty-seven clasps, which took a while.

"There's a quick-release lever if you need to get them off quickly." Ismenia showed us the recessed lever in the armpit.

The suits smelled like machine oil and were just as clunky as they looked, but the hand tongs reacted as if they were a part of me, so while their action was limited to opening, closing, and rotating, using them felt surprisingly natural. The joints in the shoulders, hips, and knees weren't too bad either, allowing for smooth movement. I could see through the helmet in all directions.

Ismenia had clearly used our measurements when she'd designed these. *How did she know them?* Still, the outfits were bulky and heavy, requiring short steps.

"Can you hear me?" When Morris talked, the mouth—a grille of blue tube lights—lit up, oddly out of sync with his voice. The sound was flatly robotic. At least it masked his voice.

"I hear you fine," I said.

Everybody grinned at me. I must have sounded robotic to them too.

We occupied ourselves for a time, practicing using the tongs' magnetic properties and clipping and unclipping paper clips until we felt like old pros.

"What's our backup plan if the fireworks don't hold Longtoe's attention?" I asked.

"There isn't one," said Hahahaha. "It has to work."

"This isn't *Mission Impossible*," I said. "Something will go wrong, and we need to be ready for it."

"What's *Mission Impossible*?" asked Nugatt.

"Leo means that a backup plan is essential," said Morris. "We need to be smart about this."

"We don't have time to be smart," said Hahahaha. "We only have time to be moderately intelligent."

"She's right," said Ismenia. "The trial is tomorrow, so we have to get moving."

"We have four days," I protested.

"They moved it up," said Ismenia. "And by the way, you have to be present, or you and humanity will be sentenced in absentia."

Nugatt held up a finger. "And you have to put the chain on him at the trial, because he's sequestered himself in his palace until then."

Morris put his tong hand to his forehead in an I-can't-get-a-break manner.

I began shedding my automaton disguise. We absolutely needed a backup plan, and I had an idea for one, but I only had the rest of the day to prepare.

Chapter Eighteen

The next day, Ismenia rolled her mobile home as close as she dared to the place where the trial was going to be held. We exited the sphere near a huge roller coaster and a pendulum ride shaped like a giant claw hammer.

"Our trial is at the amusement park?" I sputtered.

"To get better attendance," she said. "When the trial is over, the gods can eat and have some fun. This is the back side of the park. Walk through it to get to the entrance plaza—that's where everybody will be. Nugatt, God of Fireworks, will meet you at the face painting station." She left to check on the backup plan.

Morris and I were wearing our automaton disguises, but I still felt exposed, as if the gods would immediately recognize us for what we really were.

The paper clip chain was carefully shut into the compartment in my disguise's torso. I'd secreted the flask of underground lake water in there too. I still didn't know when or how the Doobie wanted me to use it; I only knew I needed to have it handy.

We marched through the amusement park. The rides seemed pretty typical of those I'd seen in life: Ferris wheel, spinning teacups, tunnel of love, carousel, drop tower, flying chairs, Tilt-A-Whirl, Zipper, and so on.

Our disguises slowed us, giving us time to examine the rides as we passed. The theme was much like human retrofuturism. In other words, what the people during the early and mid-twentieth century thought the future would look like. Some might call it 1950s sci-fi. I'd gone through a retrofuturism phase where my designs were streamlined yet comfortable, made of tubular steel decorated with chrome tail fins. It was after I'd started my own business and was doing well, and life's possibilities seemed endless.

My wife, too, was having success in her career, branching out from dog skateboard instruction to dog surfing instruction as well. Oh, Lilly! I longed to see her splashing about in the waves once more. Were there oceans here in the afterlife, or a reasonable facsimile? What about an Afterlife of the Dogs? If so, she would be incensed that dogs and humans had to be separated!

"I miss being alive. I miss Lilly. She loved going on rides."

"My students would have loved this too," said Morris. "Oh look! Bumper boats, my favorite."

"A choo choo train! Too bad it's not running—we might get to the other side faster."

But I didn't really want to get there faster. Not when I could be hurrying to my own doom.

Too soon we made it to the pink quartz entry plaza with its grand arch. From there we could see over to Longtoe's palace. I shuddered, which made my disguise clatter like a bucket of aluminum cans being tossed into the recycling bin.

Gods strolled along wearing their over-the-top haute couture. It was a Mardi Gras parade wrapped in a fashion runway inside an anime cartoon. Here a flamingo feather headdress, there bulky cupcake pants; here a cape fashioned out of sponge foam, there a necklace with jewels the size of russet potatoes.

An automaton was handing out cotton candy from a giant machine; many of the gods held pink-and-green wisps of sugary delight.

The first time I'd seen this many gods together, in the stadium-size theater, I had a lesser understanding of their power. It had been almost incomprehensible, like a bad dream. This time, I had a new and improved sense of their arbitrary caprices, the variety and scale of their powers, and the intensity of our impending peril. The bright colors and perkiness of their clothing only masked their danger.

There was a seven-story parking garage for their chariots and other vehicles, but they all ignored it and parked wherever they pleased because of their deity senses of entitlement. This was a good thing, because the parking garage held my backup plan, although I hoped we wouldn't need to put that plan in motion.

I was glad to see real automatons here and there, which would help us blend in. However, some held trays of hors d'oeuvres, as if this were a catered party. I clenched the tong hands of my robot disguise angrily. Our trial shouldn't be treated like a festival, especially not with the fate of humanity on the line!

"We need to find Nugatt," I said, but neither of us stepped forward into the midst of the gods. It was intimidating. All that god power.

"I feel like the Cowardly Lion." I wasn't joking.

"I feel like the Tin Man," said Morris. "Let's be Dorothy instead."

"Good idea," I said, even though I didn't think it was, but since Morris's suggestions often worked surprisingly well, I imagined myself with pigtails, ruby slippers, and a prairie-land adolescent's sense of justice mingled with fair-mindedness. It gave me the courage to step out into the throng. Morris was right behind me.

To my relief, none of the gods paid any heed to us, especially since we carried no hors d'oeuvres. I breathed easier.

Moonilla, God of Procrastination, wandered by in an alligator-skin business suit with a matching yellow pocket square and trouser cuffs. She spoke boisterously, as if practicing lines for a melodrama. "Humans Morris and Leo plead *guilty*. No. Wayward humans Morris and Leo plead *kind of* guilty. No. Demented humans Leo Cooper, failed furniture maker, and Morris Johnson, failed poet and teacher, plead *super* guilty!"

She clapped her hands, and a parchment with those words appeared suspended in front of her. "That's it. That's a keeper." She plucked it from the air and rolled it into a tube, which she bounced absentmindedly against her head. The gesture seemed oddly human.

As our counsel, she should be defending us, not throwing us to the wolves and maligning us. I clenched my tong hands and stifled the urge to set her straight, lest I give us away.

Morris said quietly, "Why, I oughta..." Usually he would say such a thing in the voice of Moe (of Three Stooges fame), which his students loved, but since he was wearing his disguise, it came out in robot vibrato. Unfortunately, it made several gods look at us strangely. He backfilled quickly. "Why, I oughta go clean the toilets for the god masters, whom I love and revere and who are all things wonderful. I would rather serve the gods than oil my joints."

That was putting it on a little thick, I thought, but it did the trick. They returned to their hors d'oeuvres.

We kept an eye out for Longtoe but didn't see him.

At the face painting station, an automaton was adding the finishing touches to a tiger on the cheek of a god, and several other gods waited to be painted, but Nugatt wasn't there.

We retreated to a spot where we could watch for him and talk without being heard. "Where is he?" I kept asking, the robot voice flattening my nervousness.

"He'll be here," answered Morris each time, patting me on the shoulder, which made an odd clunking sound. It reminded me of a music video Morris had made with his students using found objects like overturned buckets and old pipes.

After about ten minutes, Nugatt strolled into the plaza dressed in a red sequin body stocking, floppy hat, and black cape.

My first thought was that his garb was the perfect costume for the commedia dell'arte stock character *Pantalone* (the greedy old merchant in Italy's sixteenth-century improvised theater), except for the sequins.

My second thought was that we were doomed.

He'd brought no fireworks. Instead, he had an accordion, which was so big and heavy he had to lean back to keep his balance.

Morris shook his automaton head, or rather, swiveled it. "He's going to play music instead of shooting off fireworks. That won't be a strong enough distraction. We'd better pivot to the backup plan."

"Let's wait. Maybe he knows something we don't. Maybe Longtoe is a polka aficionado." After thinking about it, I added, "I just hope he doesn't like to dance."

"No kidding. It'd be impossible to put the chain on him while he's kicking up his heels to 'Ta-Ra-Ra Boom-De-Ay.'"

We approached Nugatt and gave him the code words. "The strata coaster has been repaired."

He responded with his own. "I will ride it from sunset to dawn."

Now we only had to wait for Longtoe to arrive, but my patience was used up. I shuffled my feet, swiveled my robot head, and tapped my tong hands. We kept waiting for him, and he kept not arriving. My nerves made me sweat like warm cheese. My automaton joints chafed my shoulders and knees. "Ta-Ra-Ra Boom-De-Ay" kept playing in my head, accompanied by hi-hat cymbal and slide whistle noises.

We kept watch on the palace, from which he would emerge. It seemed like a lifetime ago that the sentries brought us to his mosaic-covered residence, with its seven perfect Doric columns. And that perfect drapery, with its ethereal detailed embroidery. Even from the plaza I could see fantastical beasts seeming to trot among the magical threads.

I imagined his moss-green moat as a lazy river that I could ride with an inner tube. The stress was getting to me, and so was the machine-oil smell of my disguise, and I would have loved to escape to it for a while to ease the tension. *Buck up*, I told myself. *One way or another it'll all be over soon.*

"Well, if it isn't Nugatt, God of Fireworks," said a grating voice. (Think of a utensil scraping a dish at an acute angle.) It belonged to a god wearing a white linen suit. The tilt of his matching white fedora gave him a jaunty air and made him look like a long-faced Humphrey Bogart.

"Hello, Whatnow, God of Snideness." Nugatt spoke warily, shifting his stance to place the accordion between them, as if to block an attack.

That attack came quickly, but in words. "You look like you fell out of the ugly tree and hit every branch on the way down."

"Oh yeah?" Nugatt's eyes kaleidoscoped to a dull beige. He seemed desperate for a response, but came up with none.

"You haven't launched any fireworks in eons," said Whatnow. "I figured you lost your—shall we say—potency."

"Yeah, well, I haven't been in the mood."

Whatnow gave a short, sharp laugh. "Haven't been in the mood!" I hoped never to bear the brunt of his attack, because merely listening to him made me feel small and unskilled.

"Oh yeah? Take this!" Nugatt began playing. It was a jaunty song that made me think of red-cheeked maidens in polka-dot dresses holding hands with fresh-faced youths in lederhosen and knee-high socks.

"That's the Hop Scotch Polka," said Morris, who recognized it instantly because he wove both polka and rap into his lesson plans to liven the students when their energy flagged.

Some of the gods nodded their heads to the saucy beat, while others danced with their fingers. Others scowled, clearly unhappy with the choice of music, especially one dressed in a batwing cape and goth black corset.

As the song went on, I noticed that the gods appeared to be anticipating something more than just the final notes of an accordion solo. They were nudging each other and glancing upward.

Nugatt played the final chord, stretching it out by pumping the accordion bellows. More gods were agitated; a few seemed terrified, cowering as if expecting to be dive-bombed by winged trickle-trackles.

The music ended. There was silence.

Everybody looked around, even Nugatt, but nothing happened.

The God of Snideness seemed extra pleased about Nugatt's apparent failure. "Very nice," he said in a clipped, dry tone. "Do you take requests? Then I request..." He paused to slowly raise one eyebrow. "I request..." he repeated. The other gods leaned in to hear which song was so special.

Finally he said flatly, "I request silence."

Some of the gods tittered. Others made their own suggestions. "Swing Low, Sweet Chariot," called one. "Uptown Funk," shouted another. "Stairway to Heaven," called a third. "What's heaven?" asked a fourth.

All at once the world went dark and there was a noise like a thousand simultaneous thunderclaps.

My heart thumped fast and hard. *This is it*, I thought, *I'm going to die*, forgetting I already had. When I did remember, it didn't improve my state of mind, because even after a couple of weeks it was still jarring to know that I was dead. Besides, it still *felt* like I was going to die.

"The universe is exploding!" I cried, although nobody could hear me, which was just as well because it wasn't something an automaton would say.

The sky ripped apart. Gashes of pink, purple, and red shredded the firmament. The gorgeous colors were the clues I needed to jog my memory: These were the fireworks Nugatt had planned. Not just any fireworks, but fireworks worthy of the gods. Nugatt had set them off by playing his accordion.

The gods were all wonderfully distracted, absorbed by the spectacular display, oohing and aahing. But it was too soon. Nugatt had warned us that he had only ten minutes' worth of boom-boom. We would have to be quick and get the paper clip chain around Longtoe's neck as soon as he arrived.

It was difficult to watch for Longtoe in the midst of those tremendous booms and blinding flashes, but we gathered our courage and peered all around, jerking with fear at every blast. I knew that whenever he arrived, getting to him would be like going through a war zone, but I was ready to soldier up and try it, even though I was shaking so hard I feared I wouldn't be able to clasp two paper clips together. I practiced opening, closing, and twisting my hand tongs until I felt I could compensate for my tremors.

All too soon the wind-down came, and still Longtoe was persona non grata. The last bits of fireworks hung in the sky, sputtering like frying bacon.

When they burned out, I let out a moan. Plan A had failed.

Ironically, Nugatt seemed to be suffering from the same need to prove himself as I often felt. The gods were too much like humans. That would have been our downfall, except that I'd set up a backup plan, although I wasn't confident about it. I feared it wouldn't be nearly as interesting as what had just gone down.

Morris's helmet made a steady buzz. I only realized it was a noise of exasperation when he put his tong hands on his hips, saying, "*Now* he shows up."

I looked up and saw Longtoe arriving in his chariot. The sight made me quiver like well-set gelatin. My archnemesis was about to land, and I was supposed to go to him and adorn him with paper clips. My neck still hurt from his strong grip. My skin prickled as I recalled the burning pain from his golden net and his promise of unimaginable torment.

What had I been thinking when I (a mere human) agreed to this? That I could conquer a god? Save humanity via the use of office supplies? Impossible!

Dozens of vessels the size of food trucks began descending from above. What could they be?

Actual food trucks, I realized, since they featured pictures of vegetable stew, pasta in white sauce, and savory fillings in spinach tortillas. The vehicles settled to the ground. I could smell the delectable cuisine over the machine-oil smell of my disguise. My stomach growled, but even if I could have eaten, I was much too nervous.

Longtoe landed expertly, coming to a vigorous yet gentle stop without a single wobble. He stepped out, garbed in a tufted, multilayered robe that evoked an ancient civilization. Mesopotamian or Sumerian perhaps? On his head was a smart-looking gold-and-silver dome hat. A slit in his robe revealed his naked calf, turned just so to show off its muscular perfection.

A bird landed on a nearby light pole. Dakota! She was able to spot us by a mark we'd put on the tops of our helmets. Holding up both arms, I clicked my tong hands three times, giving her the signal to set the backup plan in motion. She flew off. My heart went out to her. She was risking herself for us, and she wasn't the only one. I only hoped things would go according to plan this time.

Longtoe shouted jubilantly, "Let's get this trial done with so we can feast and ride the Ferris wheel!" I don't think he saw the irony that George Ferris Jr., its designer, had been a human being.

The gods cheered. This didn't bode well. I was sure that they thought the fastest way to get to feasting and riding was a guilty verdict.

Ness, God of Just Ness, emerged from the crowd, still giving off attentive meercat vibes and seeming particularly excited about the pasta food truck. Rather than his judge's robe, he wore floral pants with a paisley shirt, an unfortunate combination. "Okay, start the trial, and make it snappy."

Longtoe raised a well-manicured hand. "The gods used to be proud and organized, until humans arrived."

I heard murmurs from the nearest gods. "I don't remember being organized" and "I don't remember before humans arrived." Their dissent pleased me, but it needed to be stronger and more direct.

"We have become petty and imperfect because of human influence," continued the god. "We can only become proud and perfect when they're gone. Plus, the space that they now occupy can become something better." He spoke slyly. "Sports stadiums." Some of the gods perked up, nodding to each other. "Race tracks." More gods perked up. There were high fives and fist bumps. "Food courts." Hurrahs and hoots. "Karaoke bar-casinos!" Wild raucous cheering.

Again I was struck by how similar gods and humans were. Not only in their pastimes, but also in their self-interest. Why did they have no empathy for two poor humans who could easily be innocent? And why rest the fate of humanity on us? It was unjust and unethical from every angle.

"Let's get to the verdict," suggested Longtoe.

"I like the way you think," said Ness.

My blood ran Slurpee-cold.

Thankfully, just then Dakota arrived. Dangling from her talons was a sloth—our friend Darby, who in turn carried a skateboard. She set him down, and he immediately began doing ollies and kickflips.

This drew the gods' attention. *A skateboarding sloth! What a novel addition to a fireworks show.* I eased closer to Longtoe, but hadn't gotten far when his attention flagged. Darby didn't have much skill yet (too bad Lilly hadn't been there to teach him), plus there were no ramps or rails for more impressive tricks.

Fortunately we had more up our sleeves than just a single skateboarding sloth. More birds began to arrive, carrying more sloths, who carried bundles. I'd asked Dakota to have the birds bring as many sloths as they could, thinking she'd bring a couple dozen, but she'd outdone herself and brought hundreds. Somehow the avians and sloths worked together to set up zip lines and trampolines, and in no time the sloths were giving a show that rivaled any Cirque du Soleil performance in originality, skill, and choreography.

They slingshotted themselves into the air and bounded on trampolines, leaping over the gods like furry cannonballs. They zip-lined every which way, whooping sloth whoops and chortling sloth chortles. They were everywhere, turning and zipping, leaping and flipping.

Longtoe was distracted by it, but not enough. He seemed to have a need for situational awareness and kept looking back. I couldn't approach him covertly.

Morris stole a tray of caprese skewers with balsamic drizzle from a passing automaton and placed himself in front of Longtoe, who batted the tray away. It clattered to the ground.

Morris backed up a step; Longtoe raised one eyebrow, then stepped forward and bent toward him, sniffing. I approached him from behind.

Morris backed up another step. Longtoe stepped forward another step. I stepped forward another step. This continued for a bit, provoking an unfortunate cha-cha-cha earworm in my head.

Morris stopped. Longtoe stopped. I took one more step, bringing me right behind the God of Perfection. Now was the time to place the chain around his neck. I opened the secret compartment; the hinge squeaked like a startled raccoon. Longtoe wheeled. With the sides of his hands placed just so to avoid reflections, he peered into my robot helmet. I could have sworn I heard his eyes *chunka-chunk* when they kaleidoscoped charcoal-gray and black.

Still peering into my helmet, his face only inches from mine, he sneered. "Leo Cooper. In pathetic disguise. You thought you could fool the God of Perfection."

He straightened, then whipped a black stick out of his robe. The smirk on his face told me all I needed to know. Whatever it was, be it magic wand or techno tool, it was guaranteed to bring me to my knees. I supposed he was tired of my shenanigans and this was his version of bringing out the big guns.

"Hey, Perfecto Schmecto, I'm over here!" yelled Morris.

Longtoe turned back and pointed the stick at him. My friend was in danger! Forgetting everything else, I automatically rushed to Morris and shoved him out of harm's way; he fell to the ground.

There was a small flash. My arm felt like it had been heated to the melting point of steel, which I knew to be 2,500 degrees Fahrenheit, but I was in too much pain to mentally convert it to Celsius. I cried out. My robot suit converted the sound into something less agonized, I'm sure.

Longtoe growled like the MGM lion, pointed the stick at my torso, kaleidoscoped his eyes, and gritted his teeth in what I could only assume was determination to put me in greater-than-unimaginable torment for the rest of eternity.

Pain kept me rooted to the spot. I was done for.

There was a flapping of wings. A crow landed on Longtoe's head. I bleated a short, hysterical laugh. The fluttering bird had given me a reprieve, however brief it might be.

He reached up to swat it, but it avoided his hand by climbing nimbly around his scalp, as if circling a bald spot, although Longtoe's perfect coif had no such thing.

This was my chance to get the necklace on him, but my injured arm hung like a long handle dipper gourd, which can grow four feet long and is excellent when used for arts and crafts but is inedible and, more importantly for this comparison, not a useful appendage.

I would have to work one-handed. Using the magnetic properties of my good tong hand, I drew the chain out of my belly compartment. He was tall, but I was resourceful. From behind, one-handed, I tossed one end of the chain around his neck.

Now I had hold of one end, while the other rested across his clavicle. All I had to do was connect the two ends.

Things seemed to go in slow motion. The fate of humanity rested on my ability to attach two bits of hard yet flexible metal to one another. Two pieces of office equipment. Or were they more of a tool than equipment? My mind struggled for the correct word choice while I attempted to join the two ends using only one tong hand.

It didn't happen as quickly as I hoped, because Longtoe began prancing in his struggle with the bird. I rotated my tong this way and that. If I could just get the paper clip on one end close to the paper clip on the other, I could press both against Longtoe's seriously firm neck muscles in just the right way to connect them.

When I'd pushed Morris, he had fallen on his back; the automaton disguise kept him grounded like an upside-down turtle. "Pull me up so I can help!"

"No!" I needed to be the one to overcome the God of Perfection. He was my archnemesis. If I couldn't *be* the God of Perfection, then I was going to *beat* the God of Perfection. And I was going to do it one-handed. Humanity would sing my praises!

"You're hurt," shouted my friend.

"I can still do it," I said.

"You can't. You're flunking."

I fumed. Morris should be a better friend. He should let me have this win. He was already better than me at languages and poetry. Ismenia liked him better, and so did Dakota. Also, now that I thought about it, our harpy eagle mom had pushed him from the nest first, showing more trust in his flying abilities than mine.

"I've almost got it," I said.

"You haven't almost got it."

He was mincing words now. Of course, *technically* I didn't almost have it, but I *nearly* almost had it.

The paper clip chain dropped to the ground, but I knew I could still succeed. I only had to scoop, toss, and attach. That would be a piece of cake compared to, say, a foxtrot, which I'd mastered in a very short time.

The crow flew down to the chain and nudged it with its beak. *It's trying to help me*, I thought. But I didn't need help. I could do this myself.

"That's the crow that stole my lip piercing!" shouted Morris.

My heart seemed to skip a beat. I flashed back to that moment when we'd first arrived in the Afterlife of the Birds. The sun glinting off the sleek black crow as it flew high into the air with Morris's shiny piercing in its beak. That bird's wing had a brown feather nestled among the black ones, and so did this one.

It *was* the same crow! And now it seemed to be considering whether the paper clip chain was worth taking. In an instant, the chain could be gone, and all would be lost.

The crow picked up the shiny treasure. The chain dangled, kinked and uneven, swinging like a defective pendulum.

I dove for it, but the bird flew off, absconding as quickly as you could say "doomed humanity." It veered toward the palace; I lost sight of it.

I had failed. Our only means of controlling Longtoe was gone.

Only then did I realize that my ego had ruined us all. In the time I'd taken to try to get the paper clip chain attached, Morris could have done it ten times over. My insides looped and coiled like a ball of mating snakes. One of Grandma T-Bone's expressions came to mind: *He's so stupid he could throw himself on the ground and miss.* That was me. I was that stupid.

Longtoe reached out and pointed at me with his black stick.

While I quailed, I imagined my wife learning that I'd goaded a god into melting me into a lump of red-hot eternal agony. She would say lovingly, "Oh Leo, you frigging idiot." And then when she found out I'd gotten all humanity relegated to the Afterlife of Biting Insects, she would repeat the phrase less lovingly, with real profanity. And I would deserve every single expletive.

Chapter Nineteen

B oth Plan A and Plan B had failed. There was no hope left. The least I could do was help Morris up so he could escape and have a little bit of time to himself before suffering in perpetuity.

I threw myself at him, spatulaed him to standing, and we both ran as best we could while limited by the clunkiness of our automaton suits. We wove among the gods. While their presence slowed us, they were also in Longtoe's way.

"Follow me," cried Morris.

I did, pleased he had so quickly developed a plan of escape, only to find that he was heading for a sloth trampoline. Now, I like jumping on trampolines as much as the next guy (as long as flips aren't required), but this wasn't just any trampoline. It was an afterlife trampoline. Although it was only the size of a manhole cover, one little jump would take us several stories high. We were bound to hurt ourselves when we fell, and then there would be no escape.

However, the gods were starting to get grabby, and Longtoe was right behind us. We had no choice but to use it to get out of reach.

Morris went first. It propelled him as if he'd been shot out of a cannon.

Distracted by the beautiful arc of his leap and the way he exuberantly stretched his arms and legs mid-flight, and also by the way the sun glinted off his automaton suit, I forgot to be afraid. I jumped onto that trampoline with the vigor of a child jumping into the first rain puddle of the season.

I flew into the air, high above the gods. I felt morally as well as physically loftier. *This is what you get for giving me a sham trial! I'm taking the high road!* I cackled at my silent wordplay.

But then I remembered to be afraid. At any moment I was going to land, and it was going to be excruciating. My automaton disguise wouldn't protect me—it would only shatter along with me. I was about to suffer a combo platter of pain types—piercing, dull, sharp, racking.

And what was worse, Morris would too, even sooner than I would. He'd reached the apex of his flight arc and was now flailing. My good friend had already suffered greatly from his broken leg, and now he would be hurt even worse. They would dump him into the Afterlife of Biting Insects, where he would be too injured to fight off bees, wasps, hornets, fire ants, or ticks. He would suffer immediate and extraordinary torment.

Suddenly, Dakota swooped down and clamped her talons onto Morris's arm. She was saving him!

The surprise of it made me jerk, and I flipped unintentionally. Luckily I righted myself midair—I'm not sure how—leaving me posed as if sitting in a dentist chair, which would be an excellent position for Dakota to grab me as well.

However, she flew away without me. I remembered she could only carry one of us at a time. She had abandoned me, saving Morris instead. I told myself it was just chance. I also told myself to focus on what was important. I only had moments to do something, anything, to save myself.

I tried flapping my arms and pedaling my feet on the off chance that my automaton suit had some hidden properties I wasn't aware of. I also said, "Initiate jet pack." That was a waste of time. After all, it was basically just a costume.

I spotted one of the sloth's zip lines below me. At first I rejoiced, but then I realized I was heading for a catastrophe. My luck (lately) and physics (always) being what they were, the zip line was going to slice me in two at the waistline, where the upper and lower parts of my automaton suit left a thin gap. I readied myself for the worst possible pain. Maybe not as bad as childbirth, but certainly a close second.

I imagined the top half of me tumbling in one direction while the bottom half of me fell in another. Would anybody think to join the two halves, and if so, would they meld together? After two weeks of death, I still didn't know certain basics about the afterlife.

I felt a sudden lurch. Not from being cut in two, but from something seizing my body. It took me a moment to understand that my sloth friend Darby had zoomed by on the zip line and caught me just before I would have become sliced Leo. I was saved! Tears filled my eyes. Such impeccable timing. My perception of sloth ability had changed so much since I'd arrived, and now it was further modified. They were super beings!

But there wasn't time to celebrate, because we were rocketing toward Longtoe's front yard, or whatever you'd call the area in front of a god's palace. Probably not the best place to end up, but beggars can't be choosers, even dead ones.

Unfortunately, my weight was too much for Darby, and I slipped from his grasp. Again my perception of sloth ability changed; they weren't super beings after all, just outstanding beings. The term vigorously capable would also fit.

And so, rather than gliding smoothly to the lawn, I was free-falling once again. My mind went haywire, but only for the few short moments before I fell into the moat.

I landed on my back with a big splash. The impact was especially painful where the edges of the automaton suit hit my lumbar spine. It was so excruciating that I wondered if I *had* actually been cut in half. I bobbed like a newly returned space capsule, not daring to move and find out.

Cold water rushed into my suit around my neck, chest, and legs. Now I *had* to move, or I would sink. I kicked my legs and wheeled my arms. It was agony, but at least I learned that I hadn't actually halved myself and that my injured arm would now work. However, my movement caused water to surge into my suit even faster.

I sank down under the surface. I had the notion that my helmet would hold enough air for me to breathe a few more breaths, but again, it was just a costume. Just as its holes had allowed me to breathe, they now allowed water to get in.

I sank ever downward, my helmet now full of water. The light came down in rays of a drab moss green that I had never used in my upholstery and vowed to continue not using, if I ever again had the opportunity not to use it. The deeper I went, the worse the visibility was, like the inside of a rarely cleaned fish tank. I couldn't see as far as my feet, so I couldn't tell how deep the moat was.

My cheeks bulged as I held my breath; little bubbles escaped my mouth. Could I die in the afterlife and go to another, more terrifying level of death? And would I then be permanently separated from Lilly and Morris?

My lungs burned. I tugged at my helmet, but it wouldn't come off. Neither would the torso or bottom. Why had I agreed to such a lumbering, useless outfit?

Then I remembered the quick-release lever under my armpit. I hit it, and the automaton suit pieces loosened. I pushed them away.

Now I was free, but the surface was only a bright patch above me. However, I refused to suck that nasty bile-green water into my lungs. I clamped my mouth shut, and my sinuses, and my eyes, and also my buttocks, because I couldn't help doing so when everything else was clamped. I kick-kick-kicked and paddle-pulled my arms. Up, up! I thought of that motivational quote: *Start your day in an upward direction, and the rest of the day will follow the uphill path.* But it was the wrong one, because this wasn't the start of the day. Now I would surely fail.

Before I knew it, I'd breached the surface and was gulping in air. The sweet freedom of breath! I would never again take it for granted.

Dog-paddling in place, gasping, and wiping water from my eyes, I lamented how psychologically frustrating it was to continually be in danger, then saved, then in danger once more. It was a pattern I needed to fix, because I was a big proponent of being proactive rather than reactive.

A voice called, "Over here!" It was Morris, at the edge of the moat. He had ditched his disguise and was beckoning. Oxygen deprived and racked with pain, I somehow managed to swim to him and pull myself out of the moat with his help.

He hugged me (yes, it hurt), but quickly, because we were now on the palace grounds, with reptilian sentries not very far away. This was disastrous. How were we going to dodge them here? I was about to suggest we swim back across the moat, but then Longtoe swooped overhead in his chariot. My shoulders tensed, and I muttered a consonant-heavy oath. Once more I was caught up in that reactive rather than proactive pattern, and I had no idea what to do.

Suddenly the sky was full of chariots, ornamented like art cars, with figurines, jewels, and trinkets in appealing patterns. Lilly would have loved them! But I wasn't so enamored, given the circumstances. They landed all around us. Gods emerged. Morris and I stood back to back. I was dripping wet, clothes clinging to me like fresh seaweed. Disguise-less, I felt particularly vulnerable.

My mind floundered about for a solution. What to do, what to do? When we'd been surrounded by giant slugs in the Afterlife of Slime-Emitting Creatures, we'd tossed them away like sleeping bags. In the water with the hagfish, we'd danced to save ourselves. Neither of those strategies were suitable now.

Longtoe approached; his dramatically slow gait magnified his air of menacing danger. A group of reptilian sentries was right behind him, gritting their teeth in what I found to be an unnecessarily unsympathetic manner. I withered a bit the closer they got.

And yet I still hadn't given up. I had one more idea, thanks to mid-century Hollywood. I wasn't happy at the thought of getting back into the moat, but it occurred to me that the sentries could be the water-avoidant type of reptilians, and that Longtoe and the other gods would be loath to dirty their magnificent outfits in the mucky water. "Bathing Beauty," I whispered to Morris to convey that we should side-dive into the water one by one like the row of beautiful women in that classic 1944 movie.

Before we could act on my idea, Longtoe let out a howl of rage that was part banshee, part jet engine.

He was looking at his palace, where dozens of sloths were climbing his drapery, perhaps drawn to it by the fantastically beautiful images. Their sharp claws were shredding it like tissue paper. Strips were falling to the ground. Clouds of fabric dust arose in front of the palace.

Longtoe would never forgive its destruction! I didn't know why this struck me as so dangerous, when we were already on his permanent shit list, but it seemed like a step too far. Something that we would never be able to undo.

"No!" I cried, forgetting to speak sloth.

"No," cried Morris, remembering to speak sloth, but it was already too late. The last shreds dropped away and the dust dispersed, revealing all that lay beyond.

I clapped my hands to my cheeks. "Wow."

"Double wow," said Morris.

There was a sudden silence so profound I tilted my head to get the moat water out of my ears, but that wasn't the cause. The gods themselves were too stunned to speak or move.

The reason for our astonishment was that in Longtoe's palace, where perfection should have reigned, there was—yes, I'll say it—a godawful mess. From where we stood it looked like a hoarder's palace, with piles of junk everywhere.

Once the gods got over their initial shock, they bustled forward for a closer look. Pressed by the fray, we had no choice but to ride the wave, up the stairs and right into the building itself.

I saw a yellow velvet baroque-style fainting couch, stained brown with grease from half-empty food containers. A plate of tomato pasta had spilled onto a once-exquisite parquet floor. Moldy artisan bread crusts were stacked like a lopsided Jenga game. Potted fig trees drooped with thirst, their brown leaves scattered about.

Dirty clothing lay everywhere. The armpits of white shirts were stained yellow. Sandals (the strappy kind that you would expect a god to wear, as well as flip-flops) were caked with mud. At my feet was a robe whose hem had been unevenly repaired with strips of duct tape.

And the cockroaches. So many of them! The opportunistic hand-size creatures were merrily climbing through old food containers and scurrying amid the rubbish. A small crowd of them gathered under an ebony Egyptian folding stool (Middle Kingdom period) to watch their kin flip one by one from the seat onto a tattered golden pillow. After each dive, there was a chorus of chirping and clicking, which I interpreted as cheering.

"Cockroach Olympics," said Morris wonderingly.

The gods murmured their displeasure. Ness, God of Just Ness, snarled, "Longtoe, God of Perfection, you expected perfection from all of those around you, and yet you yourself are imperfect."

Longtoe hung his head. The locks of his hair drooped, still perfect, but in a diminished sort of way.

But what I took for shame was really the god amassing his anger. His jaw clenched like an overtightened vise. Heat signatures rose from his body, making the air above him waver like a mirage. His eyes kaleidoscoped from red to crimson to scarlet, which, incidentally, are not the same color.

"Look what Ismenia, God of Trickery, and the humans have done," he said. "They've destroyed my palace, and the rest of the Home of the Gods won't be far behind. They're the ones who are imperfect."

He went into a long rant about how humans (me in particular) had wronged him. In theory, I didn't object to his pontification because the longer he talked the more time I would have to plot an escape. However, I was truly hurt to be blamed for something I had no part in. He had trashed his own home long before I got there. I couldn't help but think how similar he was to human beings, who often blame others for their own shortcomings.

I set aside my hurt. Once Morris and I escaped, we could become outlaw rogues, fighting for the freedom of humanity. For inspiration, I tried to think of a famous duo we could emulate. Butch Cassidy and the Sundance Kid were outlaws, not freedom fighters, as were Bonnie and Clyde. Han Solo and Chewbacca were fictional, as well as (at least one of them) exceptionally hairy.

Instead, I evaluated who and what could help us escape. Darby was on our side of the moat, but he had climbed a tree and had none of the items that would make him quick. The birds and other sloths were farther away. We could fashion disguises from the discarded clothing, but we would first have to get to them.

I silently summarized what Morris and I had to work with to save ourselves, using mental bullet points to keep it all straight:

- One slow-ish sloth.
- Various pieces of unclean god rubbish.
- That was it.

Longtoe paused in his diatribe, giving us what would likely be a last chance to plead our case. Morris made a desperate attempt to stave off disaster. "Let's break into small groups and write a short paragraph about this topic."

Longtoe interrupted. "I demand the immediate destruction of Earth and the eternal annihilation of its inhabitants—both dead and alive. I now condemn all humanity to oblivion."

Oblivion! I'd thought the biting insects thing was bad, but this made my toes curl. Everything seemed to spin; my stomach roiled. I realized that we should have emulated Butch Cassidy and the Sundance Kid after all, but it was too late now. It takes time for me to get into character.

"No," moaned Morris. "This can't be happening. I shouldn't be dead."

Longtoe added, "Along with humanity, I condemn sloths and birds to oblivion."

"Except for peacocks," shouted one of the gods.

"Except for peacocks," repeated Longtoe.

"Except for humans, sloths, and birds," I shouted.

Longtoe sneered at my sneaky attempt to counter his demand. While trying to keep myself steady, I shrugged in a manner that I hoped seemed innocent and childlike, like somebody you wouldn't sentence to oblivion. My model for doing so was a three-year-old neighbor, who had gotten away with spilling blueberry syrup all over the kitchen floor because he thought the pretty color would please his parents.

Longtoe produced a glittery orb the size of a cue ball.

"Gadzooks," said Ness. "He really means it."

Wendex, God of Obvious Observations, cleared his throat. "That is an obliviation enabler tool, also known as an OET, although nobody actually calls it that because Ohio Educational Television has the same acronym. Oh-bliv-ee-ay-tion is pronounced in five separate syllables. It will send all humans and listed species to oblivion."

His words weren't quite accurate. *Listed species* was a specific legal term for species designated as threatened or endangered under the United States Endangered Species Act. However, it was accurate if he meant the species he himself had just listed verbally. (He might have used mental bullet points like I had earlier.)

Either way, humanity's situation was suddenly quite dire, which was my fault because this had been *my* backup plan. I was the one who'd thought of bringing in the sloths. I wanted to negotiate with him—ask him to send me to oblivion and spare everybody else—but I began hyperventilating and had to bend over to breathe. Morris pounded my back, which didn't help.

I wouldn't have gotten a word in edgewise anyway, because the reaction among the gods had turned against us, and thousands of gods were now urging Longtoe to use the obliviation enabler tool.

Ness shouted, "Oblivion it is!"

Suddenly Longtoe yelled, "Ceasar!"

For a moment I was confused. Had Julius Ceasar (former dictator of ancient Rome) just arrived, and could he help us? Perhaps by giving some kind of oratorical discourse, or maybe an inspirational speech? Would I recognize him? In other words, did he look like his statue? Or was Ceasar merely the name of another god, perhaps the God of Salad? He could even be the God of Croutons, for all the sense things made here.

This sidetrack distracted me from hyperventilating, and I stood straight, peering around for edification.

Then I realized he'd actually said, "Seize her!" A wave of disappointment sloshed over me, not because I wouldn't be seeing Julius Ceasar, but because he had meant *seize Ismenia*, who had just shown up.

He began complaining about how much trouble she had caused each time she unleashed Chaos among them, which told me that it had happened not just once before, but every so often. I didn't know why, but this seemed like an interesting and potentially useful fact.

The sentries rushed toward Ismenia, but she shoved her palms outward: *Back off.* "I invoke my right to diatribe."

The gods gasped, from which I inferred that either the right to diatribe was rarely invoked or it was a powerful tool. Maybe both. I felt the teeniest, tiniest, most minuscule smidgen of hope.

Longtoe scrunched his nose like a chess player trying to stave off a checkmate, but recovered quickly, flashing a sneer of superiority. He returned the obliviation enabler tool to his robe pocket, then scythed his arm in a go-right-ahead gesture.

Ismenia rolled her shoulders in preparation. Morris and I gripped each other's forearms in manly solidarity. Could she save us?

"Lothus, God of Ruffles," said Ismenia.

A god came forward. He was bedecked head to toe with ruffles, some grapefruit pink, some banana yellow, some lime green. On his head was a Carmen Miranda tutti-frutti hat with ruffles in place of fruit. He acknowledged her with a pert nod.

"Many humans wear ruffles," said Ismenia.

He jutted his chin with sudden interest, causing the ruffles on his hat to flip-flop.

She continued. "Plus, humans do interesting things."

Lothus pursed his lips in an I-hadn't-thought-of-that manner. He marched over and examined me.

I had to prove humans were interesting, and fast! In a moment of weakness, I planted my feet and took the easy way out by pantomiming a wall. In my own defense, the fate of humanity rested on me, and it was something I excelled in.

"Wow!" cried Lothus, suitably impressed. So were some of the other gods, but one of them said, "It's an overdone mime trope."

"Mime troop?" Ness looked around. "Where?"

"Trope, not troop," clarified the god. "It means common. Cliché."

I still had plenty of gods to win over, so I broke into a moonwalk, which is really a variation on the pantomime walk-in-place trope, but always a crowd-pleaser. There were mixed reactions to that as well.

"Sammich, God of Schnauzers," said Ismenia.

A god jolted forward, pulling six enthusiastic schnauzers on leashes. The floppy-eared, muzzle-bearded dogs panted their happiness. The god's green velvet tracksuit had an odd pattern that I belatedly recognized as dog hairs.

"What does Longtoe say about your dogs?" she asked.

"He says that—" He choked up.

"Take your time," she said gently.

"He says that they don't really love me, but pretend like they do because I feed them. And that I should put them in the Afterlife of the Dogs where they belong." A tear fell from his eye.

There was murmuring among the gods, generally unfavorable toward Longtoe, although one god changed the dynamic with, "I'm more of a cat person."

"That's enough!" shouted Longtoe.

Ismenia stood tall and spoke in a commanding voice. "I haven't finished my diatribe."

"Yes, you have." Longtoe gestured to the reptilian sentries. "Take her away."

They grasped her. She fought them off with kicks, punches, pushes, leaps, and bounds. Obviously she'd had training in boxing, various martial arts, and bowling. Possibly curling as well.

While this was going down, I remembered the flask in my pocket. I felt in my bones that this was the time to use it! I could pour it onto Longtoe, and it would have some kind of effect on him. Disable him probably. I didn't know how, but it would do the trick, and it would be much easier than putting a necklace on him.

A feeling of triumph surged through my body. The Doobie was coming through for me. Finally, after all the searching, all the running, all the heartache, I was going to conquer Longtoe. I was going to wipe out all this misery, find my wife, and begin my journey through death anew!

I reached down. The flask wasn't in my pants pocket.

I felt a cold chill of remembrance. It wasn't there because it had been in the compartment of my automaton torso, which now lay at the bottom of the moat, where it was impossible to retrieve. All the gods were between me and the moat, and visibility within the moat was only a few feet, so even if I could get there, I doubted I would ever find it.

My arm fell to my side. I'd blown it. The Doobie had given me a weapon, something to save my wife, my friend, and all humankind, but I didn't have it, and now it was too late. If only I'd thought to swim back down and get it from the compartment before climbing out of the moat.

It's not over till it's over, I told myself. I would find a way to help us, somehow, someway.

Ismenia was still fighting off the reptilian sentries, but she seemed to be weakening. I couldn't help but think if she ate more she wouldn't be losing steam so quickly. I considered going to her aid, but even though she was flagging, it was still a high-speed fight. It would have been like interrupting a dance of chain saws.

I saw Morris watching the action too, giving little unsure starts as if timing his entrance into the jump ropes at a double Dutch competition.

They finally subdued her. She seemed beaten, as if she'd spent all her energy on this fight and had nothing left to give. It hurt to see her in the grip of her captors. Such a free spirit should never be held back.

Besides, this was disastrous. Our strongest ally could no longer help us.

I noticed something gold on the ground. The remote to Ismenia's house! It had fallen during the struggle, but nobody seemed to have noticed.

It was only then that I realized our backup plan hadn't been a true backup plan, but a variation of plan A. Both versions relied on distractions to accomplish the single goal of putting the necklace on Longtoe. But now, as soon as I had the remote in my hot little hands, I would have a true backup plan. A devious backup plan. The real deal.

I needed that remote. But Longtoe was striding toward me.

Now Hahahaha came out of nowhere and addressed the gods. "All eyes on me." Before I knew it, she had removed her veil and begun to laugh. It began as the sliding of a trombone, then morphed into the sound of a sparrow flapping, then became the clatter of a bowling alley.

It was absolutely hilarious. As I fell under her spell, I realized this was a last-ditch attempt to help us.

The gods who were affected by Hahahaha had an astounding variety of laughs. One sounded like a donkey, another like a crow, and a third like a ferry boat horn. Their laughter propelled them into an odd choreography. They stumbled around, clutching their sides, rolling on the ground here and there, as did the reptilian sentries.

About a third of the gods remained laugh-sober, including Longtoe, although they paid no attention to me or Morris. This was my chance to retrieve the remote, but I was hobbled by laughter, as was Morris.

To fight hilarity's power, I had to think of something terrible. It wasn't hard. My wife and friend were doomed to oblivion, and it was all my fault because I'd let my ego get in the way of subduing Longtoe. Shame banished my giddiness, giving me control over myself.

"Ceasar as well!" said Longtoe. I figured out much more quickly this time that he meant "Seize her as well," meaning to grab Hahahaha.

Nobody was looking in my direction. I dashed over and scooped up the remote, then scanned the icons on its buttons. Yes, it had what I required. Now I needed the courage for what came next.

I pressed the button with the house icon. Ismenia's sphere must have been close, because it arrived in seconds, stopping with a screech just on the other side of the moat. Everybody jumped and made noises of fright, even Longtoe.

I leapt onto a handy cast-iron bench. All the gods gazed up at me. I was still wet from my dip in the moat, and now I began to sweat. I had to hold on to the remote carefully so it wouldn't slip out of my hands. With all the bravado I could muster, I yelled, "Drop this ridiculous farce against humanity, or else."

Longtoe crossed his well-developed arms. "Or else what?"

I puffed out my chest. "Or else I will unleash Chaos upon you."

My hand hovered over a button with a little dog face on it. I had surmised that it would set Chaos free, and I must have been right, because Longtoe's eyes grew wide. He held up his arm protectively and backed up as if I were a bomb about to go off.

But then he got a sneaky look in his eyes and an even sneakier smirk on his face. His hand crept toward the pocket of his robe.

I gasped. I knew exactly what he was going to do next, and that was to get the Ohio Educational Television—no wait—the obliviation enabler tool back out of his pocket.

With his eyes trained on me and his robe being a bit floppy, he didn't locate it right away, but I had mere seconds to stop him.

"Freeze or I'll do it!" I shouted.

But he didn't freeze. His hand found the side seam of his robe and followed it down. His top knuckles disappeared into his pocket, then his middle knuckles, then his base knuckles.

My own finger hovered over the button to Chaos's den. Shivers of dread flitted down my back like miniature rolling thunder.

"No, Leo," cried Morris. "Don't release Chaos. Bad idea."

I had no time to decide. It was now or never.

I pressed the button, and the remote vibrated slightly. I took that as an indication that something was going to happen.

Grandma T-Bone wasn't there, but I heard her voice in my head loud and clear. "Holy shit, Leopold K. Cooper. Now you've done it."

Chapter Twenty

Morris clutched his head. "Leo, you screwed up big-time."
His statement cut through the tumult of my thoughts, and I realized that releasing Chaos had been the perfectly wrong thing to do. The gods already saw me as representing humanity, so they would judge all the people of the world by this one action. It was an action so profound that punishing only me—just one person—wouldn't be enough. Whether people were good or bad, boring or interesting, wore ruffles or not—none of that mattered anymore. What mattered was that I'd pushed that button. They would never forgive me, and so if we survived whatever Chaos was going to do, they would never agree to send only me to oblivion. That option was gone.

Let me repeat that: *If we survived Chaos.* My innards sloshed like pig slop. I'd just blown any chance I had of saving my wife and my friend, and humanity was doomed. Double doomed.

But... had I really unleashed Chaos? I looked past the sentries, at the sphere. Nothing was happening.

Longtoe's hand reached the obliviation enabler tool, and he held it up. It glittered like a toy, even though it was a powerful weapon. "Imperfect humans. You are, as they say, 'toast.'"

I didn't want to be toast. I didn't even want to be bread. I didn't want to be Leo standing in the Home of the Gods, about to be not standing anywhere. What had the point of my life been if it was all going to disappear? All that striving and working and suffering for nothing. And what about the good stuff? A montage of holding hands with Lilly ran through my head. In the park, on the sidewalk in front of our house, on the beach... I'll stop there because we held hands a lot over the years. Time slowed (yes, yet again), and going through the montage took a while. Even so, it would soon be over.

Then I would be cold, soggy toast, tossed into the great garbage can of oblivion.

"Whirling dervish," called Morris.

Reacting quickly to his order, I shoved the remote in my pocket and began to spin, arms outward like blender blades. My action knocked the obliviation enabler tool from Longtoe's hand. It flew high up into the air and then fell onto the quartz pavers, where it split in half with a loud crack.

I became still and quiet, but inside I rejoiced, my inner voice saying all kinds of nonsense cheers like *Ya yay ya* and *Woopie yoopie ha!* The obliviation enabler tool was no more. Now, no matter what happened, nobody would be sent to oblivion. My relief knew no bounds.

Morris blubbered, "You saved us!" and I felt as if my heart would burst.

Longtoe turned to Ness, God of Just Ness. "Hand me your glue."

Ness handed a tube to Longtoe, who gave me a look that said I'd merely put off the inevitable, and only for a couple of minutes. I feared he was right, because the tube boasted *Quick-dry!!!!* in bold red letters, size thirty-two font.

Morris blubbered, "You didn't save us after all!" I felt as if my heart would break.

Longtoe bent to pick up the two halves of the obliviation enabler tool, but stopped mid-reach because of a loud noise. It sounded like a colossal shredder that had been fed too many sheets of paper but was valiantly trying to shred them all anyway.

That noise came from Ismenia's sphere. I trembled, afraid to look, but my head swiveled in that direction of its own accord. A garage-door-size outline glowed on the sphere.

The button had worked after all. It seemed that Chaos would soon emerge.

The gods gave a collective gasp. I don't know how to describe a few hundred thousand gods gasping; I'll just say it made my nipples ache and made me want to tunnel into the ground all the way to bedrock.

I sensed something seeping through the widening crack on the sphere: power combined with madness.

My innards, which had felt like pig slop, now felt like pig slop heated to boiling.

Longtoe straightened without having picked up the obliviation enabler tool. His eyes kaleidoscoped, predominantly in midnight blue and topaz, but with orange touching in as an accent color. "What have you done?"

There was actual fear in his voice, which turned my boiling pig slop innards into full-rolling-boil pig slop innards. If a god was afraid of something, then it must be even more dangerous for a human. What had I done? I had unleashed Chaos! Any moment now Ismenia's "dog" would leap out of the sphere and we would be in great peril.

There was an earsplitting noise like hundreds of knives being sharpened at once. The door in the sphere swung open.

"Oh holy mother of insanity," I breathed. "Chaos is emerging."

"Good doggy." Morris's voice, now an octave lower, had the dull vibrato of a movie trailer narrator, which terrified me even more because bad things happen in movies.

A god shouted, "Chaos is upon us!"

Technically Chaos wasn't upon us, not yet, but the words spurred a riot. The sentries and the gods—including Longtoe—headed in all different directions, bumping into each other like pinballs and then spinning off into new directions. Some of them boarded chariots. A few of the more athletic ones leapt over the moat.

I had the presence of mind to snatch the two halves of the obliviation enabler tool and shove one into each pocket, grateful that the harem pants accommodated them so easily. Then I hit the button on the remote again, in the hope that I could close the door before Chaos emerged.

I was too late.

A giant beast—the size of a mastodon and just as furry—leapt out of the sphere. Maybe it was a dog, but it was hard to see into the wind that swirled around him. I could see random features within that maelstrom: eyes that glowed like fire opals, a hound snout with wet black nostrils, humongous padded paws with clear blunt nails that honestly could have used a little trimming, and chestnut-brown fur that looked almost cuddly in its flowing luxuriousness.

His drool was the orange-yellow of a profoundly acidic flesh-melting pool. And that growl—I could feel it in my solar plexus before I could hear it, a rumble that jiggled my upper intestines and lungs and joggled my heart from side to side.

He was the strangest creature I'd ever seen. And yet there was something familiar about him. I guessed that was because he seemed like a dog, even though I wasn't sure he was. Although I could have sworn I smelled wet dog. For sure I smelled the wet soil that was being churned up by his swirling winds.

Morris and I threw each other to the ground, each trying to save the other.

In his terror, Morris spoke somewhat poetically. "I desire sangfroid, yet have none."

"Have some of mine," I said, an automatic reply, since I couldn't remember what sangfroid meant, but I would normally share whatever I had with my best friend.

"I thank you kindly," he responded, also automatically.

Then I remembered that sangfroid meant poise under pressure, which I definitely lacked at that moment. I was sweating and nearly hyperventilating, and I might have mouthed *Mommy help me* once or twice.

Chaos loped toward the amusement park. Bits of quartz paving flew up into the air, as did three automatons and a dozen ornamental trees. When he reached the cotton candy machine, a massive swirl of pink and green appeared, blending itself into the air around him. For a few minutes, Chaos was a tempting, sugary treat.

He moved on. Other bits of debris diluted the pastels, turning him gray, then brown, then purple. His maelstrom twisted the roller coaster into one of those complex birthday present bows that are impossible to make yourself, no matter how easy it looks online. Next he reached the carnival games. Stuffed animals erupted high into the air, then fell all around us like soft, lovable hail. When I realized they were plush toy reptilian sentries, it made me briefly envision the real ones as huggable.

To escape Chaos, Ismenia's captors had let her go. She cavorted wildly, shaking her bony hips, windmilling her reed-thin arms in opposite directions, leaping, bowing, blowing kisses. She was completely and totally enamored with her dog and its associated mayhem. It was a love that knew no bounds, motherly, daughterly, sisterly, and so much more. Although her mouth was as wide as a muppet's, any sound coming from it was drowned by the cacophony of Chaos's rampage.

Longtoe rushed to try to contain him. He tossed a golden net with a practiced arc, but the dog's antics sliced it into golden spaghetti, which spun outward into a brief 3D sculpture, then dropped to the ground.

"He's coming our way!" shouted Morris.

Chaos vaulted over the moat and crossed the palace grounds. Now that he was closer, he seemed even more familiar. Why?

We wrapped our arms around a tree, ducked our heads, and held on with all our might. I wondered how bad being whipped into smithereens would feel. Pretty bad, I was sure. My senses were on alert like they'd never been before. I felt alive—and yet I was dead!

The wind battered me. Bits of things hit me, stinging my skin. I heard Morris shout, "Ow," just as something big bounced off my head, which would have confused me—could he somehow feel my pain?—except that I was already completely confused, as if the wind had torn away my ability to reason.

The maelstrom ripped me from the tree. I found myself flying through the air, arms flailing, feet cycling, heart pounding, thoughts cartwheeling. My eyes were shut tight against the bits of stuff that pinged against my face.

My speed slowed. At any moment I would stop shooting through the air, and then I would fall. No, not again! This was all so unfair. I was woefully untrained in afterlife knowledge, especially in the hurtling-through-the-air part. I should have been given a handbook the moment I arrived, listing everything I needed to know to navigate this new and dangerous place. If not a handbook, then at least a laminated cheat sheet of dos and don'ts.

But—what was this? I was floating. Things stopped hitting me.

I opened my eyes. Chaos no longer swirled, his attention taken up by some floating birds. They flapped their wings, but nothing seemed to come of it. They were suspended like the rest of us. Without the tornado around him, he looked like a mastodon-size sheepdog with chestnut fur. The sense of madness was gone, replaced by playfulness and devotion.

I recognized him now. He'd grown quite a bit, but I knew this was the dog that had been in the tunnel with me in my vision. That was why he seemed so familiar! This was a clue, but I wasn't sure how it fit with my situation, and to be honest, it was hard to think straight when I could be seconds away from crashing to the ground.

The gods were suspended around me, their eyes kaleidoscoping. In their odd and colorful clothing, they looked like toys that had been tossed up into the air by enthusiastic kindergarteners.

Longtoe was among them, looking strong and powerful, as if he had merely been caught in the act of leaping over a tall building. He caught me staring, and his gaze narrowed with animosity. He wasn't done with me. He was going to torture me severely, with great relish, as soon as godly possible.

Thankfully, some debris floated between us. I could concentrate on this strange phenomenon and try to understand it. There was no gravity. Had Chaos changed the very laws of physics?

What about Morris? Was he okay? Avoiding any sudden moves so as not to undo whatever was keeping me suspended, I looked for him and saw him floating nearby, apparently unharmed.

Darby was off in the distance, and he spotted Morris as well. Each gave the other a little three-toed wave, sharing a moment of dumbfoundedness. They didn't know what would happen next, but at least they'd made a final connection before the turbulence resumed.

Only a short time ago, I would have envied that connection, but now I was glad for them, although they probably wouldn't have this respite for long, and that was my fault. I'd pressed the button on the remote. I tried to cry out an apology, but my mouth was too dry to speak.

I felt my head lowering. To keep from going topsy-turvy, I kicked my feet and waved my arms, but it did nothing. I reasoned that I needed to coordinate my movement better to achieve stasis, and so I tried the dog paddle, the butterfly, and a head roll, among other things, but nothing worked. Soon I was upside down.

But the fear that usually accompanied inversion wasn't there. I felt like an astronaut, looking out at a blue Earth. I knew exactly where I was in three dimensions. Surprisingly, it was fun. Fun! I felt a bit of awe and even thankfulness. Chaos had made me enjoy being upside down. I would never have thought this could happen.

Chaos—what was he? Not just a dog. I wondered if he were a god, a bestial god. Or could he be the Supreme Being? No, that didn't feel right. He was merely separate from the rest of us. As if he came from a different plane of existence.

While I contemplated Chaos, concentrating on him with intensity, my mind seemed to detach from my body. It felt like a spring jettisoned it outward, but not through space. Through time. Leaving my body behind, my consciousness shot backward, passing my marriage, the start of my career, adolescence, childhood, birth. And then, back even further, passing by years as if they were grains of sand on a beach. My mind bobbled in a time way before my birth. Before I existed.

I felt my consciousness oozing into a body, like motor oil being funneled into an engine. Not into my own body, but into the body I'd occupied during my vision of digging the tunnel.

I inhabited that body more fully now than I had then. This time I could sense that my arms were long, my jaws were powerful, and my brow ridge protruded. Because the body's owner wasn't *Homo sapiens*. He was a type of protohuman.

There were other protohumans with me. My tribe. My family. Those I depended on, and who depended on me. We had heard cries for help—not actual cries, but a spiritual calling out of some kind. We were digging a tunnel, burrowing our way toward the origin of that desperately forlorn SOS.

We had brought along a dog, but not just any dog. One that could help us with our task. A special dog that jumped and twirled and created its own wind, so that the dirt we dug was flung out of the tunnel and carried away. The dog gave us energy and strength. Without it, we could never have excavated such a long, difficult tunnel through dirt nearly as hard as rock.

Chaos was the dog that had been with me in my first vision. The same dog that I had released from Ismenia's sphere. That meant something, but what?

We reached the people who were crying out for help, but they weren't people, not yet. They were missing a sort of life force, which caused them to suffer horrendously. We couldn't let that continue, so we touched them. When we did, our souls poured into them.

I felt that if I could only stay in that moment, and exist as that protohuman long enough to understand his life and sort out his thoughts, then I would understand something valuable. I would gain knowledge that was better than any handbook, more useful than any cheat sheet.

But I didn't get the chance, because my consciousness oozed back out of his body and passed further back in time, going faster, faster, faster. This was something like falling, but much worse, because falling was merely descending toward the ground, and this was being propelled toward doom. When I finally hit something, the impact would be much harder and involve the dispersion of my soul.

There was no impact. Instead there was a lurch, like an elevator stopping too hard. My mind tingled all over, but not in the clean way my mouth feels after swishing it with fluoride rinse. More like my neurons were twanging loose one molecule at a time.

I didn't know where I was, but it wasn't any place I wanted to be. I tried to get away by imagining my mind reaching out, but I was tethered somehow, and my mind began to feel like Silly Putty being pulled at both ends.

Somehow I knew that I'd reached the very beginning of time, before there was a universe. I didn't know how I figured it out; I only knew I didn't belong there. Only Chaos belonged there.

More understanding invaded my consciousness. In the beginning was Chaos. Everything sprang from Chaos, and everything would eventually return to it. Chaos was the foundation of life, its reason for being. From Chaos came fulfillment and achievement and empowerment and enjoyment, and every other state of being that ended in *ment*, plus a lot more besides.

Chaos was an instrument of change. If not for Chaos, life wouldn't have come into being. There would be no such thing as nature, no humans, no me, no Lilly, no Morris. No Grandma T-Bone.

I'd been looking for the meaning of life and death, and I'd found it. It was transformation. Humans had transformed from protohumans to humans, and there was more to come. We would become neohumans, then neo-neohumans, and then something else altogether.

But only if I survived to save us from destruction. I was now in great peril. If I stayed there in the beginning of time, there with Chaos, I would be part of what everything sprang from. I would be part of the Big Bang, if you will, although that was a simplification. Being part of creation was not a good thing, not only for me, but for everybody and everything. I was now the fly in the ointment, the bad apple in the barrel, the sour note in the melody. If I remained, I would spoil everything. There would be no Earth and no afterlife.

I felt the popping and crackling of a run-up to an explosion. Soon it would be the point of no return. "No!" I screamed. "Get me out of here!" My words were voiceless yet echoed nonetheless, the sound waves bouncing to eternity and back.

In what felt like the return motion of a boomerang swing, my mind was moving once more, this time forward in time. Yes, yes! Forward through the beginning of the universe, on to my beginning, and—finally, thankfully, mercifully—to the present. My mind oozed back into my body.

I let out a long, wobbly moan of relief.

However, I was still floating about fifty feet above the ground. Five stories high. There were two possible outcomes now. In the less likely outcome, I would float forever. In the more likely outcome, I would fall. If I gained control, what would be my best landing position? Drop and roll? More like drop and shatter, from this height. Should I land on my feet? Hands and feet? My back? Certainly not my head.

As my thoughts zigzagged, I realized that I was being lowered gently. From fifty feet high to forty-five. From here, I would only break forty-five bones, I reasoned. Whether that was right or wrong, my brain needed the simplicity of it. I descended further, to forty feet high. If I fell now, I would only break forty bones. Things were definitely looking up (although, to clarify, I was looking down). Thirty-five feet: thirty-five bones. The slow, gentle descent continued.

I was reasonably sure now that I would land comfortably and safely. But then Chaos lost interest in the birds. The maelstrom began spinning around him, and whatever force had held us suspended let us go.

I fell, and hard. There was no time to position myself; I landed face down.

The message of pain had to travel from my nerve endings to my brain, and time was still a bit disjointed, so for a precious, tenuous, welcome ten seconds, I felt fine. My brain seemed to know the message was only delayed, and it made me squeeze my eyes shut in anticipation. When the agony finally arrived, it felt like I'd fallen onto a bed of nails. My screech was hobbled from the breath I seemed unable to take, so that I sounded like a shoe being wiped on a doormat.

At first I was sure I'd broken all my bones, and from the pain in my torso, that included every rib. But I must not have, because I managed to drag myself to my hands and knees without crumpling back down. My whimpering sounded like a doorway in a horror movie being ever so slowly opened.

I surprised myself by rising to a squatting position. I could actually support my own weight! I straightened to standing. Everything hurt, even my eyebrows, but it seemed that I was intact. However, I already had bruises the color of bacon-stuffed prunes.

Others, too, were picking themselves up, but Chaos's wind began ramping up. I stumbled sideways, trying to steady myself in the growing gale. I had to stop Chaos somehow. *Think. Think!* I told myself. Surely I'd learned something during the last two weeks that I could use.

No ideas surfaced.

Chaos bounded forward, a tornado begetting dust devils that spun outward in all directions. I dropped into a horse stance, knees wide as if straddling a Clydesdale, so that when a dust devil hit me, I remained upright.

He bumped into a stone wall, then, seemingly annoyed by having done so, he made a low growling noise that was somewhere between a whine and a complaint.

I saw parallels between Chaos and Lilly's dogs, who would get wound up in exactly the same way. They didn't understand they were tired and needed to rest.

To calm them, my wife would sing to them. Her favorite tunes for this were "Somewhere Over the Rainbow," "Amazing Grace," and anything by "Weird Al" Yankovic.

Was this insight useful? They say that "music soothes the savage beast," which I hoped was true even though the actual quote was "music hath charms to soothe the savage *breast*." With an *r*.

Regardless, I sing like a broken hinge, the opposite of soothing. And while Morris once confessed to me that he sang "My Funny Valentine" in the shower, I'd never heard him because he refused to sing in public.

He did, however, perform his poetry, which could be considered musical, if you squinted a little.

He was not far away from me, also in horse stance. "Morris," I called. "You need to sooth the savage beast with your poetry!"

He replied despairingly, "It's not 'savage *beast*,' it's 'savage *breast*.' With an *r*."

"I know that, but it's been misquoted so much because it might be true. At least give it a try!"

"All right." He sucked in tremendous amounts of air to support his outdoor voice, which was quite loud, since he often had to be heard by dozens of grade school kids on field trips.

"There was a big doggy named Chaos..."

Another limerick! I nearly lost hope. But over the noise of Chaos's swirling, I could hear that certain something in Morris's tone. Regardless of its form, he was putting his all into this poetry. It made you want to listen because words of wisdom, power, and irony were sure to follow. I knew that if I didn't drop everything and listen with all my senses, I would miss out on something extraordinary.

Chaos must have felt the same way, because his hurricane swirls slowed and took on the soothing, wavery glow of a tropical ocean at sunrise.

"It's working!" I said. "Keep going."

Morris belted out more lines.

"There was a big doggy named Chaos
Whose tongue was the color of hot sauce.
We gave him a treat.
He thought that was neat..."

Before he could belt out the final line, Longtoe tackled him. The two rolled over and over, Longtoe's hands around Morris's neck.

What was wrong with Longtoe? Why couldn't he see that Morris was trying to save the day? He was wrong to hurt my friend, and what was more, in my eyes he was now far, far from perfect.

I rushed to help, but the other gods understood what Morris was trying to do. Several of them took hold of Longtoe, wrenching him away.

My friend staggered to his feet and tried to speak, but couldn't. Longtoe's grip had hurt his throat. His mouth moved, but no words came out.

With the last line of the limerick unspoken, the sense of anticipation was frustrating, to the point where I wanted to become a hurricane myself and tear things to bits. It was as if a spell had taken me over.

The same seemed to be true for Chaos. The poem that was meant to soothe him now promised to make him even more frenzied. Somehow I knew that this time the result would be catastrophic. For a short time, he had turned physics on its head, propelling me back in time to where only he had existed. Whatever he did next would build on that. Something worse would happen. Something that would truly end all existence.

We had set up a situation by starting the poem, and now everything depended on finishing it.

Morris couldn't do it. I looked to the gods for help, but they were checking their fingernails or picking lint from their clothes, avoiding my gaze. The sentries were wandering about confused, fiddling with their ear holes as if they were filled with water.

So it was up to me. I would never succeed, but I would have to try anyway, knowing in my heart that this was pointless. I was no poet! Nothing I could come up with would come close to Morris's powerful verse. I had no idea what to say, but I had to figure it out with a quickness.

Chapter Twenty-One

I spoke Morris's words, hoping that their momentum would inspire a final line.

"There was a big doggy named Chaos
Whose tongue was the color of hot sauce.
We gave him a treat.
He thought that was neat..."

Now I only needed to add the ending. *And made some hollandaise sauce?* No, that had nothing to do with a big dog. *We sold our stock at a loss?* No, this wasn't about divesting. *Then played a game of lacrosse?* A game of fetch would be better, but didn't rhyme.

Chaos seemed about to burst. I had to pick something and do it now. I blurted a final line.

"He brushed and so now he can floss."

I knew immediately that I'd blown it. The line I'd come up with was insulting, assuming he had bad doggy breath. Plus it was disconcerting; didn't dentists recommend that you floss *then* brush? And so wouldn't vets recommend that dogs also floss *then* brush? If a dog flossed at all, which many didn't.

I was doomed. Humanity was doomed. Even the gods were doomed, because the universe was going to turn to mush.

Chaos's eyes turned the light brown of a wet acorn. The winds emanating from him dulled to a soft breeze.

I was afraid to move. Was this the calm before the storm, or had the limerick actually worked?

He gave a long, rumbling, doggy sigh and rolled onto his back. This classic move for inviting belly pets was nearly impossible to resist. I approached the big beast, cautiously at first, then with verve. I stroked his side, since I couldn't quite reach his belly. His fur was as soft as morning mist, and he smelled like freshly laundered 1,000-thread count Egyptian cotton.

I gave Morris a look that said, *I can't believe it. We succeeded in calming him.*

Morris gave me a look that said, *I didn't know you were so good with words!*

It made me happy that he thought so, although I knew I had just gotten lucky.

"What have you done to my dog?" cried Ismenia, more in wonder than in dismay.

"He just needed soothing," I said.

"Don't we all?" she said.

I knew all would be well because of the insane amount of cheers, whoops, and hats being thrown into the air.

Wrong again. All would not be well.

"Seize them!" said Longtoe, and this time there was no doubt whom he meant. All of us: me, Morris, Ismenia, Hahahaha, and of course, Chaos the (currently) calm and lovable dog.

The sentries and even some of the gods leapt to do Longtoe's bidding, but Nugatt, God of Fireworks, called out, "Leave it. They calmed the dog down. The amusement park can be fixed. Let it go."

"I have made a decree. I won't take it back." Longtoe spoke so adamantly that a bit of spit came out with his words.

Nugatt backed up a step, out of fear, I thought, but then he wiped his face and I realized he was just avoiding any further flying spit. He wasn't afraid at all. He said fiercely, "You're not in charge. Just because you say it's so doesn't make it so. You got away with that for a time because you're the God of Perfection, but as we can see, you really need to work on yourself a bit more." He stopped to calm himself, hands rising and falling in sync with a deep breath. More kindly, he said, "Why don't you take a little time off, reconsider your goals?"

Nugatt's intentional compassion only made Longtoe angrier. He seemed like he was going to explode, but somehow he contained himself, saying, "Hold on to human Leo Cooper until I can fix the obliviation enabler tool."

The sentries lifted me onto their shoulders. I had a sudden memory of kicking the winning goal in a school soccer match and being carried on people's shoulders like this. Back then it had been thrilling, especially since it had never happened before that game. Now it was frighteningly disconcerting, and not only because their reptilian paws were pokey, but also because obliviation enabler tool pieces were bulging from my pockets where Longtoe could spot them.

However, my vantage point gave me the perfect perspective to notice a change. "Something's in the moat," I blurted.

The ground sloped down to the moat, so all of the gods could see its surface.

"Crocodiles?" one asked timorously.

"Bad case of algae," said another with the same intonation as *balderdash*.

I knew the answer. The flask had leaked, and now the moat showed the same reflections that we'd seen in the underground lake.

I hadn't been able to identify the shades earlier, but now, with the gods surrounding me, I could. The listless gray shapes in the water represented these gods. There was the profile of Ismenia, her sharp nose and chin. There was the profile of Longtoe, with his chiseled cheeks. There was Lothus, God of Ruffles, but without the ruffles.

I'm ashamed to admit that, rather than announcing it with solemn seriousness, I raised my hand like an eager schoolboy who thinks he won't be called on unless he's louder and sillier than all the other students in the classroom. "Oh! Oh!" I cried, nearly causing the reptilian sentries to drop me. "Those are reflections of you gods. From when you were merely shades."

Longtoe's eyes opened and shuttered like camera irises. His mouth gaped—I think in fear. He understood what I meant, and it terrified him. Then he got hold of himself. "He means lampshades. He makes furniture. Which has nothing to do with anything."

I was thinking hard, putting it all together on the fly, desperate to understand it all myself. My vision as a protohuman started to make more sense to me. I knew why we'd dug the tunnel. To get to the gods, who had been calling for help. Once we reached them, we'd shared our life force with them.

"No," I said proudly and pointedly. "Not lampshades. Ghostly shades. Three million years ago, give or take, you weren't gods. You were shades that were underground, on an island in a lake. A flask of water from that lake has just spilled into the moat, so now it shows what you all used to be like when you were underground, existing as shades."

There were gasps and cries. "It can't be!" and "Impossible!" and "Say it ain't so!"

I continued. "Three million years ago, give or take, humans saved the gods from being shades. We shared our life force with you. Because of us, you became the colorful, powerful, interesting, charismatic, style-conscious beings that you are."

I expected the gods would either pooh-pooh me or require more tangible proof, or at least further explanation, which I didn't have. I wasn't even sure myself of the complete story, or if I'd interpreted it correctly. What if it had all been a delusion, brought on by a psychedelic substance in the moat algae?

However, many of the gods were staring off into the middle distance, brows furrowed, mouths parted, looking all the world like they'd just been struck in the head by errant hockey pucks. Others were prancing and circling as if they'd just touched a hot stove.

Ismenia's eyes kaleidoscoped scarlet and gold. "I had forgotten, but I remember now. Before humans came and rescued us, we were shades."

"It's true," wailed Lothus, God of Ruffles, tearing ruffles from his chest.

Nugatt, God of Fireworks, pressed on his temples, elbows splayed. "No! Don't make me remember that. It was so horrible."

Three gods believed me. Others seemed to be strongly considering what I'd said. Had I gotten it right?

"We were ghosts," added Ismenia. "Nothing but wisps. Crowded yet alone. We looked into one another's eyes and saw nothing. We touched each other, and our hands passed through one another's limbs. It was a time of emptiness. Nothing within, nothing without."

"Stop!" Nugatt put his fingers in his ears and babbled to block her words.

She yanked his fingers out of his ears and shouted over his babble. "We were wisps of mist. And yet, every so often we could almost smell a flower, almost taste a fruit, almost feel our own skin—just enough to show us what we were missing."

"We get the point." Nugatt bent over, hugging himself.

Ismenia continued, intoning her words like a prophet with a message for all godkind. "Then humans came and used Chaos as a conduit to give us some of their own spirit. They led us across the lake and out of the nothingness of the shade land. We weren't always here in the Home of the Gods. Humans brought us here."

Morris spoke up, his voice finally working, though a bit raspy. "I think you can stop now. They're writhing."

Indeed they were. Hundreds of thousands of gods were stiffening and loosening like those little thumb-controlled collapsible puppets that sit on a plastic base.

I was still on the shoulders of the reptilian sentries, which gave me an excellent view of all their writhing. It was a beautiful, spasmodic choreography that I appreciated all the more due to my dabblings in the world of mime and dance.

Longtoe staggered forward and kneeled in front of Ismenia. "Stop, please stop!"

She continued anyway. "You were vague and flimsy. You weren't perfect. You weren't anything. A big empty ball of nothing. A vague wave of ashes, but not even that."

"That doesn't make sense," moaned Loofa, God of Semantics. "We couldn't be nothing and be something."

"We were all shades," she continued. "Moving about without purpose, wandering, disquiet. There were no days, no sound, no food, no sleep. We couldn't enjoy anything because there was nothing to enjoy."

The gods began to still their frantic motions, although they jerked here and there.

Longtoe remained on his knees. His pose held such anguish—yes, such perfect anguish, even though he wasn't perfect after all—that my thoughts paused and I could only see the beauty in his form.

"I didn't see this coming," whispered Morris.

"Things definitely took a turn," I murmured.

"It's all true," said Hahahaha, God of Laughter, not laughing. "We were smoke without fire, flames without heat. It was awful. And it was awful for eons. Nothingness was all we ever knew, yet still we knew that we were missing something, but we would never have it, never even be able to imagine fully what we lacked."

Morris nodded understandingly. "The ultimate fear of missing out."

Hahahaha continued. "But I remember once more. Humans brought me their laughter. It was so beautiful and clear and positive and wonderful that I took it inside myself. And I became Hahahaha, God of Laughter." She laughed like glass chimes in a sweet-smelling breeze. Good thing her veil was down or I would have gotten lost in it.

Longtoe seemed to rally. He stood and shook himself, as if he'd been under a spell and was now coming out of it. His eyebrows tilted, giving him a sinister aspect. He belted his words once more, speaking to the other gods. "Even if that's all true, it doesn't change anything. So what if humans saved us three million years ago, give or take? What have they done for us lately? Nothing! They're just in the way. There are too many. It's time to purge ourselves of them."

Would he never admit to being wrong? Why did I have to connect the dots he should have connected on his own? I used a palms-up, elbows-jutting gesture that meant *you're not getting this, are you?* "You can't get rid of us without hurting yourselves! We're a part of each other. Without us, you'll go back to being shades."

My statement produced different reactions among the gods. Loofa's lips pulled back in fear. Wendex's eyes went wide with understanding. Ness's eyes squinted with uncertainty.

"Blaaaaaasphemy," said Longtoe, drawing out the word as if this were an opera and he the leading tenor.

Longtoe gestured, and the sentries lowered me to the ground and began dragging us away.

It occurred to me that since gods were like humans, they would tend to believe pithy sayings rather than reasonable explanations. I needed to summarize the connection in very few words, and those words needed sticking power. They needed to be catchy.

I took a deep breath and spoke with great portent. "If humans tank, gods tank!"

Not my most eloquent statement, but it did the trick. Ness, God of Just Ness, said, "Huh. Well, if you put it that way..."

The sentries let us go. I ramped up steam, hoping to build on this gain. "We didn't just give you our life force. We used Chaos to connect you to our life force. To save you, we made you a part of us. That's why we're so alike."

"Nonsense," said Longtoe uncertainly.

"He's right," said Ismenia. "Even when we first emerged, we weren't fully formed. We've evolved along with humans. They went from protohumans to humans, and we went from protogods to gods. We've changed over time because we're connected to them. Just as they've changed over time from being connected to us."

"But humans are so ridiculous," sputtered Longtoe. "You spend all your time on things that don't matter!"

"Just like the gods do," I said.

There were denials, but I forged ahead, even louder. "You play games. You're jealous and petty. You forge alliances based on whims. But you're imperfect because we're imperfect, and so rather than get rid of us, you need us to improve ourselves so you can improve yourselves. And vice versa."

"My head hurts." Longtoe pinched the bridge of his nose.

"When humans used Chaos to connect with us, they saved us," said Wendex, God of Obvious Observations. "And we have been connected to them ever since. We forgot about it because it was three million years ago, give or take. We just needed something to jog our memory."

There were murmurs and dissents.

"It is *kind of* obvious," said Ness. "I mean, I kind of remember being touched by humans, via Chaos, and there was an influx of souls and a mixing."

"That's not obvious," said Whatnow, God of Snideness, sounding more fretful than snide.

"But Wendex said it." I spoke as loudly as I could, to make sure many gods would hear this important point. "That means it must be obvious. And if it's obvious, then it must be true."

Longtoe looked stunned. "The human is right."

There was a moment of silence while everybody took this in. Longtoe had agreed with me! I held my breath. Was he raising me up, just to bring me down like he'd done before?

He clamped his mouth shut. Apparently he had nothing more to say.

The air was filled with the sound of thousands of gods saying "Duh" and knocking their palms against their foreheads to show that they should have figured that out earlier.

"If humans get sent to oblivion, then all the gods will be sent to oblivion," said Wendex. "And what's more, unleashing Chaos every once in a while is part of the natural order of the Home of the Gods and the afterlife. Therefore Ismenia, God of Trickery, should be commended!"

All the gods cheered for Ismenia, which made me feel like leftover potato salad. Shouldn't I be commended as well, for unleashing Chaos? And also for keeping Longtoe from erasing humanity, which would have erased the gods? But my envy was momentary. I was truly happy that Ismenia was in the good graces of the other gods once more.

"I remember something else," said Ismenia. "Earth."

There were exclamations of "Oh, right, Earth!" and "That was a big deal."

"What about Earth?" cried Morris.

"The gods gifted Earth to humans in appreciation for what they'd done," said Hahahaha. "It was set up as a limited-time vacation."

"A time share?" asked Morris, confused.

"No, a period of time when they could visit Earth. Each human got a hundred years. But humans started breeding when they were there—it being vacation and all. And so now all the people that are currently on Earth have never been to the afterlife, and won't get here until they die."

"Let's review the key points from today's lesson," said Morris. "Humans started out here, in what is now called the afterlife (although I imagine it had a different name before Earth was involved). They dug a tunnel, bringing along Chaos, who connected humans to gods, which saved you all from being empty, forlorn shades. Humans merged with you, in a way. And then they went to Earth for vacation, leaving offspring behind, and Leo and I are their descendants. And we're connected with you too."

"That's it, I guess," admitted Longtoe. "In a nutshell."

"So... where's the Afterlife of the Dinosaurs?" asked Morris.

I was a little annoyed, to tell the truth. Longtoe, my archnemesis, had just admitted defeat. We were almost in the clear. Why sidetrack things with a dinosaur question? But then I was curious too, now that he'd asked.

Ness, God of Just Ness, waved to his left. "The dinosaurs are over that way." He got a sneaky look of camaraderie. "Perhaps one day you'll visit them because..." He made a big show of banging his gavel on the bench, shouting happily, "You will not be sentenced to oblivion or to the Afterlife of Biting Insects. Your case is dismissed!"

That sure sounded like everything would be fine now, but I didn't believe it. Every time I'd thought we were in the clear, something had happened to prove me wrong. Longtoe kept popping up with some justification to decimate me.

But now my archnemesis gave me a little *you won* bow. He gazed around sadly at all the gods, who were looking at him like... Well, most of them weren't looking at him at all. They didn't care about his opinion anymore. He hung his head and wandered away.

I watched him leave. The crowd closed behind him. He was gone.

I felt something vibrating against my thighs. The two halves of the obliviation enabler tool. I breathed shallowly, fearing they were about to go off like a remote control bomb. I whisked them out of my pockets, dropped them, and backed away.

They dissolved into glittery sand, leaving shimmering piles on the ground. While we watched, the sand disappeared into nothingness.

"You're free!" said Ismenia. "Longtoe can no longer hurt you."

"We're free," repeated Morris in a tone of disbelief. Then he said it like he meant it. "We're free!"

I whooped with happiness, and so did Morris. We celebrated with a chicken dance. That sounds anticlimactic, but we were still hurting from falling down, and flapping our elbows got us the most celebratory bang for our buck without sending us into paroxysms of pain.

Chaos, who had been lying calmly all this time, began to swirl again.

Morris cleared his throat and launched right into a poem. It sounded powerful and wise.

> "There's Chaos at every turn.
> He lives in the doghouse.
> Human's best friend in life and death.
> Come here, doggy.
> Let me pat you.
> Stop with the Whac-A-Moley.
> Let's eat some guacamole."

Chaos stopped swirling. Ismenia whistled, loud as a steamboat, and headed for her mobile home. "Come, Chaos."

He shrugged himself to his feet like an elephant rising from a mud wallow. As he passed me, he licked the whole side of my face with one swipe of his burgundy tongue.

My first reaction was disgust. I love dogs, but not their bacteria- and Kibbles 'n Bits-ridden slobber. I automatically reached up to wipe it off, but stopped with my hands in the air. This wasn't just any dog saliva. It felt like anticipation and smelled like wonder. That's the best I can explain it. It was a gift. I dropped my hands without wiping it off, letting it soak in.

Chaos had also licked Morris, whose face portrayed wide-open happiness. "Good doggy," he said.

Now I was free to take my vagabond shoes to New York New York and make a brand-new start of it. I was going to find Lilly. There was nothing stopping me now!

Chapter Twenty-Two

M orris and I were going to leave, but Ismenia convinced me that because of the size of the Afterlife of the Humans, the search for Lilly would go quicker with her help, using her mobile home.

"We'll start in the morning," she said. "Once Chaos has had a chance to settle down some more." Since it was getting late anyway and we were worn out from the day's adventures, I reluctantly agreed.

For the most part, the gods were happy because the trial was over and Chaos safely put away. Now they could feast (the food trucks had held up just fine) and ride the Ferris wheel, which had gone unscathed, as had many of the amusement park rides. They began dancing to Nugatt's non-firework-inducing accordion music. The songs evoked people in berets riding bicycles with baskets of baguettes and wine.

Morris and I spotted Longtoe slumped against a column on his front steps, legs and arms hanging limp. He was the picture of despondency.

Behind him was his palace, its mess on full display. Without the gods in the way, I could see more of it. It was even worse than my first impression. There was grime everywhere, and the piles of stuff were so high the building seemed almost impenetrable.

Longtoe gazed out at nothing. His eyes were dull, as if they'd never kaleidoscoped a day in his life. There was no animosity. There was no room for it among the pure despair.

"He looks bad," said Morris.

I agreed. His failure to doom humanity was the final nail in the coffin of his perfection, so to speak. In spite of all he'd done to us, I felt sorry for him.

And what was more, I saw myself in him.

I, too, had been striving for perfection. My envy of others was the same thing, merely from a different angle. I was already good with design, but I wanted to be so superior to my peers that I would win all the awards, which would have been to their detriment. I wanted to be better at words than Morris—but he was my best friend, so why would I wish that on him? I wanted to be more loved by animals than my wife... I could go on.

I hadn't tried to squash others intentionally, but that would have been the outcome. It would have meant stealing their special success away.

Of course, being better than everybody else wasn't possible, and if you'd have asked me, I would have said that wasn't my goal. But when I looked back on it, it would be hard to interpret my envy any other way.

I saw now that my admiration of Longtoe had been the culmination of my envy. I had felt that to outshine him would make me outshine everybody. I was now particularly ashamed that I'd idolized somebody who prioritized his own needs above all others.

I no longer wanted all those qualities I'd envied. I didn't want to be perfect like Longtoe was supposed to be. I didn't want to be better at design than anyone else. Or better with languages or animals.

Plus, now that I knew we had a connection to the gods and to other people, I viscerally understood that their success would be my success, and vice versa. *A rising tide lifts all boats.* I imagined a sea of rowboats, each holding a god or human waving jauntily as the water raised them.

My envy had aways lived in my duodenum, a pool of lighter fluid easily ignited, but now I felt it evaporate. A glorious feeling of beneficial purpose flowed in to replace it. Help others. Lift them up, to lift everybody up.

And right in front of me was somebody who needed lifting.

"Intervention?" I asked Morris.

During our school days, Morris and I would sometimes see another student who was anxious or depressed sitting off by themselves. We would swoop in and try to make their day better by showing them that somebody cared.

There was a big difference between then and now. Then, we were trying to improve a brief moment in the life of a lonely human. Now, we would be approaching the archnemesis whom we'd just conquered. What if he regained his mojo and began a new campaign against us?

But my newly revised sense of purpose wouldn't let me stand by while anybody, human or god, looked as demoralized as Longtoe did right then. In spite of the risk, I said, "I'm going in."

"I'm with you," said Morris.

I sat on his right; my friend sat on his left. "Talk to us," I said.

A sneer sprouted on Longtoe's face. I readied myself to escape quickly, if need be.

But the sneer was, apparently, inwardly directed. He spoke in a monotone. "I've been so busy trying to get the afterlife perfect that I had no time for my palace. Or for myself, I suppose. I was overreaching. I wanted *everything* to be perfect."

"Jeez," said Morris. "A goal needs to be achievable. If only you had LinkedIn, you would have learned that earlier."

"I've learned it now. Too late. Or maybe I've known all along. I've always been torn between my need for perfection and the difficulty of achieving it. I'm the God of Flawness, just like you said."

"Not really," said Morris, "but that brings up a point. Do you have to be the God of Perfection? Could you be the god of something else?"

Longtoe shook his head. "All the good names are taken. God of Fireworks, God of Ruffles. God of Spoonerisms." Morris raised his eyebrows at the mention of spoonerisms. I had a feeling he would follow up on that later.

"There are plenty of other names that could lead to an exciting new career." I tried to sound practical yet encouraging, without being pedantic. "You can find it by evaluating your strengths."

"But being the God of Perfection was so... so perfect. Everything else is a step down."

After some thought, I came up with a compromise. He could have what he wanted yet render it manageable. "What if you redefine perfection?"

"Redefine it?" His face took on the aspect of somebody just out of the water, wiping their face, trying to see.

"Right!" I jumped to my feet. I thought I heard music swelling, but that was probably just me getting excited. "How have you been defining perfection? What is perfection to you?"

"Symmetry, balance, beauty, size. Every aspect of a being or thing has the potential for perfection."

"That's a lot to bite off," I said. "What if you just go for eighty percent perfect?"

"Ninety-five percent," demanded Longtoe.

"Ninety percent," I countered.

"Done!" said Longtoe.

We shook on it, then he wilted once more. "Who am I kidding? Even ninety percent perfect is impossible. I have three million years of stuff, give or take. I'll never get it in order. Maybe I'm really the God of Hoarding." His voice broke.

"Nonsense," I said. "Walk with me." Not an order, but a buoyantly pleasant suggestion. Longtoe dragged himself to his feet and followed me up the steps, with Morris bounding along beside him.

I couldn't believe my own audacity. I was about to enter the home of the God of Perfection once more and walk among the possessions that he'd used daily. Yes, he was fallen and beaten, but it was exciting nonetheless. I was about to enter a place of reverence and secrecy!

We stepped over bits of tattered drapery. Inside, I was immediately struck by the bright colors of the walls, which gave the place a whimsical and imaginative feel. When I looked closely at the piles of stuff, I saw that in addition to garbage, there were things of real value. Crystal vases and jeweled crowns, along with interesting collectibles. Copper fish molds, swizzle sticks, snuffboxes, handbags, and much more. There were scrolls, partially unrolled, filled with elegant writing in a language I couldn't identify. What wonders did they hold?

We picked our way to a vast room filled with avocado art. Ceramic, paper, wooden, metal. Paintings, sculptures. All a jumble. All in disorder.

"Wow, you like avocados too?" said Morris.

"A lot." There was no spark of joy in his disclosure. "Too much."

In another room were bobblehead dolls representing various gods. I picked one up; it was Longtoe in his cowboy outfit. With its jauntily bouncing ten-gallon hat, leather chaps, and spurs that played "Home on the Range" when spun, it was a delightful example of godly kitsch. Why did Longtoe have pieces of Earth history in his very own home when he held so much animosity toward humans? It seemed that gods, like humans, were full of contradictions and not everything about them could be explained rationally.

Longtoe seemed overwhelmed and unconvinced by our attention. He went back outside and gazed out at the wrecked roller coaster. We joined him.

"I'm a hoarder," he said. "That's all there is to it."

"That isn't hoarding," I said. "It's collecting. Your problem is you've got no storage, and no way to show off your collections. It's a mess now, but your stuff would look exquisite if you displayed it correctly."

"That's true," said Morris. "You just need display cabinets."

Longtoe flipped his hand despondently. "Display cabinets are not sexy."

"Are you kidding me?" said Morris. "You're an influencer. You determine what sexy is."

"It's also a matter of rethinking display cabinets." I waved my arms enthusiastically, describing various solutions, such as rotating shelves and dust-control machinery.

Even after all that, he remained despondent.

Sensing that words couldn't inspire him in his downcast state, I gave him a mime performance instead, putting my all into it to make it a show worthy of a god. I portrayed him advancing to a state where he could learn from his mistakes rather than dwell on them. I portrayed a joyous future of god and human togetherness. I portrayed a more perfect perfection than what he'd been shooting for.

By the end of the performance, an audience of gods had gathered. Everybody was laughing, crying, and shouting "encore," so I reenacted a two-minute piece that was always a crowd favorite, in which a balloon carries me from the Eiffel Tower to the Arc de Triomphe, where I am stranded until an elephant on a man lift happens to roll underneath. The elephant and I celebrate our rescue by watching all six Terminator movies.

I knew I'd succeeded when Longtoe threw back his shoulders, crying, "There are six Terminator movies? Then I haven't seen all of them!"

He lifted his chin and boomed, "I proclaim that the Leo Cooper and Morris Johnson human trial of justice be permanently ended."

It was a little anticlimactic since Ness had already dismissed the case, but it's always nice to get buy-in, so I took it in the spirit it was offered.

There was general clapping and hooting, but then Wendex, God of Obvious Observations, stepped forward. "That's all fine and dandy, but we still have a massive problem. With so many humans arriving here every day, we still have overcrowding, which makes gods and humans butt heads. We can't seem to get along."

I perked up. As I mentioned earlier, when I was alive I'd hoped to collaborate with urban planners and architects to design whole communities, whole cities, and even whole countries. Now I had an opportunity beyond my wildest dreams.

"I'll help reconfigure the afterlife to ease the crowding," I offered.

"And I'll mediate to help gods and humans learn to live together," said Morris. "I was a teacher, so I know a lot about getting different personalities to cooperate. Plus I've worked with parent-teacher associations and interacted with school boards on topics like banned books, LGBTQ issues, and the teaching of evolution."

"Phew," said Wendex. "You're perfect for the job."

Some of the gods stepped up to fist-bump Morris. They gathered around, asking him questions, nodding at his answers,

He looked totally in his element, the way he did with a group of his students. He was beaming in a way I hadn't seen him do since he died.

He gave me a look that said he finally accepted being in the afterlife, and that he would no longer say he'd died too soon.

I gave him a look that said I was glad because his negativity had been getting kind of old.

He gave me a look that told me not to push it.

I gave him a look that said I was just joking.

He gave me a look that said he was too.

• • • •

THE NEXT MORNING, MORRIS, Ismenia, and I were in her living room, sitting at the bar counter on the stools I'd designed, eating sandwiches that tasted better than anything I'd ever eaten in life. Ismenia had already eaten two and was chowing down on a third. I was glad to see her eating finally. She wasn't twitchy at all.

Morris and I wore activewear shirts, joggers, and athletic shoes, which we thought would be more comfortable for our search for Lilly. We were about to discuss the plan to find her.

I should have been ecstatic, or at least full of anticipatory hope, but I was pensive. I'd had more time to think about our situation and to mull over the freak avalanche that had brought us to the afterlife. It was bothering me, and I had to ask about it.

"Ismenia, God of Trickery," I began, but it was hard to continue. Once I asked, I wouldn't be able to take it back. I swiveled my stool, fidgeting.

At my sudden formality, Ismenia looked at me sideways and narrowed her eyes. That made it harder for me to continue, but I found the gumption.

"You killed us, didn't you?"

Ismenia's mouth opened; she seemed about to deny it, but then tilted her head in the manner of somebody who knows the jig is up. "In a manner of speaking."

Morris sucked his cheeks in and made a noise like a tiny balloon suddenly let loose. I hadn't warned him about my suspicions, though I probably should have.

I crossed my arms over my chest. Her waffling annoyed me. Either she'd offed us or she hadn't, and apparently she had. "In all manner of speaking, you killed us. You brought snow from some other mountain and dropped it onto us while we were hiking. Then you sent us to the Afterlife of the Birds so we could make wings to smuggle you into the Home of the Gods. We weren't supposed to die. I could have gone bowling the next Saturday. I could have eaten more curly fries."

Those items weren't the most important things to me, but with my stress level mounting my brain could only grab examples of the small things in life, which, although precious, didn't make for a good argument.

Morris listened open-mouthed, hand on heart. He seemed unable to speak, even at the mention of bowling and curly fries.

"You can do all that here." Ismenia gestured widely and magnanimously, as if to indicate the entire afterlife was now at my disposal.

"You know what I mean. I could have lived a long, happy life with my wife."

Morris finally spoke, clenching his teeth so that it came out as a hiss. "You *killed* us? You made me blame my best friend for that."

"Hey, I did right by you." Ismenia's long-suffering tone resembled a beleaguered crime boss defending the use of concrete shoes.

"That's not doing right," protested Morris. "You got us sentenced to the Afterlife of Slime-Emitting Creatures."

She answered curtly. "For like, five minutes."

He raised his arms in a you-really-don't-get-it-do-you gesture. "It was at least an hour, and an hour in hagfish slime is like a million dog years."

"Dog years or Chaos years?" asked Ismenia, trying to joke it away. But it didn't soften us, so she added, "Anyway, if I hadn't shown up, you'd have been stuck in the Afterlife of the Birds."

"Because you put us there!" I cried.

"I didn't put you there. You did it to yourselves. Your theory was correct. You made it there because you ended your life making high-quality bird calls."

"You killed us, though!" said Morris. "You brought snow from somewhere else and dropped it on us and killed us."

"Ah, let it go," said Ismenia liltingly. "Everybody dies. Death isn't the end of things; it's an escape plan."

An escape plan! Only a god could compare beautiful, precious, extraordinary life to an amateur heist requiring a quick getaway. I couldn't begin to describe what a grievous error that was. All I could think to say was, "You were wrong to kill us." I kept up my accusatory glare.

Ismenia stood, put her hands on her bony hips, removed them, then replaced them. "What do you want from me? Fine. I apologize. I'm sorry I hastened your death."

I balled my fists and gritted my teeth. That apology wasn't heartfelt. "I'm leaving. I'll find Lilly myself. I don't want any more to do with you."

Morris pounded his chest once, his tone icy cold. "Me too."

We were halfway across the room when a woman came in from the hallway. She wore jeans with fashionable tears that revealed just the right amount of skin on her knees. Her crisp button-down shirt had a pattern of silver doggy dishes. Her hair was teal-colored. Her smile was big and bright and beautiful.

It was Lilly, my wife, my everything!

We rushed into each other's arms, clamping onto each other like clamps. I kept pulling back to see if she was real, then reclamping with her again.

She took my face in her hands. "I was so worried about you!"

I took her face in my hands. "I was so worried about you!"

And then it hit me. Lilly was here in Ismenia's house. Already. "How did you get here?"

"Oh," said Lilly. "I'm hungry. Are you hungry?"

Ordinarily, her diversionary tactics worked on me. There was something light and breezy and wonderful about the way she spoke that usually made me realize whatever track I'd been on wasn't nearly as special, interesting, or lucrative as hers. If I was talking about wing nuts, for example, and she brought up a trip to the beach, I would pivot happily.

But I hadn't been talking about wing nuts. I'd been asking about her sudden appearance after she'd been lost to me, so why had she changed the subject?

I glared at Ismenia, eyes narrowed. "What's going on here? Why were you hiding Lilly from me and pretending we were going to go look for her?"

Morris narrowed his eyes. "She kidnapped her."

"No, Morris," said Lilly. "She didn't kidnap me. I was just hanging out." She sauntered to Ismenia and linked arms with her as if they were old friends.

"I'm so confused." Morris opened his arms wide in a highly melodramatic yet effective representation of that confusion.

"You and me both," I said. I thought about the way my wife was cozying up to Ismenia. I thought about my stools here in the living room, which I had designed years ago. I thought about Grandma T-Bone's home here in the afterlife, which Ismenia had replicated from Earth. I thought about when Ismenia told me, "You're such a beautiful human being," just the way my wife often did.

"How long have you two known each other?" I asked.

"Ismenia and I have been friends for a while."

A while. That was vague. It could have meant twenty minutes. It could have meant twenty years.

Those last moments. When my wife was dying. She'd asked me to talk like a parrot. I'd thought she said pirate, so I'd responded, "But it's not Talk Like a Pirate Day."

"No, *parrot*," she'd said. "Talk like a parrot. A lovebird."

"Oh. Of course," I'd said. This had made sense, not only because we were lovebirds ourselves, but also because a lovebird was a small parrot, and there was very little oxygen left in the air pocket under all that snow. Plus, I certainly didn't have the strength left to talk like a macaw.

I'd obliged, and Morris must have heard me, wherever he was under the snow, because he made bird sounds as well. Lilly had tried to imitate us, but was too injured. Her attempted bird calls had sounded like whispers.

And now, in Ismenia's house, roulette balls spun in my brain, then fell into place. I squared off against Ismenia. "I don't know how you made her do it, but my wife was in on our death, and she helped us end up in the Afterlife of the Birds by encouraging us to make bird calls."

I suppose it was risky to pressure a god like that, but she still seemed like Ismenia, the skinny lady we'd befriended in the wrong afterlife. And I was fuming. She'd hoodwinked my own wife into helping with our murder!

"Now, hold on a minute," said Ismenia, but she wasn't denying it.

Morris was saying "oh my god oh my god" under his breath, his eyes wide. "Ismenia, how could you be so... so... *dastardly*?"

Ismenia's brow knit together. She seemed sorrowful, as if she cared about our good opinion but had lost it.

And Lilly—she was looking at the floor, at the wall, at the couch, at her fingernails. I hadn't figured out the full story yet. There was something else. Something Lilly wasn't telling me. And I thought I knew what it was.

I started to speak but then paused. I could do some serious damage to my marriage with this accusation. But something was up with Lilly. She didn't seem like a victim—she seemed like a perpetrator.

I forged ahead. "Lilly, was this your idea?"

She blinked at me the way she did when she wanted to look innocent. "Was what my idea?" She wasn't denying it. So was it true?

"Our death. Was it your idea to get us killed?" I enunciated so well that I inadvertently sounded like a vampire.

Morris nudged me. "Leo. That's ridiculous. She wouldn't do that to you."

Lilly looked me right in the eyes. She took my hands in hers. "Yes. It was my idea."

I made *huh* noises, the kind you make when you're completely aghast, and so did Morris. I'd guessed the truth, and both Ismenia and Lilly had admitted it. Still, it was hard to accept that my wife was the ringleader in such a scheme. Ismenia was the God of Trickery, and so you might expect her to do something deceitful. Lilly, however, was a good person. How could it really have been her idea?

Desperately hoping my wife hadn't chosen to murder me of her own accord, I sputtered, "Ismenia tricked you into this for her nefarious ends."

Ismenia held up her palms. *It wasn't me.*

"No. She didn't want to do it," said Lilly.

"Don't you see?" I said. "That's how she works. Think back to when you came up with it. She was probably dancing around the concept, giving little hints to steer you in that direction and make you think it was your idea."

Lilly gazed at me sadly. "No. It was totally and completely my idea."

When I really thought about it, I suspected she was right. She was very intuitive and not easily manipulated. Not by me, not by her clients. Even amusing commercials rarely swayed her into buying a particular product. No, she was telling me the truth.

I pulled my hands away from hers and backed up a step. My voice cut in and out. "My own wife engineered the plot to kill me and my best friend!" I didn't want to ask, but had to know. "Are you and Ismenia lovers?"

They both laughed as if the idea was ridiculous.

"Leo, you're the only one for me. You know that."

I started to melt, like I always did when she said such things, but only a little. She'd had me killed!

"I'm going to tell you a little story." She guided me to the couch, and we sat. Ismenia perched on a hassock, and Morris remained standing, eyes slitted.

My wife spoke with the soft lilt of a master storyteller. "Once upon a time there was a little girl who lived far away from other children. She was very, very lonely. One day, her fairy godmother appeared and asked her why she was so sad."

"We get it," said Morris disdainfully. "You're the little girl, and Ismenia is the fairy godmother."

Lilly ignored his attitude, touching her nose. *Nailed it.* "'Will you be my friend?' asked the little girl. And the fairy godmother took pity on her and came to play with her often."

"So what?" I asked. "Just because you've known her so long doesn't make it right that you—"

"Listen to Lilly," said my wife. I pressed my lips together testily, and she continued. "With her fairy godmother's help, she grew up into a confident and able young woman. But now she was lonely in a different way. She wanted a man. The right man. And so one day, when she was working on a photo shoot with a famous bulldog—"

"Poochie-Pie," said Morris through clenched teeth.

"Poochie-Pie," she confirmed. "Her fairy godmother kept Poochie-Pie's stand-in from arriving on the set, so that a handsome prince would have an excuse to jump on the skateboard and offer to be the stand-in instead."

I glanced at Ismenia, who looked a little too self-satisfied. Okay, she'd introduced us, so to speak. But that didn't let her off the hook by any means. I spoke flatly. "And the young woman and the handsome prince were married and lived happily ever after, until the fairy godmother killed them."

She put her hand to her ear. "Listen to Lilly."

I scootched on the couch and huffed to indicate I would listen, but I wouldn't be story-timed into thinking what she'd done was okay.

She continued. "One day, the young woman had an aneurysm and died."

My heart skipped a beat. "Wait, what? You didn't... Was that when we thought you died but you didn't? You're telling me you really did die?"

Lilly nodded. I must have looked stricken, because she scooted closer and put her hand on my knee. I let her.

Morris gasped. "You died and then came back to life. You're a zombie!"

Lilly's laugh assured him she was no such thing. "When the young woman died and arrived in the Afterlife of the Humans, she was very unhappy. She didn't want to be away from her husband. She loved him too much. So she begged her fairy godmother to let her live again."

I blinked, trying not to let myself be swayed. *She had me killed*, I told myself. *You can't let that slide.*

"Well, now," she said as if imparting a little secret. "The fairy godmother had the ability to bring a human back to life, but only once every millennium, plus she would have to give something up in return."

I pulled my head back. Ismenia had given something up to bring my wife back to life? What?

"And what she gave up was..."

"Hugs," suggested Morris breathlessly. "Chocolate."

"Close," said my wife approvingly. "Her fairy godmother gave up all food until the time that the young woman died again and was once again in her presence."

I looked at skinny Ismenia and instantly understood why she looked like she'd had a hard life. She didn't eat for a decade. She'd sacrificed her own health and comfort so that Lilly and I could be together. If she hadn't sent Lilly back to live with me, my life would have had a painful void. I would have suffered a great deal.

Morris looked over at Ismenia's empty plate, then back at Ismenia. He held his hand to his stomach. "Wow. Years without eating. I couldn't do that."

She's the God of Trickery, I reminded myself. "But... she killed us," I said lamely.

"I'm getting to that. One day the fairy godmother got banished from her home. She was only allowed to be in the afterlife of animals."

Lilly looked away. She cleared her throat. What she was about to say was difficult for her. "Because the fairy godmother was banished, she was losing her magic. She had many powers, but they were fading. She'd lost her ability to visit the young woman, and soon she wouldn't be able to communicate with her either. She needed to find a way back to her home before her powers faded away completely.

"The young woman offered to bring climbing equipment to the fairy godmother, very good equipment that would work on crumbly cliffs, so that she and her godmother could climb back to her home. But to do that, the young woman would have to die and carry the equipment with her to the afterlife of animals."

I clapped my palm to my head with sudden understanding. "That backpack full of weights you brought on the hiking trip. You told me you were building your muscles so that you could lift Great Danes onto skateboards. But it didn't have weights. It had climbing equipment." I felt stupid for having fallen for that. She wouldn't need to build muscles to lift a Great Dane onto a skateboard. The dog could merely step onto it.

Lilly nodded, then continued her story. "The young woman would normally go to the human afterlife after dying. But if she died while talking a bird language, she would instead go to the Afterlife of the Birds, where she could meet up with her fairy godmother. The young woman wasn't good at bird calls, so she needed her husband and his friend on the hike to help her. However, they weren't supposed to die. The avalanche was supposed to sweep her away and leave her husband and friend alive."

"You were going to leave me behind!" I moaned.

Lilly briefly put a finger on my lips to shush me. "She didn't want to leave her husband behind, but of course she couldn't make him die. Unfortunately, the fairy godmother's weakness after not having eaten for ten years impaired her ability to manipulate the snow with precision, and instead of just killing the young woman, it killed all three hikers."

My soul felt lifted, but my heart was as heavy as the cast-iron kettle balls sitting unused in my closet. I took one of Lilly's hands and held it to my chest. "Morris and I weren't supposed to die."

Morris sounded relieved. "You didn't take out a contract with a god to kill us."

Lilly tilted her head with love and caring. "That's right. How could I murder the humans I love most?"

She shifted back into storytelling mode. "And when the men died, their bird calls were so spot on that they died and went to the Afterlife of the Birds, but the woman went to a city in the afterlife that was many miles away."

There was silence while Morris and I absorbed all this new information.

I rubbed her hand, looking into her eyes. "So when did the young woman... when did you find Ismenia?"

"Last night." She abandoned the storytelling voice. "I'm sorry Longtoe treated you so badly. He hated Ismenia because she kept unleashing Chaos, and also because she didn't agree with him unquestioningly. He hated me because I was such a good friend to her. And so he hated you for being my husband."

It made sense. When we'd first met Longtoe it was Lilly's name that had first inspired his anger.

Morris asked, "Why an avalanche? Why not something easier? She could have jumped off a building while imitating bird calls from an app."

I winced at the thought of my wife jumping off a building.

"That wouldn't have worked," said Ismenia. "There are specific requirements for things like that. You'll understand them better when you've been here a while."

I lay back on the couch pillows with a big sigh. I had so much to learn.

"I know it's hard for you now," said Ismenia, "but your time on Earth is just a blip compared to what's left for you. And now you and Lilly have each other."

That was true, but Lilly's wording during her story had been revealing. She'd called us the *humans* she loved the most, rather than, say, *beings*, which left it open for her to love Ismenia either equally or more than me.

Also, Ismenia clearly loved Lilly, so much that she would give up food for a decade to ensure my wife's happiness. The irony of this was that I'd been jealous of Morris, thinking that Ismenia liked him better than me, while in fact both Morris and I were not even in the running for the God of Trickery's favorite human.

To summarize, Lilly might love Ismenia more than me, and Ismenia loved my wife more than me and Morris combined. That was a sure path to envy and resentment.

But I didn't tread that path. Instead, something in my soul seemed to loosen even more than it had when I'd stopped being envious of Longtoe. This knowledge that Ismenia and Lilly were best buddies helped me understand that no matter how much I yearned to come first, no matter how much I yearned for validation, no matter how much I yearned to be superior, there were just too many people and gods for that to happen.

But that was okay, because my wife's happiness was my happiness. So was Ismenia's and Morris's.

It felt much better to view it this way. It was like all my life I'd peered through a store window at my own joy sitting on the shelf, waiting for me to come in and get it. And now I had. Now I could move on with whatever death had in store for me.

· · · ·

LATER THAT DAY, MORRIS, Lilly, and I headed toward Longtoe's palace to see what could be done about the mess and come up with some ideas to organize it. The three of us were still recovering from the strain of recent events and wanted to stay local. Later we could travel and reconnect with dead relatives and friends, and meet historic figures we'd always wondered about.

Lilly and Morris were hungry so we stopped at a food truck, where the dragonflies were blowing tiny flames at crème brûlées to caramelize the sugar on top. They preferred using their fire rather than biting people, as it turned out. Longtoe had given them their freedom, so they went back to what they'd been doing before he took charge of them, which was baking, soldering precious metals to make jewelry, and lighting candles.

When we got to the palace, I noted with relief that the reflections of the shades no longer filled the moat. The lake water I'd spilled no longer affected it, leaving the surface smooth once more.

Morris had been so supportive in helping me look for Lilly that I wanted to do something he'd enjoy, so once we were inside the palace, we started by organizing one of the avocado rooms. (Apparently there was an entire wing devoted to them.)

Morris rubbed his hands happily. "Where to start, where to start?" There were avocado-themed dishes, string lights, throw rugs, candles, purses, backpacks, and so much more. I particularly admired an avocado sculpture that was nearly as tall as I was, yet appeared real enough to eat.

Lilly picked up an oil painting that had been leaning against the wall, a still life of a sliced avocado. It was beautifully depicted in various shades of green, although a black blemish marred the bulbous part.

"I've been thinking," I said.

"That's dangerous," joked Morris. He found a Mr. Avocado Head toy and plugged the eyes and ears into it. Without the mouth, its expression was one of concern.

"What have you been thinking about?" asked Lilly.

"About the meaning of perfection." I pointed at the painting she held. "I think that each being, whether living on Earth or existing in the afterlife, is perfect in themselves. We all have flaws, and yet those flaws are a part of the whole. Like this painting, which wouldn't be as good without the blotch on the avocado."

Morris spotted the mouth for the Mr. Avocado Head on the floor. He scooped it up and placed it, giving the toy a cheery grin. "That's kind of a contradiction. Being perfect, yet not perfect."

"I know," I said. "But it's like Chaos. Destruction and creation all at once."

Morris held up the toy, pretending that it was talking for him, like he might have done in his classroom. He spoke in a ponderous yet lovable drawl. "I think it's a way of looking at things, is all. Appreciating things. Not getting hung up on them, but also not giving up on them."

Lilly touched her nose to say that he'd hit it on the nose.

I sorted some things into different piles. Avocado-themed soap dishes and toothbrush holders in one, couch pillows and a quilt in another. "Honey, why didn't you tell me you were friends with a god? You know you could have trusted me."

"You would have thought I was crazy."

I would like to think that I wouldn't have. But sometimes Lilly knew me better than I knew myself, and I suppose I'd been happier without that complication anyway. I let it go.

"It fascinates me how people and gods are so alike from having evolved together," I mused. "We started as protohumans while they started as shades. Then we became modern humans, and they became modern gods. What's next?"

Morris gathered some avocado playing cards. "I guess that together we'll evolve into something different. I don't know what that will be." He paired the cards with an avocado board game.

Lilly sorted avocado bow ties, vests, and socks into a pile. "Evolution isn't necessarily a straight line toward excellence, but hopefully in the future we'll have fewer bad qualities and more good qualities."

"I wonder if evolution is the right word," I said. "So much chance involved. Maybe we need to change more intentionally now."

"Yes," said Morris. "Then we could all be more perfect."

I raised an eyebrow. "Can you be *more* perfect? Isn't that like saying somebody's *more* pregnant? You either are or you aren't."

My wife made an *annhh* noise of disagreement. "You can definitely be less pregnant or more pregnant."

"So you're saying somebody can be more perfect?" I said uncertainly.

"Not you." She tilted her head slyly. "You can't be any more perfect than you are."

I grinned like an idiot.

Using the Mr. Potato Head drawl, Morris pretended to answer for me. "Aww, you always know what to say."

• • • •

LATER, WHILE LILLY and Morris continued sorting, I took a little break. From the palace steps I gazed out at whatever you call a palace's front yard. I realized that I'd begun thinking less about what I'd left behind in life and more about what might lie ahead. The future seemed wide open, full of mystery and excitement, the way it did when I was a child. I could make of it whatever I wanted.

To do that, I needed to learn a lot more about the afterlife and the gods. I had discovered that the meaning of life and death was transformation, and I was going to transform myself through learning. I vowed to be proactive, rather than reactive. I never wanted to be in such peril again. I would be "perfectly" ready for any challenge that might arise.

For the moment though, I would enjoy the scenery. The boxwood hedges were nicely trimmed in diamond shapes. The gardens were lined with yellow-and-purple pansies and white jasmine. The green lawn looked so lush that it begged to be walked on.

I slipped off my pistachio-green espadrille loafers and shuffled across the lawn, sighing at the softness of the grass blades on the bottoms of my feet. Just as in life, in death the little things were the most precious.

I spotted something shiny on the ground. Was that a paper clip? I picked it up. More paper clips followed. I froze with the sparkling silver chain dangling in the air, barely believing what I held in my own hand.

Was this the chain of submission that I'd tried so hard to put on Longtoe's neck? The one that the crow had stolen from me? The one that would render god or human docile?

I believed it could be, because the bird had flown in this direction. If I tested it and found out that it was, then it would help me with my vow to be proactive.

I put it in the pocket of my joggers and zipped it shut. I didn't need it right now, but who knew what the future might bring.

I breathed deeply, filling my lungs with the fresh smell of cut grass and the peppery smell of jasmine, then headed for the stairs to rejoin my wife and friend.

I'd had a beautiful life, and I was sure now that the afterlife would be even better.

About the Author

Susan Whiting Kemp is the author of *Sorry, Wrong Afterlife*, *The Climate Machine*, and *The Time Philosopher*. She is a co-author of the short story compilation *We Grew Tales*. Her writing has appeared in *Bewildering Stories*, *Hobart*, *Wilderness House Literary Review*, *HowlRound*, *The Blue Lake Review*, and *The Writer's Workshop Review*. She has written or edited thousands of proposals, articles, and reports for science and engineering companies. She holds a Bachelor of Arts in drama from the University of Washington.

Read more at https://susanwkemp.com/.